BLAZE

AMELIA K OLIVER

EDITED BY EILEEN TROEMEL

INTERIOR TRICE ELLIS

COVER DESIGN DREAM COVERS BY K & L

First edition

TRIGGER WARNING

First Edition.

GLOSSARY OF TERMS

Glossary of terms

"Advanced"
General term for those who no longer have the cancer gene
& are immune to PV.

"Alpha"
Superintelligence. Large skulls to accommodate their huge
brains.

"Panda"
Zombies. White skin, black around eyes and mouth. Crave
flesh.

"Hands"
Farmers, immune to PV.

"Brute"
Super strong. Very tall and brutal.

"Mover"
Immune who deliver crops to the cities and underground colonies.

"Seer"
Super eyesight. Massive eyes.

"Evo"
Super hearing, or speed or agility.

"Panda virus" aka PV
Airborne virus. Bitten or scratched turn into Panda.

The few remaining humans that aren't immune live Underground. Unable to leave for fear of being infected, their numbers dwindle.
Breathing could kill you.
If you're bitten - you're dead.

INTRODUCTION

History tells of a time long ago when small-town scientist Dr Gordon Isaac's discovered the cure for cancer. Great right? And it was... for a time.

Those who chose to use the cure produced children who were a bit different. With each new generation, these abnormalities became fearsome, developing abilities beyond that of humans. The "Advanced" took over the world, claiming to be at the top of the food chain. Super intelligent "Alpha's" governed the cities, while incredibly strong "Brutes" became their bodyguards. With super hearing, speed and agility, the "Evo's" became general dogsbodies. Within their protective force field covered cities, they prospered.

They unleashed the Panda virus after 100 years of war. Made in a lab inside Tri-City, it was designed to target the gene Advanced no longer have; but humans do. Something went wrong and now "Panda"; flesh-eating shells driven by hunger, roam what's left of the wastelands above ground.

BLAZE
AMELIA K. OLIVER

"Y ou're a vile excuse for a person and you deserve far worse than this." My entire body shakes with the need for revenge as I stand over the man who broke me. "Thank your lucky stars I'm bored with this game," I growl at him, venom lacing my voice. He scrambles backwards in the dirt, his blood mixing with the dust as he tries to get away from the fifteen-year-old girl pointing a gun at him.

His clothes are torn, bloody, his eyes wild with madness. I tortured him for two weeks, and now, I'll end this.

"Don't! Please? I'll give you food! I'll give you my slaves?" His snivelling only serves to enrage me further. My lip rises in a snarl.

"Shut the fuck up and die!" Raising the heavyweight of the Colt 17 in my hand, I fire my last remaining bullet into his dick.

1

Blood and gore spray into the air, some of it hitting me in the face, but I don't even blink, needing to watch as this bastard suffers like he made me suffer. His screams draw the attention of several nearby Panda. His choices are to bleed out or be eaten alive by zombies. What a way to go.

"ARGH!" I bolt upright on my pile of rags. "Shit!" I wipe the sweat off my forehead with the back of my hand. It comes away dripping. For the last five years, I've had this same nightmare, a recurring memory of my past. Every night I wake up in a cold sweat, my clothes soaked through, my stomach twisting and turning like a sharknado took up residence in my belly. Fucking Tac. Fucker got exactly what he deserved. But something in me died that night and something else awoke, something dark and unforgiving. A new me was born, and she gave no quarter to mother-fuckers who dared to mess with her.

MY NAME'S KAYLA, and this is a story of how war never changes. But humankind does.

BLAZE

AMELIA K'OLIVER

I crouch on my perch at the top of one of the few surviving buildings in this area of London. The interior has all but collapsed in on itself, but the outer shell is mostly standing. There's no glass in any of the windows. The floor creaks and dips as I shift my weight to my other foot.

Patience.

I clutch onto my most prized possession in one hand; my bow. The butt is resting against my hip; a pair of eye spies in the other. I resist the urge to whip off my long black wig and claw my scalp raw. Instead, I focus on my breathing, making sure it's even. Soundless air whispers past my dry lips as I remain still.

Patience.

Dirt streaks my skin, making it itch, but I don't scratch. That would make it much worse. I desperately need to clean myself up, but I can't until this mission's complete. My clothes are riddled with more holes than I can count, but right now. None of that matters. I'm here for revenge.

My target; Reginald Masters.

The bastard who killed my mother. He had his men attacked her compound on the outskirts of what's left of London when I was a teen. Their goal; to steal all the stored crops in the barns, then set the fields on fire.

My mother and her four husbands fought back. They stopped the fires before everything burned to the ground, but a Brute caught my mother.

He murdered her.

My fathers me that when they found her body at the back of one of the big black barns; the Brute had broken all of her bones.

The thought breaks my concentration.

They wanted me to exact revenge, that's why they told me. I'm sure a normal girl would've thought it cruel to tell me, but I'm not a normal girl.

I look back at the building I've been watching for the last few weeks. I don't know what it was back before the wars, but it's a large single-story. The blackened walls are still standing, which is rare in this part of the City. Most of the buildings are in ruins here. The bombs decimated most of this area, leaving patches here and there untouched. My reconnaissance proved to me old Reggie visits here once every fourteen days.

Today was the day. I just have to be patient.

Determination to kill this mother fucker for what he did is like fire streaming through my veins. It's the only emotion I've allowed myself to have for the longest time. My cold, dead heart welcomes the flames. A noise in the distance makes me drag my eyes back to below me.

He's here. I set my eyes back to the eye spies and watch the dead man walking.

Until I destroy him, I won't stop. Even if it destroys me.

. . .

* * *

WHEN IT HAPPENED - the death of my mother; I was on one of my little jaunts. I never knew what I was searching for, but I was drawn to the empty streets, anyway. I'd scavenge and explore. Searching, needing... something. I haven't found out what it is yet, but it's out there. I knew it was.

When I returned that fateful morning, it was to find my fathers mourning, grieving, broken. Their hearts were as black as the scorched dirt. The farm was all but destroyed, too.

We laid her to rest amongst the cornfields. Her being killed was such a sad loss to the world. To never be the same now that she's gone.

Her kind are known as Hands, named so because no one wanted to bite the hands that fed them. My mother was a master Hand, with skills passed down from generation to generation. They kept both sides of the war alive with the food they grew. But Hands are rare, so they are well compensated by both the Advanced and the Scraps in exchange for crops. Technology, fossil fuel and knowledge were the preferred choices of currency. Old money has no meaning out here in the Wastes. If you want something, well, you better have something to exchange with.

They did well for themselves, as much as anyone could in such harsh living conditions. Their way of life was survival. Keeping the Panda at bay was the number one priority. The second was feeding the remaining beings on this God-forsaken planet.

My eyes water so I wipe them with the back of my

hand; creating clean patches on my face. I'm not crying. I didn't cry then; I'm not doing it now.

My mum's crops had been popular; in demand. She would see no one go hungry, doing deals with families who had nothing to give but their gratitude. Her heart was kind and full of love. Her kindness and generosity are a significant loss to this fucked up world. For what?

Greed.

I, on the other hand, have no such soft feelings inside of me. I'm tough because that's what I need to be, want to be. Being soft only gets you killed. I have no plans to die today, or any day close to now.

AND NOW HERE I AM, kneeling on what I presume used to be a balcony based on how the floor protrudes from the wall above what was once London town. Nothing about this area would make you think it was once a large, overpopulated City. But then again, nowhere in the Wastes is overpopulated anymore. Kinda the opposite. The only place that could sustain more than a few people at a time is surrounded by a force field. People like me aren't welcome there.

Tri-City. Home to only the rich and powerful.

Peering through my eye spies, I watch as Masters exits a strangely shaped vehicle. It's black and shiny, with angles that are sharp and pointy. Within seconds of his feet touching the ground, he's surrounded by thirty or so Brutes and Evo's. Fuck, I won't be able to take down that many. I shake my shoulder. My quiver only carries twelve arrows.

Behind the throng of Evo's walks a tall, thin man. Even from this distance, I can see his eyes are huge. "Seer. Shit."

If he spots me, I'm as good as dead. I drop the eye spies to my chest and retreat into the shell of a building. A weight settles in my heart. I wonder why he suddenly needs so many Brutes? Last time, he arrived with only three.

I wasn't ready then. My quiver had been empty because I'd run into a group of Panda on the way here, barely escaping with my life. And I'm not ready now. Shit. Shit. Shit!

If he has an entourage of Evo's, that means he's from Tri-City. It's the biggest colony of Advanced in the UK and lies in the very centre of old London. I've never been close. I can't risk being seen, but I've spied it from afar. A force field dome surrounds the whole place. It shines in the sun like oil spilt in water, iridescent and impenetrable, protecting those lucky enough to live within it from the toxic air and the virus. No one gets in, at least those of us who aren't Advanced don't.

I slip back into the building, carefully placing my feet on the grid-like metal floor. "Baby!" I call my pet back to my side. Baby's a huge slobbering mutt. His fur looks like it's on fire with reds and oranges throughout his coat. He weighs at least twice as much as me, if not more. Pure muscle and loyal. Vicious fucker, just like his mummy.

He bounds over to me, deftly navigating the crumbling structure, the ring of fur around his face bouncing with his movements. He skids to a stop before me and sits at my feet. "Good boy. Come." Baby follows close behind me, his body pressing against my leg. Never too far away. Baby's been my companion for the last two years. He's the only living thing I trust completely. We wind our way down the building, both of us jumping across the treacherous areas we can't climb down. I take my time; if I get injured out here, I'm fucked. People like me don't have access to real medical care. People like me die from a simple scratch.

I navigate what's left of the inside of the building, using footholds and grabbing onto anything that doesn't move. The muscles in my arms burn and sweat breaks out over my skin.

I'm fit. A person doesn't have to choose not to be in this world. One wrong foot and I'm dead.

As we reach the bottom of the gaping hole that runs through the middle of the building, I see movement out of the corner of my eye. Baby growls from above, momentarily distracting me. "Baby?" I feel something smash against the back of my head. There is a flash of brown, and then the lights go out.

***

I CAN'T SEE when I come to. The hit to my head has left my vision blurry. Blinking hard and shaking my head a few times, I try to look around my surroundings. All I see is - nothing - it's pitch black. Heavy chains are weighing me down. "Shit!" I try to pull my hands through the bindings, giving myself bruises. It's never a good thing when you wake up bound, that's not my kinda kink at all, maybe if...

A male voice comes out of the darkness.

"What's your name, kid?" I jump at the sound, not expecting anyone to be in this foul-smelling place with me.

"What's it to you?" I've roamed the wastelands alone for the last fifteen years, my first outing at just five years old. I've never been caught off guard; therefore, I've avoided capture. Now look at the mess I've gotten myself into. Trapped, hot, sweaty and lumbered with some dick-weed in the dark.

"Just asking, kid," the deep rumbling voice answers.

"Not a fucking kid." Who does this guy think he is? Kid? Nah. Big badass mofo right here.

"Sure looked like a kid being dragged in here by those arseholes."

"The Hulk would look like a child next to the Brutes. I'm not a shitting ankle biter," I snap, really irritated now. A grunt is his only response. Oh, Mr Fucking chatty box. Fantastic. "Where the hell are we, anyway? It smells like fossil fuel in here." The place stinks like it's soaked in gasoline. It burns my eyes and sears the lining of my throat. I try to swallow past the taste of copper, but I end up coughing instead. So thirsty.

"Fucked if I know, kid. What's a Hulk?"

I lay my head back down on the hard ground, not bothering to answer him. Can't believe I got myself into this shit, never lose concentration, Kay! Dammit, what fresh hell is this? A shrill scream rents the air. I bolt upright, my pity party over, for now. "Gotta get out of here. I've got shit to do."

I wiggle around some, trying to find a source of light. I need something to put between the chains and my wrists, then I can pry them off. That's it, Kay, focus. My foot catches something, sending it rolling across the floor. My hand shoots out to grab it just as someone else does. "Fuck, it's mine, get off!" I whisper-yell.

"Not likely, kid. I got to it before you did."

I tug it towards me, using what little strength I have. Whatever they hit me with, my body still hasn't recovered. He tugs it back, and it slips from my grasp. I scream inside, the sound vibrating off my skull. "I need that to get these damn chai..." Before I can finish, I hear metal clanking on the floor. His chains, no doubt. "Pass it 'ere."

"What'll you give me for it?"

"How's a punch to the dick sound?" A tut comes from the darkness.

"If you want to break your hand, go for it." Cocky mother fucker.

"Yeah, that's a negative, asshole. Don't know what I'd catch. Give. It. To. Me." Frustration wells. I hate relying on others. Right now? This bitch holds my way out of here. My head could explode any second.

The man chuckles softly. This isn't a game, mother fucker. "Please," I grind out between clenched teeth. The pipe hits my outstretched leg and I snatch it up. I jam it down into the space between my skin and the chains, the sharp edge scratching the soft skin on the inside of my wrist. Bollox. I twist it, but the gap's too big. Damn it! I can't get leverage.

"Need my help, kid?" He's much closer now. I can feel his breath skim over my heated face. Why's it so bloody hot in here? I still can't see him. My mind conjures up a stick-thin guy with buck teeth and maggots in his beard. Yuck. His voice sends shivers down my spine, though. What the fuck, Kayla? Hello! You're trapped with a stranger, he's now free and you're stuck. If I could hit myself over the head right now, I would. "Fuck no." I sound flustered. Damn it. Show no weakness. Jesus, Kay, concentrate. I try for a few more minutes, leaving behind bruises and scratches, but I just can't get the right angle. "I can't quite get... ugh!" I stare dejectedly at where the irons on my wrists rub my skin. My arse is going numb.

Moments pass in silence until I feel rough hands around my ankle.

As I'm pulled across the floor, I let out a little whimper. I'm glad my ass is numb because, after this, it's probably going to hurt for a bit. Calloused hands appear in the faint light from what I assume is the door. A way out! They use the pipe to pry off my restraints.

His rough skin gliding across my own sends a bolt of something down to the apex of my thighs. Ignoring it, I wonder where Baby is. It'd be a stupid move calling out to him. His massive body and deafening roar would attract too much attention. No, I can get out of this myself. Plus, he could be hunting, and mamma needs to eat. Or he could be hurt? Whoever attacked me is probably in pieces by now. Nah, we've been through worse. He'll be fine, I know it. My thoughts are scrambled, my mind working overtime to deal with the amount of pain that swirls through my head. I've got to get out of here. My nose itches from the fumes and my head's pounding. I need to get out. Like right now, before I'm sick. I stand as soon as the chains hit the floor, wobbling a little. So hungry. So thirsty. My thirst burns in my throat and the hunger gnaws at me.

"My pleasure," His words whisper past my ear.

Oh shit. He's right behind me. The heat coming from his body makes sweat drip down my spine. I suppress a shudder. Here I am, stuck in a dark room with a stranger who has an attitude and I'm getting turned on? Yeah, I've officially lost all my marbles. I stumble around with my hands outstretched, trying to find a door.

"Yes!" I say as my hands find and wrap around a handle. Pressing my ear against the wood, I try to determine if there are guards on the other side. Nothing. No breathing, no footsteps.

Caution.

I push the handle down, taking my time so it doesn't make noise. I open the door just a touch, then further when I don't hear footfalls running. The light's blinding as I step out. Oh, dear Lord, where am I? I've seen nothing like it before. The entire building in front of me is shiny and white.

Nothing's white in the wastes. If it was it's now grey, or so caked in dirt it's black. But I don't see a single streak of dirt on this strange building. Fuck, aliens? I sigh. I mean really, Kay? You've lost your mind, girl. Aliens, ha.

The stranger stands behind me, far too close for my liking. The only people I've ever interacted with willingly were my parents. My Dads were rough men. No patience for ankle biters. Except for Klaud. He was kind to me occasionally when I ventured back home. So, being this close to someone new has my insides slithering like snakes in a barrel.

"Could you be any louder, kid? This place is crawling with Evo's."

I turn to face the man from the dark. I wish I hadn't because... Hot damn!

Just short of six feet tall, ripped and tan, with no shirt on his torso, he looks like one of the guys in my mum's magazines from before the wars. She'd let me take them out of the plastic once in a while when she would tell me stories passed down to her. This guy's sex on legs, and he knows it.

"Shh!" I scold him for being loud while being too loud myself. He rolls his odd coloured eyes at me and I'm speechless. The left one's brown. Rich and earthy. The right is blue like bright blue. Freaky. Yet intriguing.

Square jaw, pouty lips, arms laced with tattoos I can't

even describe I'm so overwhelmed by him. They snake down his arms, stopping at his knuckles. The ridges of his muscles have my fingers twitching to touch. Hot. As. Fuck. He's a beast. My mouth waters as I stare like an idiot. Not wanting to miss a single hard inch of him, my eyes greedily drink him in.

You just don't see guys like him in the wastes. Most of them are half-starved walking skeletons in skin sacks, or so dirty, you can no longer tell what colour their skin should be. Neither appeals to me. But this guy... He must be from the City, which makes me want to gag but also climb him like a tree to sniff his hair.

"Move aside, kid. I have places to be." He roughly pushes me to the side. Rude! What the fuck? Anger rolls in my belly.

Obviously, he's an immune like me, otherwise, he'd be dead 'round about now. Except he's not dead, nope. He's very much alive. Good. Lord.

I should kick his arse for pushing me, though. As he walks away, my eyes flit to his rear. My mouth drops open. I'm pretty sure drool just landed on my foot. Hoo boy. Bubble butt rude mother fucker. Why'd he have to be a cock gobbler? I wouldn't mind a slice of that ass. Maybe the whole pie. Yum.

He stomps like we're not in the middle of escaping hostile territory surrounded by Evos. Every Advanced in this place can surely hear his footfalls, or you know, by the aliens.

Pulling myself out of my funk, I tiptoe to the side of the spacecraft. Because let's face it, this ain't a building. Too clean. My hands go to my shoulder and hip, only to realise my eye spies and my bow and arrows have been taken from me. Bastards! They got my precious blades too; even the small ones I keep strapped to my inner thighs in case of emergencies. Fuck a duck, I'm defenceless! You don't mess with a bitch's weapons!

"Don't follow me, boy. This is not the time for play, run along." He shoos me with his hand, never once looking at me. Well, fuck you, mister. I skirt around the side of him and make my way down the wall of the shiny thing beside me. My eyes scan the area in front of me, not just for Evo's but for Panda, too.

Panda; the result of a virus the Alphas created in an effort to kill off the few remaining humans. Named as such because the skin around their eyes and mouth turned black while the rest of their skin became white as ghosts. They mindlessly crave flesh. Human. Animal. They're not picky. Slow, but deadly in groups, Panda wreak havoc in the Wastelands, infecting or killing anything with a pulse.

This area's probably packed with the rotten buggers; they're everywhere. Only a few thousand people were immune, less so now as it mutates and new strands become stronger, clever.

I have to be very careful extracting myself from this situation. It would be a ball ache to fight off any Panda without my weapons. I mean, I can do it... of course... but why churn butter with your hands when there are more efficient ways of doing it?

I stop at a corner. Tendrils of my golden hair have escaped from under my wig. It would be a mistake I couldn't make twice if I were to roam with my natural hair flowing freely. I'd be dead quicker than I could sneeze. My mother would cut it short when I was a girl to keep it from escaping like this.

"Never let them see, Kayla. They'll take you from us if they see it."

The memory of my mother assaults me, simultaneously filling me with grief and anger, temporarily distracting me. For the split second that I'm frozen, the beast has enough time to sneak up on me.

"Move it! Seer over there." He grabs my chin, jerks my head toward a wooden shack in front of the spaceship behind us and doesn/t let go. Shit. The feel of his hand on me sends shivers down my spine. Down, girl!

I tear my chin out of his grip, push off the shiny white surface at my back and run as fast as my legs will take me into the streets of London towns Wastes.

After about twenty minutes of navigating Panda and street debris, I end up in an area I recognize and can make it home from that point on. Home. Yeah, it's an old bus. Big, yellow and rusted, but watertight. I'd found her when I was a child, ripped the rotten seats out and made her my Wastey home. She's not much, but she's mine. A precious commodity out here. I press myself up against the brick wall that faces my bus, Old Yella. Listening, watching.

This is protocol, always. Always check for enemies before entering your home. Failure to do so gets you killed, or worse... turned into a Panda. The sound of a rock scuffing the ground makes me spin around. My hand comes up and is just about to connect with a handsome face when the fucker easily catches it and shoves it towards me.

"Don't be stupid, kid. I killed three Panda who were following you. You owe me your life," the beast of a man growls at me. My mouth pops open. There was no Panda following me. I don't get caught by Panda. Dude's confused from the lack of water. I shake my head and give the area one last scan. "Fuck off, mister."

I bolt away and run into the makeshift door of my bus,

yanking it shut behind me. I slink down to the floor and use the looking glass I placed on the roof and the attached one in the footwell so I can see outside without being seen myself.

Beast is casually walking towards Old Yella. His body's relaxed, his gait loose and sure. He's not even looking around him for Panda! Idiot. He's gonna get himself killed. Or worse, me. Three loud clangs rent the air, forcing me to jump to my feet. "You'll attract zombies, you freaking idiot!" I stage-whisper through a small open window.

"You gonna let me in, kid? I saved your life. You could at least give me some water."

Nah. Take a note, big guy, Kay doesn't share. Shaking my head, I move further back into my bus. I'm not letting him in, and I ain't sharing my water. Grabbing the canteen I always keep for emergencies, I slip the little device I love so much into my pocket. I found it when I was fourteen. I don't know what it's called, but it's my favourite thing in this fucked up world. Except for Baby, of course. Black, sleek and sexy. The screen's cracked a little and the solar charger's been repaired so many times it's now all tape, but the things on it keep me entertained when nothing else does. Like; Books about a kid and his two friends who are all magic. Their school's full of perils unheard of, but the boy always prevails. And music sung by a young boy. His hair over his eyes, singing about his "Baby". And photos. Lots and lots of photos of small creatures. They appear to be the same species but all different colours. Apparently, they enjoy knocking breakable things off surfaces and sitting in small spaces. It's hard to believe these things were real before the wars.

I plop myself down on the dusty settee in the middle of

the small space and take a long sip of water. Ahh, liquid gold.

"Let me in, kid. You don't want me to bring Panda to your door, do you?"

Bitch has a point. I huff and rise slowly, making my way to the door without haste. When I finally get there, the look on his face has me both squirming and hot at the same time. Unlatching the rudimentary lock, I step back as he pushes his way in, almost knocking me on my ass.

"Water?" He raises an eyebrow at me, hands on his hips like a mother. I snigger inside. Pansy. It's safe to say that in the Wastes, there isn't an abundance of sexy males to choose from. The Hands and mercenaries who call the barren land home are rough, moody and often brutal. I've mostly kept my distance from them.

But this guy? His clothing has no holes in it. His stone coloured pants are tight around his legs, the top half of him is naked for the world to see. Beautiful artwork graces the toned muscles of his arms that beg to be licked. I think I'm in heat or something. Why is my body reacting so strangely?

Shit. I throw a bottle at him; not to him, but at him, because I'm not his friend. If it happens to hit him upside the head; I'm ok with that.

He catches it midair.

The smirk on his face makes me want to throat punch him and kiss him. I'm not sure in which order. As he drinks the entire contents, I'm mesmerized watching his throat work. It has me licking my lips. What the fuck is wrong with me? Why am I drooling? I wipe my chin. With the imaginary drool removed, I shrug at him.

I pull my hood up and concentrate on my feet. I can't get distracted here. He'll be gone before I get the chance to even learn his name. At least I hope he will. Finishing the water, he gasps softly, making my eyes flick up to watch as he wipes the back of his hand across his plump lips.

"What's your name, kid?" I glare at him from under my lashes as he eyeballs the place I call home.

Over the years I've collected scraps of fabric and pinned them to the walls, creating a cacophony of colour and texture. The bits of furniture I've scavenged are well used, dusty and repaired multiple times. I built a stove of sorts into the sidewall, its chimney poking through the dented roof. The floor's bare. I used to have rugs, carpets, and rags, but I couldn't keep them clean. So now it's bare metal.

"Cat got your tongue, kid?"

Cat? What's a cat? I shake my head and push my hair back under my wig. Can't be too careful. I can't wait to take it off. It itches. "No," I answer. Smooooth like ice. "I've got nothing to say, that's all. Just leave!" I'm a social butterfly. Anger bubbles in my stomach. I need this guy to leave. If my mum found out…. Except, she won't, will she? She's dead. Emotions I normally don't allow myself to have; rise to the surface, forcing tears to leak from my eyes.

"What's the matter, kid? Where're your parents?". With that, I break down, my body heaving with sobs.

"Ah, shit." I hear him move as tears stream down my face unchecked. I don't know where it came from, but I wish it would stop. There's a stranger on my bus. I can't show him weakness. He attempts to comfort me as I curl up into myself and mourn the loss of my mother for the first time since her death.

"There, there, kid. Everything's going to be ok."

No, it isn't. It'll never be ok again. Closing my eyes, I see my mother wrapped in an old sheet, oddly flat and floppy in one of my dad's arms. Shit. Pull yourself together, K! I angrily swipe my tears away, then shift so the stranger's hand falls from my shoulder.

"It's good to cry a little sometimes. Listen, I know of a small tribe just south of here. Follow me and I'll get you to safety." A sarcastic giggle leaves me, unbidden.

"I'm safe. Just leave." I rise and walk away from him, picking up my stuff as I go. I can only rely on myself to keep me safe. Others aren't to be trusted. I intended to get him to follow, and as soon as he's out the door, I'll close it behind him and lock it. Only, that's not what happens. What happens is so terrifying; I scream. It echoes around the metal space of my bus.

"Come here!" Beast grabs my hood and with it a handful of my wig and pulls, hard, revealing my golden blonde hair. Without thinking and going against my instincts, I scream as my heart pounds in my chest.

"What the fuck?" Beast stands there with my wig in his hand, staring at it like it's a new species of animal. Scrambling, I pull my hood back up, but it's too late. He's seen it. I'm dead.

"Oh my God. It's you!" His face is full of shock, mouth open, catching flies.

I duck my head and dash out the door, barely grabbing a spare sword on the way out. I run headlong into the city streets as I strap it to my back. Shit. Shit. Shit. He saw! I'm so fucked right now. For almost twenty years I've hidden my hair. Within a half-hour, I've exposed my weakness, and he's seen my bloody hair! Now I'm running around London for the first time without my wig! Way to go, K!

BLAZE

AMELIA K'OLIVER

I weave between mangled cars and piles of rubble away from the threat behind me. My goal is to get to the hiding place just down the next street, but I trip and fall, landing face-first in the dirt. I hit hard and my breath leaves me. I lay here panting, barely able to breathe through the dust. What a newbie move.

Always take care when running. A fall could end your life.

I hear footfalls behind me. Wheezing and spluttering, I turn on my back and swipe my hair from my face. The sun shines on it, making the near-white locks shimmer so bright, I'm almost blinded.

"Here, put this on. We've gotta get you out of here. I smell Panda." Beast thrusts my wig towards me. I slip it on with uncooperative fingers. His mismatched eyes never leave mine. Is he going to kill me now? I mean, why give me the wig if he's just going to kill me anyway? What's his game? Fuck, I'm lying on my sword and can't breathe.

"I'm Connor. You're Kayla, right?"

Hold the fuck up, how's he know my name? My head spins and I dry heave. I push off the ground, shove my wig back and stalk away. He follows. Damn.

* * *

"How'd you know my name?" It's already getting dark, the air reeks of death and rot as we walk. I set a fast pace. I pull my bandana over my mouth to block out the smell. It doesn't work. My black jeans and jumper help me blend into the night and keep me warm.

"Kathryn." He says my mother's name like he knew her. Like he'd said it a million times before.

He knew my mum? I stare at him, my jaw hanging open all attractive like. I'm so stumped by her name on his lips I slow down enough that he gets ahead of me.

"Your mother and my father had known each other for many years before you were born. Kayla, don't you know who you are?" He stops and turns to me. I skid to a halt mere inches from his body.

"I'm Kayla." Giving him my best 'well duh' face. Obviously, bitch. The one and only!

"Yes. But you're more than that." Beast takes hold of my elbow and drags me into the nearest building. This whole day is fubar, and I can barely even think, let alone stop him.

It's pitch black in here and I stumble and trip over debris, but he never lets me fall, his grip on my elbow punishing. Depositing me near the door, he builds a small fire, breaking pieces of furniture and scraps around the space and piling them up. The flames cast just enough light to see his features. He looks at me with narrowed eyes. I pull down my bandana and take a deep breath of stale air. My head swims with information and confusion. How is this even possible?

"Kayla, my dad's President Keeper." The breath leaves my lungs. His dad's the freaking President of the UK? As in the richest, both in monetary and food value, man on this island? My confusion must show on my face because he slides his hand down my arm then grasps my hand, lacing his fingers with mine. I look down at them in confusion, not mentally present enough to think about the fact my hand's encased in his.

"You're Connor Keeper? As in, the son of the guy who runs Tri-City?" My hand automatically reaches behind me to toy with the twine wrapped hilt of my blade.

"Yes, love. The one and only. Sit." It's not an order but I still bristle a little. Folding my arms across my chest, I lean against the wall. His face breaks out in a huge smile and he laughs. I can't help but smile too. I don't laugh though. The last time I laughed without sarcasm was a long time ago.

"Ok, precious. You make your stand, I get it. I do. The Wastes... they're harsh. Survival of the fittest. But, honey, I would never hurt you. Quite the opposite, actually."

Ok, so now I'm getting freaked out. No one's ever spoken to me in such a... a ... I don't know what way. My vocabulary's severely lacking when it comes to emotions.

"What's going on?" My voice raises the more I speak. Sweat forms on my brow. I drop my hands and once again I'm dismayed to feel empty holsters. The presence of cold steel is comforting to me, without my blades, I feel lonely.

"I... we..." He stumbles over his words. It makes him adorable and I hate him for it.

"Spit it out, man!" The words are harsher and louder than I intended. He shifts uncomfortably. I decide to sit down, fearing what he's about to say will make my legs turn to jelly. I park my bum on a pile of rubble. Sharp edges bite into my flesh, but I ignore it. My arse can wait.

"We're promised. Not just me, " he begins.

Promised? No freaking way. Nah ah. I am not marrying this beast. Not happening.

Outdated laws mean that when a woman reaches the age of twenty, she must marry those she's promised to. But my mother never once told me they had promised me to anyone. I thought I'd escaped those archaic rules.

"Your mother and my father grew up together, Kayla. We... we played together as kids. Those marks on your shoulders?" He points a finger toward me. Instinctively, I raise a hand to press on one scar I have on my back. How does he know about them?

"Those are from Panda. Listen, we don't have time now. I need to get you back to safety. You need to sleep and I need to hunt."

He walks away as I sit here open-mouthed. Does he know about my scars? We played together as kids? I've never met another child in my life. They're so rare. And how could a Panda have scarred me? I'd be infected or dead. Once scratched or bitten, immune or not, you die. I'm so exhausted, my mind and body are playing tricks on me. I take my jumper off and roll it into a ball for a pillow. Unable to continue to think for another second, I lay down and fall headfirst into sleep.

"Con! Come chase me?" I run from the boy in front of me. My little legs pump as I speed away. My head turns to watch the cute boy chase after me, excitement on his face. The sunlight catches his golden hair, the same colour as mine. The sound of giggling echoes inside my mind.

"Gotcha! You're so pretty, Kay." Our eyes meet, his one brown one blue, so full of love. He's a little older than me and much bigger. He tickles me relentlessly. Our laughter is loud and carefree. I feel alive. And loved. I love this boy.

Suddenly, a huge explosion rents the air and our small bodies are thrown, landing hard on the packed ground. My head bounces off a rock, and the sound of screams pierce the buzzing in my ears.

"Holy shit!" My body comes to life. In one swift move, I find myself standing in front of Connor. His face is a mask of concern and something else I can't place. His hands are on my shoulders. The heat from his palms calms my shock.

"What's wrong, Kay?" He uses the same nickname as the small boy from my dream. I'm so shocked, I almost pee a little. Damn, he knows me? Well, knew me. Shit. Or maybe he planted the idea in my head and my subconscious mind turned it into a story like those I read on my device.

I pull my shoulders free from his grip and move to the empty doorway. The early morning sun glimmers off pieces of metal within the rocks and stones littered everywhere, causing me to squint. When the bombs hit this site, they didn't do as much damage as intended. There were a lot of buildings still standing, a bounty to be plundered for scavengers like me. But after so many years, they're all ruined and barely standing. Their contents eaten by the remaining wildlife or taken by survivors. Mother Nature's taken over any space she can, giving London a wild look it didn't have back before the war. Trees, grasses and wild-flowers sprout from carcasses of old motor vehicles, what's left of buildings, and between the bones of long-dead creatures and humans. It isn't uncommon to see skeletons while roaming the city and the surrounding areas.

Wildlife's a rare sight, though. Should you see an animal on your travels it's terrible practice to kill it for food, but most still do. When you're on the brink of starving to death it's hard to resist meat. The animal population never recovered because the food's so scarce and the Panda eat whatever they can catch. Except for rabbits. Those things are everywhere.

"I won't hurt you, Kay." I don't jump at his words. Years of fighting for survival have attuned my senses. I'd felt the air shift behind me alerting me he was near.

"You couldn't if you tried, Connor." I step away from the entrance and begin my journey. Where to, I don't know, but I walk anyway. I have to leave here. The rotten stench of Panda makes me want to vomit. They're close, and always hungry. I move faster through the tall grass, brushing the tips of my fingers through it. Connor follows me, making more noise than necessary. I don't want him near me. Panic rises like flames from my gut as I replay my dream over and over.

How can this be real? He'll get me killed before I find out.

"Kayla, wait! You're going the wrong way!" Connor struggles to keep up as I masterfully navigate my way to the vehicle wreckage. I need to reach the other side.

One of my dads used to call this a "motorway", that the humans before us used it to travel far and wide. Their journeys took mere hours instead of the weeks I take by foot. Four lines of burnt-out vehicles stretch as far as the eye can see. It's beautiful in its own way. Two rows point north, the others pointing south, front to back they line the road.

"Kay, if you don't slow down," A Panda screams, stopping us in our tracks. Shit. With so many places to hide, we won't see it until it attacks.

"Get on the tallest thing here!" I shout the order while clambering up the side of a rotten pole. I need to know how many they are. Splinters stab my hands but don't penetrate through my roughened skin. I reach the top in seconds. Years of practice means I'm adept at climbing. I watch in horror as at least four Panda come pouring out from between cars. One appears out of nowhere right at the side of me, screaming and clawing at the base of the pole to get me. The noise will bring more. I have to kill it. Sliding down the wooden pole, I land on its shoulders. I slam the heel of my boot into its skull, bits of its brain splatter my face. Yuck.

Looking around me, I realise I'm in a suitable spot to pick these fuckers off. Hoping to draw the zombie's attention my way, I cup my hands around my mouth and shout, "Over here! Come get some meat!" Reaching back, I grab the hilt of my katana and draw it out. Just as more than one Panda answers my call, I see Connor sitting on top of a huge vehicle on the opposite side, a shitty smile on his face.

Mother fucker!

The first Panda reaches me. Slashing my blade, I sever an arm. It drops to the ground with a thud. The beast screams its anger and launches its rotting body at me. Practically all bone and small chunks of flesh, its weight isn't enough to take me down. Instead, I swivel on my heel, my hand on its bony shoulder, and send it crashing down. Its protruding bones clatter against the ground. This one's old and weak. Easy kill. I bring the heel of my foot down onto its skull, ending the long years of its torture in a spray of bone and matter.

Two more emerge on my right. These two can't be more than six months old. Their bodies are almost fully intact. One's missing an eye, the gaping hole left behind is oozing. That one climbs onto the top of a vehicle and waits. I cock my head to the side, studying its strange behaviour. Usually, Panda just attack.

Essentially brain dead from the virus, their bodies are on autopilot. Their only goal is to feed. Panda don't have the capacity to think or to attack with efficiency. They just pounce without thought, their decomposing bodies barely able to put up much of a fight. Yet, this one crouches and stares at me while the other rushes head-long at me. It bumps and scrapes itself against the structures on either side of us, leaving behind chunks of skin that flap in the wind. The Panda on top of the car turns towards where Connor's watching. Like a beast, it springs from its crouch. It flies with more grace than many Scraps or Advanced can muster. Roof to roof, it jumps as I watch.

I've never seen a Panda move like that before...

A body crashes into my side, breaking my train of thought. We fall to the ground. I land hard and my blade is knocked from my grasp. Ouch. Twisting, I bring my hands up and push at the Panda's shoulders as it snaps and snarls, attempting to take a chunk out of me. I move one hand to its throat while I snake the other between us to pull a smaller knife from the holster at my thigh, only to find it empty. Damn it! Fuck. Shit.

My fingers sink into rotten flesh and liquid oozes out between them. I gag and dry heave. My vision blurs as my eyes water. The Panda reaches out its arm and just as it's about to slash pointed nails across my face, a deafening roar breaks through the pounding in my ears.

Baby.

The Panda suddenly jerks and is torn from me. Panting and bruised, I sit up just in time to watch Baby tear the zombie's head from its body. Even after all the years killing Panda, the sound of ripping flesh and breaking bone still makes me cringe. As Baby continues to eviscerate the Panda, I push myself off the ground. Picking up my katana and sheathing it at my back, I jump over the aisles of wreckages and make my way to Connor. My hands are slippery with gore and I barely manage to not fall on my face as I slide over hot, rough metal.

When I reach him, I almost lose my mind. There on the tarmac is Connor and the Panda who showed signs of brain function. Its teeth snap inches from Connor's face as he struggles to keep it at arm's length. Without thinking, I pick up a rock and launch it. The stone hits the Panda on the side of its face, not enough to kill it or even break the skin, but enough to hopefully distract it.

As the rock makes contact, the Panda pauses in its attempts to take a bite of the man beneath it. It swings its eyes to me and what I see there is frightening. Cold calculating eyes stare at me. I reach up for my blade, its milky gaze following my hand.

My fingers wrap around the hilt, its eyes flick to mine. It's waiting to see what I do next. That's.... new. And freaky as fuck. Connor rolls the Panda off him. With it beneath him, he punches it in the face over and over. Blood splatters everywhere and the sound of bone crunching reaches my ears. It's then I remember Connor doesn't have a blade. Shit.

I purse my lips and whistle. An almighty roar answers

me. The Panda rolls, taking Connor with him. Its legs are on Connor's arms, pinning him to the earth. My eyes stay fixed on the creature above Connor, unable to comprehend what I'm seeing. The Panda turns to look over his shoulder, into my eyes and then down at Connor who's still trying to push the beast from him by bucking his hips. Connor's has no luck; the creature's bigger and has the advantage.

"Kay! Kill it," Connor grinds out, sounding like he's having trouble breathing. For a moment I just stand here, utterly shocked.

There's something different about this Panda; he isn't even trying to bite Connor now. Bite first, can't ask questions later, that's what they usually do. I'm normally more than happy to end their existence. But as this one watches Baby jump onto the car next to us, my body refuses to move. I stare at my dog with my mouth hanging open.

His flame-like fur is streaked with blood, his sharp teeth are exposed as he growls at the Panda. It's enough distraction for me to shoot my hand out and jam my blade into the Panda's temple.

Its body instantly dies and drops onto Connor. I finally breathe, not realising I was holding my breath.

"Ugh!" He pushes the body off him and rolls over to spit onto the ground. He's lucky it's not crawling with maggots and flies. Been there, ruined that t-shirt. Many, many times.

I grab the Panda by the collar of its shirt and pull as Connor stops heaving to watch. It flops to the side, landing in the dirt. I take a knee at its side and gaze at it, barely aware of the fact that Connor's cursing up a storm about almost being eaten.

The Panda looks fresh. Months old, maybe even weeks.

It has small patches of peeling skin across its arms. I can see an infected bite wound through a rip in its brown cargo pants. Looking around me, I find a twig and use it to expose more of the bite. I've seen thousands just like this, human teeth don't make a wound as you'd think. Our teeth and jaws aren't strong enough to take chunks out of flesh, especially after death, rotten teeth make terrible chompers and tend to just fall out. But we can break the skin and leave behind a whole mess; the result is gnarly. The edges are black and peeling, goo runs from it, dripping onto the ground in blobs. It stinks so bad Connor retches behind me. I breathe through my mouth and try to not taste the funk in front of me.

God, there's no way I'm promised to this bitch. I've spent five minutes with him and already I know there's no way I'm marrying him. We'd be dead if it was up to him to protect us.

"Are you alright, Kay?" Connor's now standing next to me, wiping his bloody fists on his pants.

Am I ok? Is he for real? I drop the stick, stand and place my fists on my hips. "Listen, mate, this ain't gonna work. You're a liability. You'll end up getting me killed."

"I knew you had those Panda beat. I thought you didn't need my help!" Frustration pours from him, his odd coloured eyes boring into mine.

"I didn't," I jerk my chin towards the body on the ground. "But you needed mine. So, if you don't mind," I whistle one sharp call and in a flash, Baby is standing in front of me, growling at Connor, "I'm leaving. You won't follow. Get it?"

Turning, I walk at a fast pace away from him towards the countryside. Baby's mane brushes against me and I lay my hand on top of his head. "Good boy." His fur's sticky with blood and goodness knows what. We need to bathe.

"Kayla, wait!" I hear him running to catch up, but I don't stop. He's dead weight. I won't take care of both of us. He's on his own. I pick up the pace, needing to put distance between us.

"Kay!" His voice is far behind me now and so I break into a run. Baby's feet pound the dirt, kicking up dust in the air behind us. We're leaving dumb-dumb in our dust. The thought has a giggle escaping me. The sound makes me slow down. I can't remember the last time I giggled. I halt. Baby flops his big ass down and cocks his head at me.

"Am I being inhuman, Baby?" I look back at where we came from and there is no sign of Connor.

Has a Panda got him? Mercenaries? Shit. Why do I care? So, he says we're promised, or we knew each other as kids. It's gotta be lies. Even if it was true, a lot of time has passed and I'm not a kid anymore. I don't owe him anything.

I turn back to Baby; his golden eyes hold judgement as he raises his top lip over his teeth. "Don't look at me like that, you dog!" I grumble while kicking at the dirt. "He's dead weight. He'll get us killed." I brush away the cloud of dirt that floats up into the air. "I won't risk you, boy. I won't." I suck my bottom lip between my teeth and bite down. Not hard enough to draw blood but hard enough to make my eyes sting. Shit.

I turn and start running back to where we came from, Baby follows. The sun is high in the sky now, it's hotter than hell out here. Despite this being the UK, the wars messed with the ecosystem, making the country a hotbox most of the time. Winters were nuclear. Temperatures dropped so low, if you stood still for too long you'd freeze on the spot. But most of the time, it's the height of summer.

I see a figure sitting on a boulder up ahead, legs folded in front of him, his head between his knees. Silent on my feet so he doesn't hear my approach, I'm able to stand by his side for a few minutes, silently listening to him grumble and curse himself. He's creative with it. It's so hard to not laugh, I have to bite the inside of my cheek to stop the bubble from working its way up my throat.

"Bloody overpowering, mongo! Why you gotta be so fricking dumb, Con? Way to chap her ass and make her hate you before you've even taken a shit!"

It's not until Baby slides up onto the rock and nudges his giant head against Connor's side, almost knocking him off, that he notices he's no longer alone. His head jerks up and the horrified look on his face makes me burst out laughing. I bend double, huge guffaws coming from me. Falling to my knees as I clutch my middle, I slap the ground while struggling to get a breath. It takes me by surprise and my usual silent approach to being out in the open like this disappears.

"What's so funny, Kay?" Connor's indignant voice pulls me from my fit.

I barely get myself under control enough to say, "Your face!" before I drop to the floor and roll around like Baby does when he's getting belly rubs. I've never seen anyone look so shocked, relieved and scared at the same time.

By the time I've pulled myself together, Baby's snoring softly and Connor stands a good distance from him. He stares at him like he expects my dog to pounce on him and eat him alive. I push myself from the dirt. I've got a stitch in my side and my mouth is dry.

"He's a... a... LION!" I flinch when he screams the word like it should terrify me.

I glance at my boy, bending to stroke his soft face. A lion? No way. Baby's a dog. A big dog, I'll admit. His paws are bigger than my face and his muscles have muscles. "He's a dog." My face aches from laughing so I stretch it out. My jaw creaks and cracks. The silence between us is deafening. "See," I pick up one of his floppy ears then let it go, "dog." As if his ears explain it all.

My mum explained what dogs are, Baby fits the description.

Connor shakes his head, his wide eyes on Baby. I turn and watch as my dog opens his mouth in an enormous yawn, exposing sharp, bloody teeth.

I found Baby when I was just sixteen. Abandoned as a pup and on the brink of death, I'd taken him in and raised him. It was the first time I'd ever loved anything or anyone other than my parents. Baby grew quickly and transformed from the small little pup I'd first taken home. He's colossal. Pure muscle and viciousness. I named him after my favourite song on my device.

"Why are you just sitting here, ain't you got somewhere to be?" I quote what he'd said to me at the spaceship. I don't care what Baby is. He's mine, and I'm his. End of story.

"I..." He lets out a breath. Looking down at his hands, he continues, "I grew up in the wastes, Kay. With you and your family. My dad, he... he didn't want to admit I was his. He was ashamed that I was half his. He sent for me when I turned six. But my mother was a Hand, so we survived for a while. I've lived in the city for fourteen years but I'm not a liability. I'm no longer used to the harshness of these lands, sure, but I've learnt a lot recently. I can take care of myself."

AM I WRONG ABOUT HIM?

Huh. That Panda was different from any other I'd seen, perhaps it was stronger? That's why he couldn't fight it off. Maybe I judged him too quickly?

"Why are you out here?" I spread my hand out to indicate our surroundings. This is no place for someone who's bathed in the lap of luxury for so long. He'd have to prove to me he could handle Panda before I thought him capable. "You need to go back. I can't carry you, Connor. I don't play nice with others."

"I'm here for you, Kayla," he throws at me.

I flinch. For me? "Huh? I'm just a Hand's daughter. A nobody."

"Look at your hair, Kay. You're not a Hand." He rubs the back of his neck. "Listen, we must get you back to the city. I've been searching for you for six months. My father will think..."

"Oh, hell no! I'm not going to the city." We? Nah. Not happening, how'd he even survive six months out here? I almost turn and walk away, but he stops me before I can make a move. His soft warm hand wraps around my wrist. He tugs but I don't pull away or go to him.

"You should let me go, Connor." Baby's snarl punctures my words. I want to throat punch him and throw myself into his arms all in the same moment. It confuses me so much, I end up signalling Baby to stand down, but my knees bend into a slight crouch, ready to pounce. My hand toys with the hilt of my blade behind my back.

He brings his other hand up in surrender, palm out. "Easy, Kay. I mean you no harm. I swear."

Unbidden, a snarl lifts my lip and I growl low in my chest. He lets me go and even though it was what I wanted; I mourn the loss of his heat.

"Please. Let me find us some shelter." He looks around us and realises that's not gonna happen. This area's bare of anything other than nature. He's out of his depth out here. It'll be me who has to take care of us. At that moment, his stomach growls loudly and we both look down at it. I click my fingers and Baby bounds away.

"Come. And be fucking quiet, will you?" I turn, knowing where we can go. "Like a baby elephant!" I scold him. Without acknowledging it, my mind decides we need to take Connor back to the city and get him out of my hair once and for all. Looks like I'm on babysitting duty.

BLAZE
AMELIA K'OLIVER

We walk for miles. Hours pass, but Baby doesn't come back. It'll take time for him to find something for us to eat. As we move, I gather edible flowers, popping them in my mouth to settle my hallow stomach. Connor drags his feet and constantly wipes his hand across his forehead.

"Here." I throw my water skin to him. He barely catches it and I roll my eyes at him. The city's a five-day walk from here. At this rate, it'll take twice that many. Not that I'm going. But Connor is. I'll get him close enough so that nothing can eat him, the book it.

"Thanks, darlin'. It's so fucking hot," he rumbles.

"The aliens take all your supplies?" I ask, venom in my voice.

"Aliens? Those buttholes didn't even leave me with a knife. I'm not usually so...."

"Inept?" I don't allow him to finish.

"Yes." He looks at the ground and swings his foot back

and forth before continuing, "I've learnt a lot out here, Kay. I'm not as skilled as you but I'm not a liability. I swear."

Huh, I wanna believe him but... so far, he's nearly been killed and he's taking up all my supplies. He never stops talking, constantly chatting and being loud. This guy's a fool. But he's the one who saved me from the spaceship, has great reflexes and has survived on his own for six months. So maybe he isn't so bad. Maybe.

We stop when I spot small, green shoots growing from the dirt. I bend to dig at my feet. Score, Tates! I sink to my knees and dig around, looking for more. These babies are amazing. They fill your belly up for hours and mixed with buds and meat, taste amazing.

"Want my help?" He asks as I scoot around, digging for gold. I look up at him with a raised eyebrow. I find myself torn. This time, between swiping his legs from under him or throwing a Tate at his head. He confuses me so much. "Those potatoes are big," he tries again when I don't respond.

I hold the Tate in my hand. It's bigger than my palm. I could eat one whole and be full all night. Nodding, I keep digging. I mean, why not? His help will save my nails from being broken to the quicks. I find a sharp rock so I can stop using my bleeding fingers. The dirt's dry and compact, but a rock makes the job easier. I ignore him, having nothing to say. I tune him out because he keeps trying. He bends down and digs too but comes up empty every time. If it wasn't for me, he would be dead in a single day. Maybe.

BY THE TIME we reach the small shack on the edge of London that I sometimes use on my many travels, I'm about ready to strangle this guy. He talks incessantly, blabbering on about mundane things. I know he's attempting to start a conversation with me or even get to know me better with all his annoying questions, but I blank him out. He won't be around long enough to know me. I'm dropping him off back into the lap of luxury he grew up in, then, I'm a ghost. Gone. Invisible. Outta here. See ya later alligator.

Just as we enter the shack, Baby comes strolling towards us, something dead and delicious in his maw. He trots to me, ignoring our unwanted guest by pushing past him. Baby drops the rabbit next to the small fire pit on the outer wall and curls up on the pile of rags in the corner, his eyes never leaving Connor. I busy myself with preparing the evening meal.

"You build this place, Kay?" Connor asks while looking around the area I only use in emergencies. I shrug one shoulder. "Of course, you did. When we were kids you were always building forts out of scraps." He smiles warmly at some made-up memory. I curl my lip at him. I can't wait to be rid of him and return to my life of solitude.

"When did you last have company?" I bend to rummage through a box of cooking implements in the room's corner. My bowls and pans are made from battered metal sheets, bent and shaped by my own hands. I pick out a deep pan for the Tates and a flat one for the meat.

"Never." I put everything back into the box when I have everything I need. Glancing over my shoulder at Connor as he just stands there, waiting for me to continue. "Start the fire." I look him in the eye, my eyebrow raised in challenge. "You can light a fire, can't you, Connor?" I say, knowing full well he can start a fire. He's irritating me, and I feel snarky. His mouth stretches in a thin line. Putting all the Tates in the deep pan, I head outside to wash them.

There's a large tub to collect rainwater and I dip the pan in it to wash the Tates. I scrub the dirt off each one; they don't taste good with mud on them. Once they're clean, I pour the dirty liquid onto the ground. Adding clean water from the smaller bucket next to me, I head back inside.

I place both pans on the grill over the fire Connor's built. Small but effective, it'll do. He disappears through the front door so I allow myself to relax a little. Returning a few minutes later with an armful of sticks, Connor adds some to the fire. Despite growing up in the city, he can make a decent fire at least. I skin the rabbit just as Connor finishes stoking the flames.

"I've never done that." My head snaps towards him, mouth dropping open in surprise. His dad is the president, so I guess I shouldn't be. They don't need to prepare their own food. I nod because I have no idea what to say. He sits on the floor near me and watches, flinching as I pull out the guts and place them in Baby's bowl. My dog... err... lion, lifts his head and sniffs the air. We eat together, always. Or never.

Soon the shack is filled with the smell of our feast as I add the meat to the Tates. My mouth waters, my stomach growling and gurgling in anticipation. I sit on the bare floor and watch the flames, my mind wandering to times past.

Dancing to the beat my fathers play on upturned barrels as my mother laughs in the lap of one of the visiting mercenaries. Killers for hire, they do the cities' dirty work. Keeping the hands of the rich clean while eliminating those who dare cross them.

Playing coin flip with an errant Mover.

My first kisses. Shared with a group of underground boys.

My mother had encouraged me to choose boyfriends, but I wasn't interested. Boys were stupid. I'd rather explore the city than waste time with lads.

"Kayla." Pulled from my daydreams of happier times, I realise the pan has started to boil over, the liquid sizzles against the flames. I rise and take it from the grill to prepare the bowls of food. Connor watches me, his eyes never leaving me as I move around the shack.

I hadn't wanted to start a relationship, especially with a Mover. Movers are how Hands ship their crops to the city and the Underground. They use wheeled trucks pulled by powerful men using straps. It's a harsh job, but well compensated. They don't stay in the same place for long, meaning relationships are impossible. I still want nothing to do with guys, least of all the guy whose eyes have yet to leave me since we arrived.

"Are you ok, Kayla?" Ignoring Connor, he needs to stop asking me that, I pour the food into two bowls; the Tates and meat mixture is thick and cooked to perfection. I pass one bowl to Connor. "Thanks," he says excitedly.

Baby pads closer and takes his place next to me as I sit on the rug in the middle of the space. Usually, I'd eat half the pan myself, keeping the rest in a plastic tub in my backpack. The one the aliens had stolen from me. I need to find another. But now, I have to share with this guy. Mother fucker. I dig in using my hands to scoop up the edible heaven. They're relatively clean from washing the Tates. Connor watches me with open distaste.

"What the fuck now?" I growl. Man, this guy is annoying as fuck.

"Nothing. I'm sorry. It's just," His eyes flick to my dirty

fingers then to my food. I shrug, not caring that there's dried blood and dirt under my nails.

"Ain't nobody got the spare water to keep their hands clean out here." He nods as if he understands, but, he doesn't because he just looks down at his own hands and winces. Tentatively, he dips two fingers in his bowl, scoops and licks them.

"Hmm, oh God. This is so fucking good," he says around a mouthful of chow. Not too bothered about using his hands anymore, he scoops it up and shoves it into his mouth, moaning around each bite. That's right bitch, chef extraordinaire out here in Panda land.

We eat in relative silence, which is bloody fine by me. The gluttonous sounds of Baby eating his rabbit innards are the only noises to be heard. Several times, Connor seems like he wants to say something to me. His mismatched eyes flick to mine then his mouth opens and closes, like a fish, but he says nothing. Between mouthfuls, I study him. I notice the roots of his hair are lighter than the rest. Intriguing.

He catches me looking and I jump to my feet. Busted. I head outside. The cool night air soothes my soul as I fill my lungs.

If I were a Scrap, I'd be inhaling the Panda virus right now and then I'd be dead on the floor, soon to rise as one of them. Thank god I'm immune to the airborne virus. No one's immune from a bite though. If you're bitten, you're dead within forty-eight hours.

A hand touches my shoulder. Instinctively I grab it. Lifting it over my head, I duck and twist the offending arm behind his back. With more force than necessary, I press Connor against the wooden door frame. "Quit touching me unannounced, Connor. You'll end up dead if you keep that up."

"I'm sorry," he grunts as I press his arm into his back a little harder. "I'm used to touching people! You looked like you needed comforting."

Comforting? Is he for real? "No thanks." I let him go with a shove. Do I look like the type of girl who wants or even needs comforting? Not just no, but hell no.

"Shit." He stands there cradling his arm, rubbing the circulation back into the appendage. A smile on his handsome face like he didn't expect me to do that.

He seems unable to get angry. There's not a single sign he wants to retaliate on his features or his body language. His stance is loose, he's smiling. Huh. Gotta test that out one day.

No! Not much longer and I'll be free of this D-bag. Thank God he's the only one I've been lumbered with.

"I'm not the only one!" he blurts, spittle flies from his mouth and lands on my chest.

I stare down at myself. Ew. Say it, don't spray it, dickweed.

"There are two more." Connor throws his arms in the air and blows out a big breath.

"Two more... what?" I narrow my eyes at him. Did I say that out loud? Losing my mind out here.

"Two more of us. Looking for you." He smiles triumphantly. Well shit. Spank my ass and call me Sally, there are another two motherfuckin' assholes from Tri-City out here looking for little old me? Shucks, I'm flattered. Not.

"They won't last long. I'd bet my katana on them already being dead." He looks at me, his mouth open wide.

Seriously, who sent this peach and two of his friends out here to die?

"We came of our own volition. To find you."

I baulk. His words make my legs turn to jelly. Did I say that out loud? Seriously losing my mind.

"Nope." His smile makes me want to kick his shin.

The fuck? Nah. He's pulling my leg. Has to be.

"I'm not pulling your leg, Kayla. I can read your mind. It's my gift."

Gift? Gift! I wouldn't call that a gift. But hey, who am I to judge if he's crazy? Because clearly, I'm crazy too.

"It's both a curse and a blessing." His words are so sarcastic, I giggle again. Damnit! Why am I laughing like an idiot around this guy? Shaking myself, I stare at him.

"Listen, buddy. I don't know what game you're playing but I want no part of it, ya hear? If you think you can hear voices in your head... you've got issues." I roll my eyes and point my finger to my temple. Mindreader... Riiight. "Now, I'm tired from saving your arse all day. So, if you don't mind ..." I walk back into the small space I call home once in a while and lay down on the rags.

Motherfucker's lost his mind. Although... he replied to things I didn't say out loud. Hmm. Maybe it's true? Fucking Panda are walking corpses, would mind reading be such a stretch? Or maybe I'm crazy and he isn't even here? Maybe I made him up just to torture myself?

I don't take my clothes and shoes off for sleeping, because who undresses in the middle of nowhere when zombies roam the earth? Idiots. That's who.

***

. . .

I don't know how long he stays out there, but it's almost completely dark when Connor walks back in. Closing the door behind him, he pulls the wooden bar across the back, locking us in. He just stands there in the faint light, looking at me. Shit, does he want a medal or what? Ooh, look at the big city boy being brave standing outside in the dark.

"Kayla.,"

"Sleep. Tomorrow we walk faster. Keep up. Or die." I roll over, effectively ending our little chat. Instead of taking the hint as a normal person would, he continues talking.

"I can read your mind, Kay. Only fragments, not full thoughts, yet, that takes time. Bonds need to be built. Me and my brothers, Crowley and Charlie, we've been looking for you all our lives. See, it's not just me you used to know. But them too. We need you, Kayla. We..."

"Shut the fuck up, Connor," I growl and sit up. "I'm not interested in your stories! I didn't know any kids. They're too rare. Put a sock in it and let me sleep. My anger bubbles over, my voice getting louder as I speak. I throw myself back onto the makeshift bed and cover my head with a blanket. Four kids in the same camp? He's having a laugh. Not a chance. The shack goes silent so I let my eyes close. Sleep comes quickly, but the peace I so craved doesn't

"Come catch me, pretty girl!"

"Yea, come catch us!"

"She's mine, Charlie!"

"No, she isn't!" Two boys in front of me start to fight. Tiny fists flying, short legs kicking.

"Simmer the fuck down, lads! Your mothers are trying to draw up the plans. Now, Kay Kay, tell the boys here that you

like them all." One of my dads, Keith, looks at me, humour in his voice and a smirk on his face.

"Nope. I don't like boys! They're smelly!" I run away from them all, needing to be alone. What's wrong with them? Why can't they just leave me alone? I run into a large, sunny room, straight into the arms of my mother. Her long black hair shines in the light, love radiating from her beautiful face.

"Hey, sweetie. What's wrong?"

"Con, Char and Crow are fighting again, Mummy. Why'd you gotta pick those three for?" My childish mind couldn't comprehend the reasons. I knew there were some but didn't understand why.

"Sweet girl, you're all gifted. And together, you'll fix this world. Now, go bond with them, Kay. You'll be together forever."

My dream changes and I'm flying. Pain spreads through my entire body as I land hard on the ground. A flash of light so bright, it burns my eyes, illuminates the world around me. Like blinking, the movie in my head changes once again. This time, a woman stands before me.

The same woman I called Mummy.

"Kay, who am I?"

She points to herself, her face full of hope. Her eyes hold concern as they look down at me, making me feel small. My head hurts. I turn to look around the room. My dads gather around us, much younger than I remember them being, their faces full of fear. "I don't know." At my words, my mum bursts into tears and one of my dads takes her shoulders to lead her away.

Another flash and I'm in Conner's arms.

"I know you don't remember me, Kay Kay, but I love you. I have to go away and I won't be coming back." His boyish body's soft and warm against me. My head's heavily bandaged. It's so dark, I can barely see who it is.

He's ripped from my arms by a tall menacing man whose name I can't quite recall, his face one I can't place. A sob leaves me, and fat tears roll down my cheeks.

My body starts to shake violently, and my eyes burst open, landing on one blue eye, one brown.

"Kay Kay, what the fuck? What's happening?" Blood pounds in my ears so loudly, I can barely hear him. I shake my head to clear my thoughts.

My memory... I lost my memory in an explosion! I push off the floor and stand chest to chest with Connor, we breathe each other's air as he explains.

"That's right, Kayla. They attacked us at your mum's farm. An explosion threw you through the air and your head crashed into a boulder."

So, he can read my mind! Holy shit. What he says can't be true though, can it? I mean, wouldn't someone have told me I'd lost all my memories? "Your dads made everyone swear to never tell you. Because, well," He sighs, his warm breath fans over my face. "Kayla, your brother died in that explosion. And so did one of your chosen." He finishes in a rush.

My brother? My chosen? Oh, this is fubar! I need air! When I rush out the door, the heat of the morning makes me itch all over.   ♦

"I don't... I didn't..." My legs collapse under me and I fall to the floor. Connor tries to catch me but my descent is too swift. My knees meet the dirt, but I don't feel it. Brother?

"Kay, I'm so sorry. But you must believe me when I say the person who did this will pay. We need to reach Tri-City. We're running out of time." His hands on my shoulder. I don't shrug it off. I'm too numb to react. They took my brother from me and then my mother. Could the two things be connected?

"We believe so, sweet face." I look up and watch as his eyes roam the wastelands around us. Overgrown, empty and not a building within sight except the shack at our backs. He sniffs the air; I smell it too. Panda.

"We need to move, Kay. Can you walk?"

I scoff and pluck a bud from a nearby flower. Bringing it to my nose, I breathe its soft scent into my lungs, letting it soothe my soul.

I have no right to cry over a brother I can't remember having, or a promised I didn't want in the first place, but a tear escapes nonetheless.

Connor can read minds. That's ... freaky, but kinda cool.

"I'm not injured, Connor, of course I can walk." I lift my gaze to the sky. The sun is at its highest, which means it's time to move.

I return to the small room to collect our stuff. Our? When did I become, we? Ugh. We walk in utter silence with Connor taking the lead. I amble behind him with Baby at my side, barely aware of my surroundings. For the first time since I was a child, I pay no mind to potential threats. Baby wanders off, constantly in search of something for us to eat and then I'm alone again. He'll be back, but I miss him already.

Despite the lack of sustenance, my body feels alive with energy. Having grown used to the feeling of hunger, I don't even think about the fact it's been a long time since we ate until Connor's stomach growls loudly.

"Baby!" I shout louder than I should out here. But the need to sate our growing hunger overtakes my good sense. Turning back to Connor, I can't help but giggle a little at the look he wears. Confusion, his brows drawn down, and something else. I can't put my finger on what it is, maybe desire? The two emotions warring against each other looks funny. I want to both kiss him and sever his Achilles heel. A smile spreads across his face and I roll my eyes.

It is exhausting to be so confused. Jeez, am I - am I softening towards this fool?

"You remember my brother?" I ask as we continue forward. Baby could take a while to find us something and the leftovers from last night won't feed the three of us. I need something to bulk it up, eating once a day has become my norm. Hunger's my constant companion, but Connor won't be used to it.

His hunger bothers me.

"Yes. You were twins, except his hair was the darkest black." That's interesting. I often wondered why mine was bright blonde. A freak of nature or science, I don't know. My mum wouldn't talk about it, so I stopped asking.

I wonder what life would've been like today if he'd survived? Would we have roamed the wastes together? Perhaps he would've preferred to stay on the farm and maybe I would've followed suit. Would our mother still be alive today if my brother had lived to protect her?

"What was his name?" I focus hard on the ground, pretending to be fascinated as it turns from dry dirt to scorched earth as we skirt around a three-mile crater. Bombs didn't hit the countryside much during the wars, not enough of a population to warrant the attack. But when they hit here, they devastated this place, turning it into a hole in the planet.

"Kyron."

Kayla and Kyron. Mum liked the letter K then, huh? Her husbands', my dads', names all started with K too. Her name was Kathryn. Their names are Keith, Klaud and Kitch. Mum would tell me stories of how she met them. Rescuing her from a sure death, Brutes had caught her while trying to kill someone who'd tried to rape her. They had reached her, their promised, just in time to save her.

At just nineteen, she took them as her own. They set up the Kaleidoscope farm and together fed thousands of Scraps across the UK.

"He was promised to my sister, Albania." He smiles to himself, lost in a memory. "Together they created chaos. My dads would say if those two ruled the lands we would all starve." Shaking his head, he wipes the back of his hand across his face, smearing dirt across his cheek. "Someone kidnapped her shortly after your brother died. We never heard from those who took her. She just vanished."

His face crumples and his bottom lip trembles. Suppressing the instinct to roll my eyes, I reach out a hand and place it on his shoulder. Unknown to me, this must be some sort of social signal because he practically throws himself at me. He wraps his arms around my waist, pulling me towards him in a tight embrace. Awkwardly, I press my chin into his shoulder, my arms hanging loose at my sides.

"There's so much I want to tell you, Kay, but I'm frightened. My brothers will tell it better than I can." I raise an eyebrow at the crack in his voice. He's close to tears and emotional. I've never seen a man act this way. My fathers are gentlemen, patient until the sunset and then they'd disappear along with my mother. It wasn't until I hit my teens that I understood what them disappearing meant. Ew. No one likes to think of their parents that way. That was until they killed her, then my fathers turned wild... like animals.

BLAZE

AMELIA K'OLIVER

The sun beats down on us and Conner gives no indication of letting me go anytime soon. So, I decide to settle into his embrace. Relaxing against him, I lift a hand to rest it on his hip. The material there is rough against my skin. They must drive him nuts walking around all day in this heat. I make a mental note to find him another pair. A softer pair. And a shirt, because his torso is going to get me killed with distraction.

"Kay," he says my name on a moan which shoots to the apex of my thighs. I shift uncomfortably, the foreign feeling confusing me. I'm not a virgin. In the conventional sense, at least. Fifteen and too cocky for my own good, I'd been caught stealing ammo from a mercenary convoy. The farm got attacked by Panda regularly and my family used homemade rifles. Bullets... well, they're scarce. I got caught. The first and last time I let that happen. The guy who'd caught me was young but not as young as I was. Instead of turning me in or simply beating me to death, he raped me. He was shocked to discover I was a girl; he almost kept me for himself. Luckily for me, but definitely not for them, he already had four slaves with him and no patience to teach another. He'd beaten me a little, used my body, then sent me on my way. Scarred, bruised and minus my innocence, but alive. He'd let me leave and I collected the ammo I'd stashed before being caught. I was never the same again.

"Shit, Kayla!" Connor's hand snakes to the base of my hair to wrap around my neck. His other hand cups my face so he can look into my eyes, searching for some semblance of feeling there. Finding nothing, he leans his forehead against mine.

"I'm so sorry, sweet face. I should've been here to protect you from that." Laced with regret and sorrow, his words echo in my mind. Could he have protected me? He seems so ... inept.

"I would've gutted that bastard, Kayla. With my bare hands." He's so earnest and full of passion, I'm half tempted to believe him.

"I took care of it. The next night I followed the convoy. For two weeks, I hunted him. As the memories assault me, I take a sharp breath. As he watches with me, I can almost feel his rage.

It was a cool night. I was able to find Tac's tent by scent alone, even though the moon provided little light. It forever embedded the smell of putrid peaches and rotten corpse in my mind. For the last thirteen nights, I tortured my rapist. I started by stealing the ale his horse carried. Weighted down with the foul stuff, the horse looked at me with appreciation as I poured every drop onto the tent Tac called home as the gaggle of Tri-City mercenaries set up camp.

That night, I set fire to his only shelter, causing white

smoke to plume into the night. The smoke was visible for miles as the flames burned the ale. Panda attacked the camp several times because of it. A small but nice victory. I stood hidden amongst the broken buildings, watching, but taking no joy in the chaos I created. I'd killed several zombies who got too close to Tac. I needed him to survive. I wasn't done with him yet. I wouldn't let a Panda take that away from me.

The next day, I followed on silent feet as the group tore through farms and small shantytowns filled with Hands too old or infirm to work. They pilfered and plundered like thieves in the night, showing no mercy to the vulnerable people. I gave those arseholes no quarter as I moved from shack to shack, barn to barn behind them, slitting throats and stabbing any fucker who dared to prey on the weak. Their blood painted the shantytown by the time I was through. The group's numbers had been cut by half by the end of the night, my blade had dulled and my body ached.

The next night, I decorated Tac's new tent with the innards of his brethren after letting them sit in the scorching sun all day. I could smell the rotting flesh for days, the stench stuck in my nose. He cursed and fought his fellow troops, accusing them of the act. His fury stirred my own. The memory of his weight on me and his dirt-caked hands on my skin fuelled what happened next.

For the next two nights, I filled his new tents with bugs and dead animals. Tac garnered no information as to who was doing these heinous things to him. He took it upon himself to pay two men to stand watch as he lay under a piece of tarpaulin tied between two trees, a bed of rags on the dirt floor for his bed.

The first cracks in his facade appeared.

A few nights later the group took off to the nearest lake

to gather and boil water for their journey, I snuck into their camp. I was small enough to pass as a boy with my wig, no one paid me any mind. I dug a small hole next to his rags, just deep enough to bury a leg up to its ankle. I placed dead leaves over the hole and climbed the tree next to where he would lay. High in the branches, no one could see me, not unless they were looking for me. Hours later he'd returned, drunk, about to rape one of the male slaves, when his foot fell into my trap, snapping his ankle in the most satisfying way, causing him to scream over and over in pure agony. And still, I felt nothing. No relief that he was hurt.

Every other night I created chaos for him. Stealing, setting things on fire, leading him to slowly lose his mind. If I wasn't so broken, it would've been fun to watch.

Only, I was broken, and no matter how I tortured my rapist, I felt no better. Justice for his crimes, not just against me, but also against his slaves, had yet to be exacted. This wasn't enough for me. It wasn't enough for my mum.

On the fourteenth night, I planned to end this. Justice would be mine. Would it fix me? I hoped it would. I'd watched as Tac lost his mind, convinced one of the group was trying to off him. He'd grown paranoid and secluded himself away from the convoy. Sleep deprivation added to his madness. He laid on the mossy floor clutching knives and guns, his ankle bandaged and useless. His black scraggly beard was hacked into, his clothes stained with urine and faeces. Tac couldn't fall any lower than he was at that moment.

As dawn broke that final morning, I set his slaves free. Two women, a young man and one whose age I couldn't determine. They were bloodied, bruised and suffering from near starvation. They stood there, waiting for instructions.

Clearly immune, I sent them to the only place I knew they'd be safe: my family. They wanted to follow me, but I told them I had no plans to form a crew. I was always a lone wolf.

Perched on a branch above my rapist and gripping matching swords, I leapt on him. I planned on taking this slowly. We were out of hearing distance from his fellow mercenaries and I had the opportunity to torture this sumbitch to my heart's content. But something broke inside me the day he'd forced himself upon me. I felt nothing. I didn't have it in me to slice him up the way I'd wanted to.

Screaming, Tac scrambled away from me. He begged and pleaded for his life and it only served to make me more determined. Dropping my swords, I pulled the gun from the holster at my hip and shot Tac in the dick. His wails and screams drew the attention of nearby Panda and I left him to bleed out or be eaten. I didn't stay to see which.

"Fuck! That cunt!" Connor narrows his eyes at me, an emotion I can't decipher on his face. I need to learn more emotions other than pissed-offness.

"I won't touch you, Kayla. Not until you give me express permission. I swear!" His hands drop from my body and he steps away. I almost cry out at the loss of contact and heat. It hadn't felt completely terrible having him hold me as I relived the horrors of my past. I wanted to ask him to hold me and never let go.

Instead, I shrug and glance away, unable to look at the pity in his eyes. At least, I think it's pity.

"Let's move," I say. I turn and walk away. The heat will dehydrate us if we don't find a clean source of water soon. My waterskin is almost empty with us both sipping from it. Now, I'm pouring my heart out to him like we're friends? Why didn't I leave him in that field? What the fuck, Kay?

HOURS LATER, my feet are sore, and my clothes are soaked with sweat. We haven't found a source of water yet and Connor's driving me crazy.

"Kayla, look!" I turn just in time to watch as a deer and her fawn sprint across the blackened ground behind us. "Wow. I haven't seen a deer in forever." I turn towards him; his blue and brown eyes sparkling in the sun. Gravity seems to pull us together, but I resist and keep moving.

We walk in silence again. For reasons unknown to me, I'm the one following Connor now, my thoughts scrambled. I trail behind him, humming my favourite tune from my device. Once it's in your head, you'll never get it out: the one Baby's named after. Shifting my feet across the dirt, time slows to a snail's pace. My throat's so dry, I could start a fire with my tongue.

He's silent as he leads us God knows where. I just hope he knows somewhere with water and we arrive soon before we both start feeling the effects of the heat.

"You know where we're going, Connor?" My words make him jump. He was lost in his thoughts. His mismatched eyes meet my blue ones and my breath leaves me. I know this look, or something similar.

Fear.

"Where?" I spin in a circle, trying to find what danger he's seen or heard. I see it. There in the tree line is a mountain of a man.

"Crow," Connor mumbles as I squint my eyes to get a better look at the potential threat.

His dark hair's cropped close to his scalp and tattoos

peeking out from under the rolled-up sleeves of his black shirt, too far away for me to see the details. Muscled arms and broad shoulders take up the space between two oak trees. Impeccably clean black pants strain over thick thighs. He's so out of place in the wastes that if I didn't know better, I'd swear he just walked out of a picture.

"Crowley," Connor shouts like the idiot he is. Even if he knows this hunk, I mean guy, it's foolish to scream like that so close to the trees. Who knows what's lurking beyond the trunks? As the mountain man stalks towards us, Connor and I move too. We close the distance in no time. Meeting in the middle, the two guys throw their arms around each other in an embrace. I glance around awkwardly holding my katana, seconds away from calling for Baby. The show of affection has me looking down at the ground, kicking at the dirt.

"Crow, I found her! This," my head flicks up, eyes locking onto dark green ones, "is Kayla!" Crowley's eyes roam my body from head to toe, taking in my dirty wig, face and clothes. He wrinkles his nose. Rude.

"Kayla isn't a boy, Connor." Yeah, look again, big guy. With my small stature and the wig, I'm easily mistaken for a male. Which is the whole idea.

"It's a wig, Crow. Here." Connor starts to reach up towards my head, but when my eyes flick to his hand he stops short and raises them in the air. "Sorry!" His face crumples as he retreats a little. "It's ok, Kayla. He's my brother."

"So?" I scowl at him. Brother or not I don't know him from a stick.

"You can trust him. He knows you too, remember?" I squint my eyes at the man before me, trying to get a read on him. His arms are folded across his broad chest, but he seems relaxed. I see no weapon. It's foolish and good news for me. I reach up and push back my short black wig, revealing a small patch of my golden hair.

"Shit." The look on the new guy's face tells me he wasn't expecting that. But recognition dances in his eyes. "Kayla?"

"Yup, that's my name. Listen, guys." My eyes scan the trees. The sun's already going down, we've got maybe two or three hours of daylight left. We need to find food, water and a place to lay our heads. "I need supplies." I look at the brawny man's green eyes "Do you have any water? Give me some and I'll be on my way." My voice is croaky with thirst.

"Yes. And shelter. We've been waiting." He spins on his heel and walks back into the forest. Turning to Connor, I raise an eyebrow in question.

"You'll see. You'll see." I was expecting to see Baby on the horizon but found nothing. My feet follow Crowley as Connor strolls by my side. I'll get some water and then ghost.

We weave through the copse, dodging branches and fallen trees. None of us says anything, but Connor and Crowley share a lot of knowing looks. If I didn't know better, I'd say they were having unspoken conversations. A few metres ahead is a clearing and as we enter, all the air in my lungs comes rushing out of me and I almost fall to the floor.

The trees surrounding the area have been felled, or rather torn from the ground if the fresh mounds of earth are anything to go by. In the centre is a large fire. Heat radiates to where I stand. To one side, the tree trunks have been sawn and chopped, fashioned into benches and a table. On the other side, a man with long golden hair stands in front of a pure white building type thing. My mind fails to come up with an explanation as I stare open-mouthed.

Oh, my God. His hair!

"It's called a Campo. A pop-up mobile home. One of Charlie's inventions." Connor gestures to the guy with the hair when he says Charlie. Damn, I have envy for this guy's hair. It's past shoulder-length, wavy, frizz-free and so shiny the sun glancing off it makes me squint. My hand unconsciously goes to my bound hair. I haven't washed it in weeks. It's too dangerous to take off my wig. I'm forever paranoid about being seen.

Connor strolls over to Charlie and they hug for a long period. The feeling of Crowley's eyes on me has me turning to face him.

"What?" I bark, not knowing how to respond to all this newness. He shakes his head, his eyes not leaving mine.

"I can't believe you're here, Kayla. We've-"

"Not now, Crow. Let's get some food and drink, then we can discuss things with our guest," Charlie says. Without even a glance at me, he breaks away from Connor and enters the Campo, leaving me with Connor and Crowley. The hairs rise on the back of my neck as both their eyes lock onto me.

"Shall we?" Crowley asks. Turning to the mountain man, I nod and move to the tree benches, perching on the end of one of the thick trunks. They exchange more looks and I lose my temper.

"What the fuck is happening here? What is that?" I jab my finger towards the white monstrosity Charlie disappeared into. "You two are freaking me out with the looks. Are you aliens?" I drag a breath between my chapped lips. "Spill the beans before I leave." I glance from Connor to Crowley as I speak. Their faces are masks of emotions that change so fast, I can't keep up. Crowley speaks first.

"Connor, Charlie and I are, for lack of a better word... yours," Crowley answers so casually, it takes a second to sink in. My mouth gapes and my eyes widen. Mine? Like, for keeps? I giggle inside my head. Connor barely conceals his chuckle, joining me in the madness. He continues, ignoring the fact that my face displays how funny I find this situation. "That," he hooks a thumb over his shoulder. "Is home base. Erected eight weeks ago when we landed in this Godforsaken wasteland."

Charlie exits the - home base - as Crowley finishes speaking. He has two large platters covered with a dome of metal in his hands which he places on the rough sawn table. Lifting the lids, he reveals a feast upon each. Meat, vegetables and Tates on one; bread, seeds and fruit on the other.

Covertly, I pinch my leg under the table. My flinch makes the three guys look at me with concern. This can't be real. That food... I've never seen so much in one place before. Despite growing up on a farm, food was still scarce. Over ninety per cent of our crops were sold or given away. The meagre leftovers had to feed the five of us.

My mouth waters and my stomach rumbles. Unable to stop myself, my hand shoots forward and snatches up a roll. I bite a chunk out of it before I can even blink. My eyes roll back in my head as my mouth has a party around the fresh bread. I haven't had bread in years. Flour was too difficult for farmers to grind; they send the wheat whole to the city to turn into flour. All three men sit and watch me devour the roll and wash it down with cool water. Actual real cool water. Not even warm. How'd they keep it cool? Between bites, I pop seeds into my mouth, the satisfying crunch drawing moans from me. Every time I look up, their eyes flick away from me, pretending to look at anything other than the skin and bones girl in front of them eating like an animal.

I eat from the platters until I can't fit anymore in my stomach, and then I unbutton my pants and scarf down another roll. I don't care if it's unladylike, shovelling food into my mouth like this. I'm way beyond caring. When you're presented with food only featured in your dreams, you dive in headfirst, coming up for air only when absolutely necessary.

"More water?" I look up into Charlie's brown eyes and swallow the last piece of bread. I nod as I watch him. Charlie's around six feet and has narrow hips covered in blue jeans with holes in the knees, but they're not old. His black t-shirt is clean and hole-free. His face is kinda long, with a scar running down the side of his cheek. It looks like a burn mark if the spider leg-like marks coming from it are anything to go by. He's handsome, but not as built as the other two. He stands to fetch more water and I can't help but watch. His bubble butt makes my mouth water. Despite being thinner than the other two, he looks strong. Good looking, too.

"Spent much time around men, Kay?" My eyes snap to Crowley's grass-green eyes. The colour keeps changing and I can't settle on what colour they are.

"Nope. Ugh, I'm so full." I lean back and pat my round belly. That last roll is calling me." They both laugh, their eyes twinkling with some feeling, making me frown. I watch them wearily as I munch on the last bit of bread. Charlie comes back, places the full pitcher in front of me, then sits down. His handsome face breaks out in a huge smile as he looks at me. Something stirs in my belly as our eyes meet. He seems familiar in ways that can't be possible.

"You and Char had a special bond when we were kids," Connor says, reading my thoughts. This could get dangerous. My cheeks heat as I remember the things I've been thinking on the way here.

"Picture a wall. Solid, made of stone, and I won't be able to hear you." My eyes flick to his brown and blue ones. He doesn't look like he's joking, his face is set in a non-expression. Closing my eyes, I concentrate on forming a wall inside my mind. But all I can picture is the three men in front of me naked. My eyes pop open as an image of me naked between them is projected into my mind's eye. I gasp.

"Sorry. I didn't mean to... well..." Connor stutters around the words. Embarrassed?

"Did you do that?" I ask with narrowed eyes.

"Yeah, sorry 'bout that. I can project, but I have little control." Connor says with his eyes on the table.

Crowley pipes up, "Yeah, he can project many things into your mind."

I jump from my seat. "Did you project those dreams?" My hand reaches for my sword, my plan to sever his head from his body.

"No!" Connor stands too, his hands out in front of him in surrender. "I can't do that. Only when you're awake and allow me into your mind, I swear." The earnest look on his face has me letting my blade slide back into its sheath. "I wouldn't do that. I haven't done that. I swear to you, Kayla."

"It's true. He can't change or add memories." My head whips to Crowley. His eyes bore into mine. Thick black eyebrows grace his broad forehead. Light lashes frame his green eyes. His lips are kissable. Plump, but stretched out in a thin line. I study him as he drinks me in.

His eyes linger on the scar above my eye. A building fell on me around four years ago. My head cracked open and the scar never faded. Luckily, I made it to the farm before I passed out, otherwise, I'd have been Panda food.

"Lucky to be alive," Connor mumbles, almost to himself. We all shoot him confused looks. I'm sure mine has more than a little pissed-off-ness. Is that a word? It is now.

"So, gifts huh? Care to explain?" I ask. The three men before me shift in their seats. Their eyes cast around the area, leading me to think they're uncomfortable talking about it. I sigh. I don't have patience for games. None of this can be real. I'll humour them until I leave, then I'll go back to Old Yella. Hopefully with a stash of food.

"As you know, Connor can read thoughts, send images and his own thoughts into others' minds. Me? I'm - I'm a Brute." I gasp at Crowley's confession. He sure isn't shaped like a Brute. Usually, they're very tall. Crowley's tall, but not over the seven feet Brutes get to. Their arms and legs are trunk-like with muscle, and while Crowley is muscled, he isn't overly so. Not in the way you may think. I'm as strong as them, but I'm less noticeable. I blend in"

I eye him, checking out the straining material across his biceps. His ink looks like the same design as the tattoos on Connor's arms. I turn to Charlie, the shortest of the three of them. His golden hair and brown eyes make him appear angel-like. White lashes frame his unusual eyes. Cleanly shaven, he looks younger than he is. I turn to Connor and take him in, wetting my lips. All three of them are gorgeous.

His eyes draw me in. The blue of his right eye is stark

against his dark lashes. His left brown eye is earthy. Both sparkle in the fading light. Almond-shaped and large, they appeal to me in ways I never thought eyes could. His nose fits perfectly on his handsome face. The shadow of facial hair is a little wilder than when I first met him just a couple of days ago. Lighter than the hair on his head, it looks soft. I stop myself from reaching out to check.

BLAZE
AMELIA K'OLIVER

I frown at Crowley. His wild, black hair sticks up at all angles; he has that just rolled out of bed look popular in magazines before the wars, reminding me again of those precious magazines of my mums. God, I miss her.

Did he style it that way? Or does he just let it be, falling as it may? He frowns back at me, but it doesn't stop me from staring. His strong brows pull down over his emerald green eyes.

"What do you see, Kay?" Crowley asks.

I blink out of my reverie. Each of them is so different, yet so similar. I can't put my finger on what makes them seem... so alike. "I don't know," I answer Crowley's question. I don't know what I'm feeling. Curiosity? Lust? I've never lusted before. Do I... want them?

A roar echoes around the trees surrounding us. The guys all jump to their feet. Me? I sit and sip my water. It's getting cold. I run my hands down my arms as Baby makes his presence known by roaring loudly, repeatedly.

"Con, get Kayla into home base. Charlie with me." Crowley sounds semi panicked. I giggle, the sound shocking two of them enough they turn to face me, freezing mid-step.

"Oh God, is she mad? Did the wastes break her mind?" Charlie's words make me tut. Mad? As a hatter, my mother used to say.

"No. She just knows what that is." Connor's expression is what I now realise is his mind communication face. All frowny and serious. He's telling the other two I have a lion as a dog, no doubt

"No fucking way," Crowley and Charlie say at the same time. Turning as one, which is freaky as fuck, they both look to Baby at the same time. Standing tall and proud, my boy prowls towards them. His teeth showing, the look of murder in his golden eyes.

"The fuck, man? Should we kill it?" I jump to my feet at Charlie's words.

I close the distance between us quicker than should be possible. Nose to nose, I say, "You touch one hair on his head, and I will skin you alive. Ya hear?" Charlie swallows audibly as Baby presses against my hip, his energy wrapping around me. I feel protectiveness roll from him in waves.

"Okay! Okay. Back off guys. That thing has no issues ripping heads off for Kayla. I've seen it." Connor says.

I move my eyes from Charlie's face to look at Connor. That's right lads, me and Baby take no shit, give no quarter to no mother fucker.

The two men back away. Crowley frowns, Charlie lifts his hands up in defeat. Again, I giggle. Five minutes with three gorgeous men and I've lost my mind.

"Down boy." I pat Baby's head and he sits on his butt.

"He won't harm you unless I tell him to, or you try to hurt me. I'd suggest you don't think about hurting either of us," I say loud enough for the three of them to hear. Mistakes could cost lives. I need to make sure they know we don't mess around when it comes to each other's safety.

***

BABY and I sit at the edge of the man-made (Crowley made) clearing. Connor and Charlie disappeared around an hour ago. I didn't question where they went. It's none of my business. Crowley circles the perimeter, passing me several times without so much as looking at Baby or me. Which is just fine and dandy with me. They left me with lots of questions. I needed to be alone. They all seem to respect that. I spent most of my life alone, just Baby and I for the last few. Idle chit-chat and small talk are just not my forte. So, I sit and stare out into the trees.

A state-of-the-art alarm system laced between the surrounding trees ensures we won't be caught unaware should Panda stumble upon our little camp. Our? Eek. I want to go back to me, myself and I. All this *we* bullshit unnerves me.

On his third pass, Crowley stops a few feet from me, arms crossed over his broad chest, he stares at Baby laying in the grass cleaning his fur of blood and gore.

"He won't bite," I whisper. Crowley's eyes flick to mine, a dark brow raised. "Baby," I coo. The animal rolls over, his side hitting my hip, legs in the air as he begs for tummy rubs. I oblige and scratch the thick patch of fur between his front legs. My dog's so soft, yet vicious. I love him with every ounce of my useless heart. Crowley sits at my other side, opposite to where Baby lays. Why are these guys so scared of a dog? Baby's protected me for years, never once hurting me. I roll my eyes and settle against the tree at my back.

"So..." Crowley starts. "A lion, huh? That's.... different."

"Yup. Lion. Dog. Four legs and a tail. That's my Baby," I answer. Different? Maybe.

"Badass." He sounds impressed.

"I didn't choose him. He chose me. But yeah... badass," I watch Baby peel the bark off a tree stump with his claws. A solitary bird chirps a song above us. I let myself smile a little at the beautiful sound.

"I remember that smile. You loved music when we were kids," he says fondly.

Seems everyone remembers me, but me. I sit up and squint my eyes at the mountain attempting to start a conversation with me. "Yeah, so about that. What happened?"

He leans back on one arm. "Connor's dad sent his men to bring him back to the city. He needed an heir." He shrugs his muscled shoulder; I barely stop myself from licking my lips. "Took the three of us with him. Your parents fought back. So did ours. Things got out of control and a grenade was thrown."

Damn. Grenade? What the fuck.

"We tried to come back sooner, Kayla," Our eyes lock. I see regret in them. I wonder what mine holds. "But it was impossible until you turned twenty."

The legal age of adulthood was twenty. At that age, you could marry, have children and choose as many partners as you wish. My mother chose three. Her mother before her had nine. How she managed nine men was beyond me. I don't even want one, do I? Out of nowhere, Crowley produces the thickest magazine I've ever seen.

"I found this book several years ago." My crew are on scavenger duties. I remember you loved to read when we were kids. So, when I saw it, I kept it." His face gives nothing away, blank of all emotions.

Book? Like the ones on my device? Wow. Did he keep this for years, hoping to find me one day and give it to me?

Something foreign stirs in my chest. Something unsettling. I run my hand over the cover. The picture reminds me of the wastes I call home with its burnt trees. A simple design, yet I'm drawn to it, even without knowing what it's about. Day Zero. It's beautiful despite all its flaws. The edges have been nibbled on and the pages are crinkled. It's one I've never read before. My device only has a handful of books. I can't wait to read it. I finally drag my eyes from my new pretty to stare into Crowley's. His bright green eyes are darker in the moonlight. They hold some kind of emotion I don't have a name for. I love my new book.

"Thank you." My voice is soft and small. A smile spreads across his face as he stands and walks away. I hug the book to my chest. I can muster feelings for a book, but not a man? Perhaps I'm more broken than I realised.

I just want to murder the man that killed my mum. These three are in my way. Now Connor's with the others, I really should leave, but I can't seem to make myself do it. Baby wanders over to me and in true Baby style, throws himself onto the ground like his legs are suddenly gone. "Hey, handsome." I run my fingers through his fur, the motion soothing. "So, lion huh?" He lifts his golden eyes to me and lets out a small whine. "This is fucked up, boy." I tickle his ear and his back paw comes up and bats the air. His tickly spot. "Those men?" I jerk my head to the side, indicating the camp behind us. "They say I'm theirs. That they have these freaky powers." My body slumps a little as I relax. Baby puts his head on my knee, and I rest my forehead against the top of his. It can't be right though. Can it? I mean... this isn't a book. Special powers can't be real.

Looking around to make sure nobody is near; I take my device out of the pocket on my thigh and turn it on. The photo that greets me lifts my spirits. It's Baby and me after we'd just taken down a deer. Our faces are gaunt and bloody but we're smiling so broadly, that all of our teeth are showing. How a dog, I mean lion, can smile is beyond me. But he is. His teeth were bloody with bits of fur caught in them. We feasted on that carcass for months. I smoked it and then dried it out in a shack at my mother's farm. She'd been so proud of me, her love pouring out of her and I soaked it up. Unlocking the screen, I pull up the gallery and scroll through the photos I took since finding this thing. Mum said it was a mobile phone, but I'd never heard of it. Apparently, you could call people on it. And send textual? Textile? Something like that.

"It's very old Kayla, be careful with it. It could be the last working one on the planet."

My mum made sure no one outside of our family saw it. They'd take it from me, then I'd have to kill them. After I was raped, and I killed Tac, my mum said; I changed. I never told her what happened, but my trips away from the farm got longer and longer. She probably guessed, but she never seemed to be happy. Now I know why.

My brother's death.

Tears sting my eyes as I flick through pictures of my mum, my dads and the farm. I close it down and open the reading thing. There are books on my device, I'd read them a million times over, never getting bored with the stories.

Seven by the same person. Magic books. All set in the same school, each story a different year as they grew older. Fascinating. The ginger one's my favourite. He's a little bit of an idiot but loveable, nonetheless.

One of the other books has a bright purple cover, the redhead on it shining on the background with her back turned to us. Never Ever. The Queen of the sea was a girl who thought she was a human. Her men had various powers. Lots of sex. Oh my, the sex. I'm pretty sure there should be another because it ends without the full story being told. I wonder what happened to that girl? And was she indeed pregnant?

The last one with its black background and a hand holding an apple is about a normal girl who goes to live with her father where she meets several supernatural characters including the love interest, Edward, who's a vampire. She befriends a werewolf too. No sex in this one. Unfortunately, danger follows when rogue vampires become interested in her. Again, I'm pretty sure there was another because it ends oddly.

Just as it starts up and words appear on the screen, a twig snaps to my left and I drop the device like it's on fire.

"Kayla, you ok doll?" It's Charlie. I shuffle my foot until my holey boot is covering the screen.

"Yes." Clearing my throat, I fake an itch on my ankle and slip the device into the side of my old leather boot.

"Can I sit with you? Connor and Crowley are going to drag some water back for boiling," Charlie says with a ghost of a smile.

"There's a lake near here?" Please say yes.

"Yup. It's not big..." Before he finishes, I'm on my feet.

"Which way?" I ask, hopping from foot to foot, my eyes wide.

"Err... I'll take you." He frowns but I take no notice. Bloody hell! Water!

I FOLLOW Charlie through the trees in silence. He, however, won't shut up. Not hearing a word he says, I watch his hair blow in the slight breeze as the moonlight makes it appear white. It's so dark I can barely see where I'm going, but my senses are well-honed from so many years living in the Wastes on my own. I make it to the water without breaking anything or falling. When we get there, Connor and Crowley are standing in the small river. The black and silver liquid reaches to their hips, their torsos are bare to the moonlight.

My mouth hangs open, catching flies. Imaginary drool running down my chin as the faint moonlight highlights the ridges of their abs. Oh, fuck me. Crowley is using some sort of pan to scoop water and pour it over his head. Droplets run down his tattooed chest as he shifts, exposing two hollows that run down either side of his stomach. My eyes follow their direction to a patch of hair. A gasp leaves my mouth before I can stop it, making all three men look at me.

Ground... take me now.

"Kayla..." someone says. I'm not sure who since my heartbeat is loud in my ears, drowning out all noise. My mouth goes dry. I don't even blink as Crowley wades out of the river towards me. With his eyes on mine, he makes no move to hide his body. I lick my lips as he steps onto dry land, my eyes roaming his body without my permission.

"Like what you see, Kay?" Huh? Did he say something? I can't... His dick... My thighs clench. Blood roars inside my head. Unable to swallow, I try to speak. What comes out is a little squeak. The smile on his face gets bigger. Thick, long, wet. The veins on it are like snakes running down its length. Huge. The sight of it makes my pussy clench. He'd tear me in two with that thing! Nah ah, that's too big to fit in here.

"Are you ok, sweetie?" Charlie asks.

I peel my eyes away from Crowley's enormous cock to look Charlie in the eye. His long golden hair catches the moonlight, drawing my gaze away from the mountain man's third leg and reminding me the wig is still on my head; itchy, dirty.

"Take it off, sweet face." I turn to Connor, only to be met with his naked body. My knees nearly buckle. "We don't bite," he says with a lopsided grin. The hard ridges of his body do things to mine that I can't explain or put a name to. The designs on his arms glint with wetness, his nipples are hard. He's hair-free. How does he do that? I want to lick every inch of him.

"Not hard, anyway," Crowley adds. Damn. These two are so comfortable with their bodies, standing before me naked doesn't seem to faze them. I flick my eyes down to Connor's cock, immediately wishing I hadn't. A moan forces its way out of my lips as I stare at his huge appendage. Just as I'm about to take a step towards the men in front of me, images of Tac slash through my mind. I cringe. My arousal darts away like a spooked bird.

Charlie brings me back to reality.

"Take the wig off Kayla. Wash your hair while you can, here." He holds his hand out to me, a square block of white in the palm. "It's soap." Huh? My mum makes - made - this flaky powder stuff that smelled like acid when I was little that she called soap. It didn't look like this thing. I try to reach out for it but my hand is shaking, so I push it behind my back.

I remind myself I'm no longer that young girl. Tac can't hurt me, or anyone else, ever again. If these three guys think they can take advantage of me, not only will Baby tear them to pieces but I'll chop off their dicks and feed them to the Panda while they watch.

"Smell it, Kay. It's good." To punctuate his words, Charlie sniffs the block, hums low in his throat then thrusts it towards me. Hesitantly, I reach up to my wig with one hand and take the soap with the other. I bring it to my nose and without even having to draw in a big breath like Charlie did, I can smell something sweet. That's all I need to whip off my wig and shake out my golden hair.

It comes to my waist in loose waves from being tied up so tight all the time. It's greasy and dirty. It looks nothing like Charlie's. I run my fingers through it only to get them caught several times.

"We'll leave you alone Kay. Shout if you need us," Charlie says as I open my eyes, not even realising I'd closed them when my locks were set free. Fear rolls in my stomach. No one other than my parents has seen my hair, at least not that I remember.

"Yes, shout if you need anything, Kay." Crowley walks past me, then Connor behind him. My eyes watch as their cocks bounce against their thighs. I swallow thickly as they leave, a fully dressed Charlie behind them.

Looking at the soap in my hand, I make a decision. I'm not weak; I have the power here. It's mine, and I own it. I won't allow what that monster did to me to colour my future. I bend and peel off my boots, untying the rope on one and slipping it off, my device drops into the boot. The other one is tied with a piece of wire. I wrapped my black socks in plastic to keep them dry. I take them off with the knitted material and shove them into the boots, too.

I look around me, making sure no one hides in the trees. Even if they were, I couldn't see them in the faint light. I sniff the air like Baby does, and I can't smell any Panda. Unlatching the wire holding my pants up, I let them fall from my hips, my holey knickers follow. I roll them up and place them on top of my shoes, then remove my strappy top and jumper at the same time.

When I am bare, I look at my body for the first time in a while. Bruises are dotted here and there. My skin's pale, dirty and marred with scratches and scars. Life in the Wastes isn't for the faint-hearted. I can't help but wonder how Connor survived, but then again, I think I've been wrong about him. I run my hands over my ribs, the protruding bones making me wince. I could count them if I was so inclined. Food's scarce out in the Wastes. The condition of my body makes that obvious.

Walking into the cold refreshing water, I take my time submerging myself. I use the soap bar to scrape off months of dirt, dried blood and grime, washing until my skin's red.

"Kayla!" Up to my neck in the river, the sound of my name being called makes me slip on the rocks under my feet. I plunge into the inky blackness. Large bodies of water are so rare that unless you're camped right next to one, there just isn't a need to learn how to swim. Mum's farm was close to water, but it wasn't deep or clean enough to swim in, so I'd never learnt. My head goes under and I panic. I kick and flail, my arms pinwheeling as I sink further. My body is pulled deeper into the expanse of water like a leaf on the current. Surrounded by darkness, my mind can't comprehend what's happening. Instead of my brain telling my body to fight to the surface, it goes limp. I drift further into the depths of my watery grave. The urge to draw in a lungful of air takes over, and my mouth opens against my will, allowing water to rush in. Twitching several times my body jerks, my eyes feel like lead. I close them and my world blinks out.

BLAZE
AMELIA K'OLIVER

"Kayla! Fuck!"

Where am I? Is this the hell my mother taught me about? Cold, so cold.

"Doll, breathe, please."

The voice sounds like it's coming from miles away. I feel like I'm being dragged across sharp rocks and broken metal. The skin of my arse screams in pain as another sharp rock slices me. Pressure on my chest forces air into my lungs, soft plump lips cover my own. I realise I'm being kissed. Instinct takes over. Coughing the liquid from my body, I sit upright, aiming my forehead into the face of my assailant. Connecting soundly, I reach out, taking hold of a hand, twisting it while I stand. I throw the mother fucker touching me through the air in a circle, letting go so he lands on his back in the shallow water.

"Umph," a masculine voice sounds. Water splashes me in the face, making me open my eyes. When I do, it's to see Charlie clutching his stomach with one arm, the other cupping his nose, gasping for air.

"Shit, Charlie!" I bend down next to him. There's nothing I can do to help him. The air's been knocked out of his body. He'll recover and I see no blood, so I didn't bust his nose.

"Ugh, god, Kayla. That was," his face scrunches up in pain. "A badass move, Doll," he says between gasping breaths.

"I felt your lips on mine. I... I panicked." He seems able to breathe better now as he pushes off the rocks and sits up. I move back a little to give him space. His eyes drink me in, and I remember I almost died. "You... you saved me?" Why would he save me? He doesn't owe me anything. Soon he'll go back to the city. He'll be safe and well-fed, and I'll be a terrible memory.

"Yes, you were drowning. I was trying to force the water from your lungs and replace it with air." He laughs while dragging out of his face. Drawing up a leg, he rests an elbow on his knee, his head in his hand. "Damn near knocked me out, Doll. Who taught you that?"

"My Dad, Klaud. When I started to roam the wastes as a kid someone caught once me or twice. He said I needed to learn how to take down a grown man." My eyebrows pull down. Why am I telling him this? "Anyway... thanks for saving me," I say awkwardly. Possibly the first time I've ever thanked anyone other than my parents. The words feel foreign on my tongue.

It's then I see where he's looking. I'm about to punch him in the throat when he moves them back up.

"Sorry! I'm not... I'm not looking where you think I am. I swear!" He holds his hands in front of him as fury spreads across my face, heating my cheeks. I drop one hand to cover between my legs, the other I wrap around my flat chest.

"That mark on your stomach, next to your belly button." I look down at the scar he mentions. It's as long as my small finger, thin and white. The edges are jagged and raised. I do not know how I got that one, I have so many it's impossible to keep track.

"I did that." His head dips, looking at his bare feet in the water. "We were playing chase with sticks, pretending they were swords. I raced around the barn and so did you. We crashed into each other and my stick jabbed you. Man," His handsome face splits in a huge smile, "your mum ripped me a new one, Kay. "Hurt my daughter and pay!" She screamed so loud, my dad heard her at the other end of the field." He shakes his head and drops his hands onto his knees as I watch him relive a past I can't remember.

"Your mum was fiercely protective of you and Ky. Black and Gold, that's what she called you," Charlie says.

My heartbeat speeds up. Kay and Ky. Black and Gold. Blonde and black. My head swims, so I sit crossed legged in the water in front of Charlie, no longer concerned with my nakedness. The water's deep enough that it obscures between my legs, so I draw my knees up under my chin to hide my tiny breasts. Charlie gets as comfortable as possible and peels his shirt from his body, revealing scars across his chest.

Of its own volition, my hand reaches out and my fingertips gently run across his puckered skin. He looks down and his hand comes up to cover mine.

"The explosion." Charlie's voice cracks and something inside me pings. I press my knees harder into my chest to quell the feeling building there. Even though I shouldn't, I feel safe with Charlie. "I wasn't far from Ky when it went off. A homemade grenade my dad said." His eyes shine with unshed tears that sparkle in the moonlight. Sucking my bottom lip between my teeth, I bite down hard enough to taste blood. I look out at the water as he continues.

"Ky and I were playing, you were with Connor and Crowley near the barn. Kayla." My name on his lips makes me turn to look into his eyes.

"Kyron passed instantly, he didn't feel any pain or suffer." Relief courses through me. At least he didn't suffer. "I took shrapnel to the chest, some to the face." His fingers trace the raised edges of the scars slashed across his otherwise perfect skin. My eyes follow his actions. My mind tries to imagine what it must have looked like when it happened.

"How did you survive that? It must've been close." A wound like that on his chest in the Wastes is a death sentence.

"Connor's dad. He took us to the city. We were only meant to recover there. But when Con and Crow got better, he told us we were to stay there." He shakes his head sadly. "None of us wanted to stay. You hit your head and couldn't remember any of us. Your mother was a mess. Mr Keeper, he brainwashed us all, Kay. We wanted to come back to you." He takes my chin between his thumb and forefinger. "We missed you." Closing the gap between us, his bare chest touches my knees. "I missed you." Just as our lips meet, Baby jumps into the water, splashing us both.

"Baby!" I scold him. We move apart, the moment lost.

"Let me wash your hair, Doll, turn around." Shocked, and more than a little confused, I turn. Shocked because no one's ever taken care of me like this before, except mum. I'm confused because I want Charlie to do it. With my back to him, I spread my legs out in front of me, washing my legs again as he pours water over the length of my dirty hair.

"Pass me the soap, oh wait." His hands disappear, I hear him splash out of the river. Turning to watch as he rummages in a bag on the bank, I frown.

"What's that?" I ask as he settles behind me again. I caught glimpses, but I don't know what it is.

"A brush. It'll get the knots out of your hair." Huh?

"Brush," I say, testing the word. Usually, I just run my fingers through it until it's a little more manageable, then tie it back with a bit of cable and shove my wig over the top.

Charlie works for a long time, washing and then rinsing over and over until the strands squeak with cleanliness. I relax my body; his motions make my eyelids heavy. It feels nice to be touched like this after so long without human contact. Although I'm naked, Charlie makes no move to touch me sexually. Which probably saves his life.

"There," he says softly, pulling me out of my trance. I reach up to feel he's braided my hair down my back. Much like my mother used to do when I was little, so the wig sat flat on my head. I couldn't master it, so I just scrunched it up and tied it. "Beautiful," I lean back a little and he moves forward. His arms come around my waist, my back to his chest. Letting my head fall back onto his shoulder, I draw in a big breath.

I own the power, it's mine.

"Thank you." I feel more relaxed than I've been in, well, forever.

"You're welcome, Doll." He rests his chin on my shoulder, his lips next to my ear "You would let me play with it for hours when we were kids. You'd braid mine, and I'd do yours." Humour laces his voice. "The other two would poke fun at my girly hair." The breath leaving his mouth tickles my ear. "But you never did."

"I like it, Charlie," I breathe. For reasons unknown to me, I feel more relaxed and safer in Charlie's arms than at any other time of my life. We fall into a comfortable silence as he holds me. Baby rolls over, soaking his fur through, washing himself in the now soapy water that surrounds us. Both of us taking advantage of the rare opportunity to get clean.

"Haven't seen a lion in years." Charlie breaks the silence.

"Oh? I had no idea he's a lion. I thought he was a dog," I reply sleepily. Charlie's chuckle vibrates against my back, the sound is familiar. Gently, he leans me forward and brings a leg to rest against mine, the other doing the same until I'm seated between his legs instead of against them. I'm naked, but he has pants on. It feels intimate but safe at the same time. I don't feel threatened or have the urge to stab him.

WE SIT like that for a long time, it feels comfortable to be in each other's silent company.

"Let's get back, Doll, tomorrow will test us all." Tomorrow. I don't know what's happening for them. For me, it's when I leave these three men who claim to know me. Who stir long-dead feelings and emotions inside me. I cannot wait. Or can I?

CHARLIE STANDS and turns around to give me privacy. Having no other clothes, I put my dirty ones back on before we head back to their camp. It's pitch black now and because I don't know this area, I trip and fall some on the way. Charlie takes hold of my hand, keeping me from falling on my face. By the time we get back, Connor and Crowley are sitting at the tree table with metal bowls in front of them. The area's lit with flaming torches strategically placed around the camp.

"Want some, Kay?" Connor asks as he stands and strolls into the Campo. Crowley stares at our joined hands, a strange look on his face.

"What?" I ask him while trying to sit down, which is difficult since Charlie seems very reluctant to let my hand go.

"Nothing." His grin's lopsided. "Have a good time at the river?"

"Not like that, Crow," Charlie says, a light warning in his tone.

"How then?" Crowley hedges.

"I washed her hair," Charlie replies through his teeth.

"Annnd?" Crowley draws out the word, wagging his eyebrows up and down. I don't know what's happening here.

"And nothing. She's just met us. Put it away." My head swings between them as they talk, confused by what's happening.

"Sorry, Kayla. We've... we've waited a long time to find you," Charlie apologises.

Like their wait for me explains this odd behaviour. At that moment, Connor appears in the corner of my eye, making me jump. Caught off guard! What the fuck? I've become too comfortable in their camp. I need to get out of here before I lose my edge. He gives Crowley a look I can't decipher and places a bowl in front of me.

"What is it?" I touch the white gooey stuff with a finger. It burns.

"Porridge." Connor answers like that explains it.

"What's porridge?" I ask no one in particular. He passes me a metal scoop type thing and I look at it in confusion. What should I do with this?

"It's a spoon," he provides as he sits opposite me. Charlie lets go of my hand, so I wrap them around the bowl and lift it to my lips. All three men stare at me as I try to pour this porridge stuff into my mouth. Only it doesn't move, it just stays at the bottom of the bowl.

"Use the spoon, Doll." I turn to look into Charlie's brown eyes. The flames of the fire reflect back at me, making them dance.

"Spoon?" I frown. He points to the scoop Connor passed me.

"Scoop it up with the spoon. Like this." Crowley shows me. I emulate his actions, scooping up the awful smelling gloop and shove it in my mouth. I feel like an idiot, I know what a spoon is, but not having used one in such a long time, I'd forgotten about them. Some days, I barely feel human.

"Yuck," I say after I shovel the entire contents into my mouth and lay the bowl and spoon down. "Where am I sleeping?" I ask.

Connor answers, his brows in his hairline. "There's a space in the Campo," he says absently, his mouth open slightly and a look of confusion on his face. I look to Charlie and Crowley; each wears the same look

"Food's scarce. Even if it tastes like shit, I still eat it. Charlie," I turn to him. Reaching out a hand, I close his mouth. "Show me where I'm sleeping? I'm exhausted." I stand, not waiting for him to follow. I walk into the white building-like structure. Inside its tent-like, the walls and doors are made of shiny material. Three doors are in front of me and one on either side.

Which one's me? One across from me is open, revealing a large trunk. It looks old and has many battle scars on the front. Interesting.

"This one, Doll." Charlie appears at my side and unzips a doorway, places his hand at the bottom of my back and gently guides me into a small yet warm space. I like the way his hand feels on me.

"Wow. It's... clean." Looking around me, I realise these guys have it made. My shack and Old Yella are awful compared to this.

"What's that?" I ask, pointing to the metal thing along the back wall, at the same time something clicks in the back of my mind. A bed dumb-dumb. Have I completely forgotten how to be human?

"A bed. You sleep on it instead of the floor. It's soft, see?" He walks over to the bed and sits on it, bouncing a few times. When I stayed at the farm with my family, we slept on the floor. In Old Yella and my other hideaways around the wastelands, I collect rags and made my bed out of them. But it was still on the floor. This is raised off the ground and covered in a dull black material with legs and a thick creamy coloured... thing on top of it.

"Mattress," Connor provides from behind. I don't turn as he slips into the space. I'm too curious to look away from the bed. My legs move me forward, I sit next to Charlie. I bounce as he did. A giggle slips out as my bottom jumps up and down on the soft mattress thingy.

"Wow! It's soft. And bouncy!" I lose myself for a few moments and just bounce my arse off the bed. I get to sleep on this thing? I can hardly wait. The guys watch me with a mixture of emotions on their faces, ones I don't know the names of. Once I've had my fun, I clear my throat. "Um, guys? I really need to sleep now."

"Of course. Here." Connor thrusts a pile of cloth at me. "Clothes. We brought some from the city for you. We didn't know... we figured..."

"We thought you might appreciate new clothes, Kay. The city produces them in large quantities." Charlie helps by explaining. I lift the top piece from the pile and let it unfold. A short-sleeved t-shirt with a picture of an animal on the front. Not just any animal, but one of those on my device. It's pink with bright green trim.

"Thanks!" I say excitedly. Clothes without holes? Score! Without thought, I slip my own dirty, hole-ridden top over my head and drop it to the floor. Just as I pull the new t-shirt over my head Crowley walks in.

"Bloody hell," he breathes.

"Crow," Charlie says firmly as I tug the hem of my pink t-shirt down to cover my small tits. Seriously, they're small and have more nipple than tissue so they shouldn't be affected by them. My body doesn't have an ounce of fat on it. For that, you have to actually eat.

"I keep forgetting I'm not alone. I'm so used to just... undressing quick, in case of Panda." I duck my head and sit back down. You gotta be quick if you want to survive in this world.

"We don't mind. Shit. Sorry, Darlin." Crowley rubs his hand across his beard. "We've been out here six months looking for you, it's been rough."

"Oh," is all I can masterful" I know sex is an important thing to men, and I also know it can be pleasurable for both the male and the female. But having never experienced that, I can't tell him I understand. The thought of sex scares me, but I own the power. His leering pisses me off though.

"Yes, it has. But we understand we should take our time." Charlie says softly. Nothing but kindness in his eyes.

"Listen, guys, I'm just not interested. I'm tired. Can you leave me alone?" My words come out softer than I wanted. The exhaustion I feel leeching any anger I have towards Crowley. Besides, they're just boobs. I couldn't stop staring at his and Connor's dicks at the river, so fair's fair.

"Ok, Doll. We'll see you in the morning. My room's across from yours if you need anything." Charlie stands and kisses my hair. I let him because I feel no threat from him at all. "Just come and wake me up, okay?"

I nod numbly, beyond tired. My stomach's full for the first time in forever. Now my body wants to shut down. I lay my head down before they've all filed out of the space. The softness of the mattress sinking under my slight weight has me suppressing a moan. The last thing I hear is Connor's whispered, "Sleep well," as he lays something soft and warm over me.

BLAZE
AMELIA K'OLIVER

"Why are you doing this to your mother, Kayla? You're killing her!" A tall man shouts at me.

"Leave her alone Kitch, she can't remember anything." Turning my watery gaze from the shouting man. I look to another one, only this one seems upset, not angry.

"Sure she fucking can, Klaud! She's just playing it up because that fucking arsehole, Leonard, took away her boys!" He turns to me, grabbing the collar of my t-shirt, lifting me off the rags I'm lying on and shakes me roughly. "Tell me what you saw!" Spittle sprays my face as he screams at me. I don't know what he means. Not understanding what he wants me to say, I cry.

"Let her fucking go, you brute! If Kath saw you now, brother, she would fucking slit your throat!" Klaud screams, the fury on his face makes me wince.

The man drops my shirt and I scramble under the covers, trying to get away from the shouting. Squeezing my hands over my ears to drown them out. The woman who says she's my mummy is in the next room. Curled up similar to me now, only *she won't stop crying. The three men say that someone died, someone the lady loved very much. Apparently, I saw who did it. They blame me. It's all my fault.*

"Kayla! It's ok. It's ok Sweet face." I come around to someone stroking the side of my face, but I don't open my eyes. It's an odd sensation because the rough skin slides across mine. Like it's wet.

"Mummy?" My voice is thick with sleep. I'm in that odd place between sleep and awake, where nothing seems real.

"No, Doll, it's Charlie." The bed dips and a sudden heat envelops me. "Shhh. I'm here. Please, don't cry." Thick powerful arms wrap around my waist and I fall back into a dreamless sleep.

When I next wake up, I'm alone. Maybe I dreamt Charlie came in and held me? Wiping the sleep from my eyes, I push off the mattress. Stretching, my bones click and groan after last night's brush with death, my body aches and my lungs burn. Just then, I catch the smell of meat in the air. I bolt from the bed and out of the Campo before I'm fully awake, shoving my feet into my boots as I go.

When I emerge, Connor and Crowley are sitting at the table while Charlie's standing over a fire. A flat pan on top, sizzling meat inside giving off the most amazing scent.

Charlie says, "Morning Kay. Bacon?" His smiling face forces one to appear on my own. Bacon? What's that? "It's not real of course, but it tastes pretty good." Charlie's smile is infectious. He's adorable.

"I don't care what it is, gimme," I say, reaching out for some.

Charlie chuckles, making me almost swoon. "Sit. I'll bring you some." His smile gets impossibly wider.

I jog across the clearing to sit on the opposite side of Crowley and Connor. Their plates are already full of the meat Charlie's cooking and I eye it hungrily. Crowley passes me a piece and I snatch it up, shoving it into my mouth. I let out a loud groan. Their eyebrows shoot up and Connor grins. Crowley grunts while watching my lips.

"Oh, yes. It's like heaven in my mouth," I say while chewing. The juicy substance makes my mouth water like crazy and my eyes close as I swallow.

"Don't get much meat out here, huh Kay?" At my name, my eyes pop open to stare into Crowley's. His rugged face is so handsome, I pause my chewing to take him in. He's wearing all black, his t-shirt is tight across his muscles. His closely cropped dark hair matching the hair on his face. Straight white teeth greet me as he smiles. Connor clears his throat, drawing my attention.

"Sleep well, Kayla?" They're are so nosey. Always with the questions. Usually, it's just me and Baby. No questions come from my dog... lion. Whatever.

"Yeah. That bed's amazing. Never slept so well," I half-heartedly reply as Charlie places a plate in front of me and sits down next to me. His leg rests against mine. I look down. I half remember dragging my pants off during the night but when I smelled the cooking food just moments ago, I didn't think to put them back on. Luckily for me, I always wear knickers. I wash them each morning, they're a grey colour and at one time they had a pattern on them. Baggy around my butt, holey. You know, the sexy kind.

"Um, any chance you guys brought some underwear

from the city?" I ask them shyly while stuffing the meat in my mouth. It's so fucking good. Fake bacon stole my heart.

"No. And none of ours would fit you. We can get some there. All eyes flick to Charlie. When we get there? Oh hell no. I planned on leaving before daybreak this morning. But I slept so well, I didn't wake up.

"Guys," I begin, "I'm not going back to the city. I have a life and a home out here." I jam another piece of not real bacon into my mouth. So bloody good.

"Kayla, I think it's time we told you one reason we're here." Crowley laces his hands under his chin and pins me with his eyes. Damn. Before my mind wanders off into uncharted territory, he continues, "We three are part of the rebellion, Kayla. Connor, despite his dad being the president, plays a pivotal role in our plans."

"And those are?" Not that I want to know. I don't know why I ask, but both Connor and Charlie are wringing their hands. Is that nervousness?

"The rebellion believes all of earth's inhabitants should be allowed to live in safety." It's Charlie who answers my question, his voice harder than I've heard it so far. "Advanced or not, we should all be afforded safety and food."

He has my attention now. While it's an interesting thought. I can't help wondering if the immune has lived too long in the wastes? Try and cram them all under barriers and...

"It'll be carnage," Connor finishes my thoughts out loud. I have to work on that wall.

"We've thought of that, and we have a solution. It will require a lot of hard work and patience. And," Connor sighs and drops his chin to his chest. "We're going to have to kill my dad."

Kill his dad? Wow. That, I was not expecting. "Won't that incite a war? Your dad's the president." My plate's empty now so I take a hearty swig of my water. I want more meat, but I'm too shy to ask for more.

"Probably. But Kayla, look at you." Crowley motions his head towards me. I look down. My new t-shirt's clean but hangs from my slight frame, my bare legs are thin and boney. "The leading cause of death in the wastes? It isn't Panda. It's not the Virus. It's starvation. We see it every day in the Underground camps we visit. The dead are lying in the dirt. Bones sticking out of their skin. Hungry children beg their mothers for more scraps, like children aren't rare enough. They die horribly." I can almost taste his anger, and it calls to my own. Crowley's seen some shit; I can tell.

Well, I didn't expect that either, that's awful. How will you accomplish that? What does that mean for me?" All three of them look fascinated with the grain on the table-top. Crowley, who seems to be the leader of this little group, answers me.

"Kayla. The three of us, we're... special."

"Ookay," I drag the word out, giving myself time to think. "And that means what, exactly?"

"Well, we're not sure yet. We don't know how we do the things we can. We have a scientist working for us, but he needs all of our DNA to work it out. Including yours."

"What's DNA?" I suck my bottom lip into my mouth and bite it. All these unfamiliar words and feelings are giving me a headache, but I want to know more.

"What makes you, you Kayla," Charlie answers, something I don't have a word for in his voice. He sounds sad and serious at the same time.

"Ok. So, let me guess... I have to go to the city in order

to give this guy, who I don't even know, my DMA and then what?"

"DNA. Yes, that's basically what we need to do," Connor replies, his face serious.

"Riiight. I'm just a muggle though." All three look confused so I elaborate for them, "Normal. I'm just human. Well, immune but still just an average being. I have no special abilities. My family line never used the cure." I shrug my thin shoulders, I'm just normal.

"They did Kay." Crowley looks to Connor and Charlie who both nod their heads. "The scientist who works for us tested our DNA. Our great great great grandads, they were the very firstborn without the cancer gene."

"Right. But what do you need me for?" I'm so frustrated.

"We believe your ancestors were of the first wave too, sweet face," Connor explains. We have to get you to the scientist. Your hair?" My hand unconsciously goes to my head, just now realising I'm not wearing my wig. It's been years since I walked around without it, and even then, it was because my mum had been experimenting with coal. She would mix it with a little water and plaster my hair with it, leaving it for several days so it coloured my blonde locks. It worked for a while until my scalp started to blister.

"We all have golden hair."

I cock my head at Connor. "Correct me if I'm wrong here guys, but ah, your hair," I point to Connor. "And yours," I hook a thumb towards Crowley. "Is black, like the rest of the world's inhabitants." I'm not colour blind.

"That scientist? He developed a dye to hide it..." Connor says, but I interrupt him.

"But Charlie..."

"We ran out two weeks ago, we didn't think it would take so long to find you. I have to use two portions on mine because it's long." Charlie explains why his hair is golden like mine. Huh. That's interesting. If I could get my hands on some of this dye, I wouldn't have to wear that awful wig anymore!

"It washes out. Charlie's obsessed with his clean hair." Connor chuckles. I look to Charlie, searching for any signs he's mad, that being the only genuine emotion I can recognise. His face is peaceful. Can nothing shake him? Hmm, I'd like to test that. Both he and Connor seem so level-headed, but Crowley? He's a hothead, I can tell.

"We need to take you back, Kayla. We have no choice." I'm recognising that tone in Charlie's voice; sadness.

"It's time to eat, Kayla, do you like spicy food?" Connor asks me, suddenly standing. He smacks his hand onto his head. "Sorry. You'll like it I promise." With that odd behaviour, he disappears into the Campo, leaving me with Crowley and Charlie.

"What happened?" I turn my eyes back to Charlie, confusion rolling through me.

"Connor doesn't want to take you back to the city," Charlie answers, his brown eyes searching mine.

"None of us does, not really. But it's the only way, Kayla." Crowley reaches across the table and pushes my plate to the side, taking my hand in both of his. Our eyes meet. "We'd like nothing more than to stay out here with you. Get to know you, in relative safety." The gust of air he lets out fans my face, washing my senses in mint. "But the rebellion needs us." His hands are warm around mine, roughened like a Hands. Like he works with them. His green eyes stare straight into mine; into my soul. That feeling stirs in my belly again. My darkness connects with his.

"You feel that, Kayla?" He breathes. "I do." A low moan rumbles through his chest. I'm pretty sure my cheeks are red because they feel like they're on fire. Crowley stands just as Charlie walks towards me, and together they sit to either side of me. Turning to Charlie I try to tell him with my eyes that I'm out of my depth. That I do not know what's happening and I could use his help to escape this.

I mustn't do a good job because Charlie leans in, resting his hand on my knee. He whispers into my ear.

"We've got you, Kayla. We won't hurt you; I promise." A hand taking hold of mine makes me turn to Crowley. He smiles, not a full smile but a small one. I think he's trying to tell me something, but what, I don't know.

"Guys!" I stand, ripping my hands from theirs. Their mouths pop open. I never claimed to be smooth, nor did I say I was feeling anything for these people. "I don't know what this is. But I want no part of it." Lifting my leg over the seat, I accidentally kick Charlie with the toe of my boot. He falls back like someone threw him. "What the fuck?"

"Whoa, whoa. Easy Kayla." Crowley raises his hands in front of him as he stands.

"Ouch," Charlie moans from the ground. "Crowley, can you give us some space?" Charlie asks while picking himself up, holding his hip. His face contorted in pain. I shake my head, confused as to what just happened. Nodding Crowley walks away, heading into the trees.

"It was an accident. I..." I try to explain I was just getting off the bench, but Charlie holds his hands up in front of him.

"It's fine, doll, I'm a big boy. I can handle it." He walks

over to me, his hands still in front of him. Like one might do with a rabid animal.

"The fuck Char! I was just moving! My foot..." I try to explain that I don't know why he took such a hard hit. My stomach is rolling.

"Kayla..." Putting his hand on my shoulder, he uses it to pull me towards him. I go willingly. The connection I feel with him is stronger than should be possible. Our bodies touch from chest to knees, his warmth bleeding through the light material of my t-shirt. It's then I realise my legs are cold.

"Sweet doll, it's all a bit too much isn't it?" His arms snake around my waist, mine hang at my sides. I don't know what to do with my hands.

"I need to leave, Charlie. I have to get revenge for my mother. Masters killed her..." Charlie pulls back to look into my eyes.

"Masters? As in Reginald?" Shock clear on his face. But he doesn't let me go.

"Yes," I say excitedly. "Do you know of him? Where can I find him, Charlie?" I don't mean to do it, but I find myself joggling him. His head nods back and forth as a look that's becoming familiar to me spreads across his face.

Surprise.

"You're stronger already, Kayla." He steps back from me, not by much, but enough so we're not touching.

I have been with the three of you for less than 24 hours. The closeness... it's too much." Even as I say it, I already miss the feel of him against me.

"I understand, doll, I do. This," he takes my hand and places it on his chest. "Stopped me from letting anyone close to me for a long time. You're the first to see them. His voice is so low, I only just hear him. I angle my chin so I can look up into his face. "I've dreamt of your eyes every night." Running his hands up my body to cup my face he leans in closer, our lips a hair's breadth away. "The blue in my dreams wasn't as pretty as it is in real life."

Blinking, I try to calm my breathing. I'm panting.

"I don't know how to do this, Charlie." I lean my forehead against his and take a deep breath.

"Me neither," he replies softly. He leans in, our lips a whisper away. His breath fans my face and snakes slither in my stomach. I want to kiss him.

"Arrgh!" A shout in the distance makes us jump apart.

"Crowley?" Before I realise what I'm doing, I run to the trunk I saw in the Campo last night and break open the lid. Inside is a mixture of weapons. Perfect. I drag a sword from the top. Slamming the lid shut, I run towards the direction of the scream.

"Where are you?" Charlie shouts from somewhere to my left. I don't slow down. My legs are pumping as I run. I dodge trees and jump over branches until I emerge in a small clearing.

"Shit." Counting in my head as I move further on to the patch of blackened earth, I see twelve Panda. Connor and Crowley are in the middle; weaponless. "Don't move!" Skirting around the edge, not a single Panda looks at me, nor do they attempt to advance on the two helpless men in the middle. Well, maybe not helpless, but fucked, nonetheless. A masculine roar comes from the trees behind them and all the Panda turn to watch as another strolls from the trees.

"Fucking hell." Charlie skids to a stop as he takes in the scene before us. The Panda, who looks like he's very fresh, walks towards the circle. The back row moves, merging with the others while the inner circle shuffles to let him through. He stands in the middle. Connor and Crowley assume fighting stances.

"Leave!" The Panda says in a gravelly voice.

"Oh shit," I mumble to myself.

"Fuck me." Connor curses.

"What the actual fuck?" Crowley asks no one in particular.

"Jesus on a bicycle," Charlie utters.

The Panda surrounding the two guys disperse quicker than I've seen them move before, leaving just the one who talked. I race the rest of the distance between us and slide to a stop in front of my guys. Yeah, my guys. Because suddenly my mind believes they belong to me, and I to them.

"You talk?" I ask it. Him?

"Yess," he hisses between cracked lips. Holy crap. His dark blue eyes focus on me, locking me in place.

"How?" I'm so confused right now I barely register when the Panda in front of me winks. Turning from us, he walks at a slow but sure pace back into the trees. Like he knows we won't attack him. Turning to Crowley I ask, "The fuck was that?" Then to Connor, "He just talked right? I haven't lost my mind?"

They both stand there, open-mouthed, saying nothing. Taking a step to the left, I look at Charlie who wears the same expression as Connor and Crowley. Fuck sake. "Snap out of it lads! There are at least twelve Panda in this immediate vicinity. One of them speaks! We need to move. Now." Without waiting for them, I dash back to camp faster than I did getting to Crowley and Connor. Motherfucker told us to leave. A Panda talked, and it looked a lot like he controlled the others.

Back at camp, I yank off the t-shirt the guys gave me

and put on the one I arrived in. Charlie had washed it at some point last night and hung it over a piece of rope between the trees. It feels clean but rough against my skin. Just as the three men arrive, I'm sitting on a bench, lacing up my boots with some cable I found in the Campo.

"What are you doing?" Connor asks as Crowley kneels in the dirt at my feet. He looks up into my face, eyes bright and clear.

"Darlin, what happened back there, it's unexplainable. But it changes nothing." His hand rests on my knee, massaging it gently. It's then I realise I haven't even put my pants on. Fuck sake.

"Guys, that freaked me out. That is not the problem, I need to leave. I have to get back to Old Yella." Standing, I pace back and forth in front of the white Campo. "I've been gone too long. The bugs will have moved in or these new bloody Panda!" Suddenly, I can't breathe, the world spins around me.

"Sit doll, before you fall." Gentle hands guide me to the benches. Sitting next to me, Charlie wraps his arms around me.

"Fucking freaky. Pretty sure I saw him wink at you, Kay. What the fuck was that?" Connor's pacing where I'd just worn a path on the ground.

"I've never seen anything like it. I've been doing missions outside of TC for years, never heard a Z talk before." Crowley keeps running his hand through his short hair. "One held me by the arms from behind while another sniffed my neck. Didn't even attempt to bite me," he continues.

Oh, the world has gone crazy. Panda who don't bite, but talk and demand we leave? What fresh hell is this? "What does it mean?" I ask no one in particular.

Crowley answers me, his face as rigid as stone. "We go to the city tomorrow, first light. Pack up everything and leave. We need to take this info to Doc." At his words, the guys move around in a flurry. While I sit here, I come up with a plan. While they're distracted, I take the opportunity to slip away.

BLAZE
AMELIA K'OLIVER

I casually walk into the room I slept in, grab my things and put on my pants, almost falling over as I pull them over my boots. I take my device out of its hiding place under the rags on the bed, putting it in the side pocket of the bag I took earlier. Then the water skin I came with and the food I stashed from last night. I want my things back; I want my home too. I need the normalcy I've grown used to. Zipping it up, I slip it on my back and walk from the Campo. I guess the guys think I'm just preparing to leave because they pay me no mind as I slip out of camp and climb over the wires between the trees.

As soon as I'm clear of the woods, I break into a run. A sharp whistle brings Baby to my side. Pounding the earth, his huge paws rip into the ground, sending a cloud of dust and dirt into the air behind us.

I have to get away. There are so many reasons like what's happening between the four of us. My attraction to the three of them is growing. I can't handle it. I figured out

I'm attracted to them pretty quickly. Each has something about them I find myself wanting to keep.

Charlie with his sweetness, he's got the kindest soul I've ever been around.

Crowley with his no fucks to give attitude but I think he's secretly a good guy, too.

Connor, he's really sweet in a roundabout way. He isn't at all what I first thought he was. But it's not enough to make me go with them to Tri-City.

Baby peels away from me as I pick up speed, no doubt off to hunt for food to eat when we get back home. My legs pumping under me, I run faster than I've ever been able to. My feet devour the distance. The wind rushes past my ears, and it's only then I remember I don't have my wig. Shit! I skid to a stop at the side of the motorway where Connor and I were attacked by Panda. Removing the skin from my pack, I pour some water onto the dirt and use my hands to create a gooey mess of mud. I scoop up two generous handfuls and spread it over my hair. I have nothing to tie it with, so I tuck it into the back of my t-shirt and wipe my hands on my pants. Just as I replace the bag on my back, Baby joins my side. His large body presses against me, almost knocking me over; his mouth empty. I'm sure I'll be able to find something once we're home. He pushes against me harder. "What is it, boy?" I swivel my head to glance around but see nothing. So, I climb onto the first car, its roof hasn't rotted through yet. My head itches like crazy, by the time I'm home it'll be blistered. Shit. What a dick you are, Kayla! How could you forget your wig?

On my knees, the metal beneath me dips a little, the noise quiet. Finally, a break. All I see is empty shells of vehicles and no sign of Panda. Sniffing the air, I don't even smell death. All clear. Sliding back down the roof, my feet hit the dirt silently. "Come on boy. Time to go home." I skirt around the cars and make it to the other side. Baby cuts through and prowls down the opposite side. We don't run into any Panda the whole way back home.

As we approach the bus, we move on silent feet. I've been gone two nights, who knows what's in this area now. Pushing my body flat against the wall, I shimmy towards Old Yella. Just as I get to the edge of the wall, Baby uses his body to pin me against it.

What the...? Looking down at my dog, lion, I cock my head to the side in question. His golden eyes show no fear or anger, only sadness shines in them. Why is he sad? I blink and by the time my eyes are open, he's peeled away from me, heading back the way we came. Huh? Where's he going?

The area must be clear, otherwise Baby wouldn't leave me like this. Right? I press myself back against the wall, having leaned forward a little when Baby took off running. My body's instinct to follow him is strong. No! I must get back home, get my weapons and resume my search for Masters. I'm going to end this, soon. I peek one eye around the corner of the building at my back; the scene before me makes my blood run cold.

Panda. Lots of them.

I snatch my head back, the wall behind me seems to move and the ground spins. Shit. Shit. Shit. Around twenty Panda surround my bus. The katana on my back scrapes against the bricks as I peek my head around the side again, doing a quick scan of the area. I'm horrified to find way more Panda than I originally thought. At least thirty, their dirty torn clothes stark against the yellow metal. But that's not what scares the shit out of me. No. It's the single Panda that's crouched atop my home that sends ice through my whole body.

Pulling back, my breathing picks up. If they spot me, I'm as good as dead. I can't fight that many at once, not by myself. For the first time in my life, I wish I had someone at my side. Another body to have my back. Did Baby not smell these fuckers? If so, why did he abandon me? Mother fucker!

An idea pops into my head as I scrape across the wall and back around to the front of the building, slipping inside its blackness. There are only a few window frames on the back of it facing Old Yella. Making my decision to find one, I silently move further into the building. Climbing up the solid stairs, I make my way up into what was once a post office. At least that's what all the barely readable signs say. I wonder if my Hogwarts letter got stuck here? It's dark as I move through the building. My destination? One of the frames that's highest above my home. Luckily, I know this building well. Bombs didn't hit in this area, but the shock waves sure did a number here. The ensuing years took their toll, making the climb precarious. Chunks of the ceiling and interior walls are scattered around the steps. One wrong move and I'll either fall down them or break my ankle at best.

Running down the narrow walkway, the window frame within sight, I crouch to my knees then lay my belly flat to the floor. I crawl the rest of the way. Once there, I poke my head above the window frame, just my eyes and forehead, and look out. The Panda are shuffling around, the one on top of the bus looking down at them. It's the same guy from the woods. The Panda who told us to leave.

Shit. What's he doing here? And why's he on my bloody bus?

I turn and let myself slide to the floor, the bare brick wall scratching my back. Unable to comprehend what's happening, I just sit staring down the hall. The dirty wooden floor is littered with chunks of the roof, bits of wood and other debris. The fact that a Panda could talk is in itself mind-boggling and now, trying to come up with an explanation of how this specific Panda ended up where I live, is making my head hurt. My face scrunches up in thought as I go over the plausible explanations.

Perhaps, it's a coincidence? They could just be moving through the Wastes. They happened upon this area and thought it looked like a good place to stop. Do Panda need rest? Of course, I know what they eat. Flesh. But they won't find any around here.

I've called my bus home for years now. The passage of time doesn't mean much out here, so I don't know how many. I don't keep track. But I know this area like the backs of my hands. It's like a small town within the city limits. Its streets filled with half-standing buildings that have been picked clean long before I was born, all the buildings empty or burnt out. Smaller than those structures still standing closer to the city's centre.

I've seen no wildlife, not even rats. So, they won't be finding anything to chew on here. Finally standing; I stretch out my now aching body and move into a room next to the window. Removing the pack on my back, I drop it to the floor and unlace my blade, propping it against the back wall. There's no window frame here, but from the position of the sun on the way in, I'd say it's close to evening.

My mum would tell me about the different seasons

when I was little. Explaining that there were once more than just the two types of weather we get now, below freezing or blistering heat. She tried her best to explain milder weather, but my young mind couldn't grasp the concept. I hadn't ever known it to be cool during the day unless snow was on the ground. And today is no different, the sun's heat makes the room stiflingly hot. But I lean over and close the door behind me anyway. It won't stop a Panda, but it makes me feel better. Leaning my back against the wall behind me, I have no ideas for going forward. I hadn't even thought about what I'd do if I couldn't carry on with my life as normal. I assumed once I got home things would continue like before. I let out a sigh. Fucked up, that's what this is. Picking up my back-pack, I slide down the smooth but dirty wall, my arse landing on the floor. If I wait long enough, maybe they'll leave?

Opening the metal zip of my bag, I check my supplies. One full skin, the other is half empty. It'll last me a day but that's all. The heat will dehydrate me quickly in here. Two plastic tubs of leftovers from the guys' camp, meats and Tates in one. Rolls and seeds in the other. A couple of days, that's all the supplies I've got. Fuck, I hope those rotten fuckers leave before then. Everything I hold dear to me is on that bus. Even if I can't call it home ever again, I want my things.

It gets dark. No window means I can't tell what part of the day it is. My device is in my side pocket. Pulling it out, I place it beside me and lay my head on the bag. Hot, hungry and thirsty, I might as well try to get some sleep. I have a feeling I'll be here for a while.

The ground's hard against my body. After only one night, I already miss the mattress. I press the button on the side of my device and its screen comes to life. The light's bright, making my eyes close. I struggle to get them back open, all that running has taken it out of me. A journey which should've taken me two days, I managed in one.

Huh. Not bad Kayla.

I blink against my will. This time, losing the battle. Having navigated the device many times, I find the music part without opening my eyes and press play. The only singer on it fills the silence. Placing it under my head so only I can hear it, my body relaxes. The singer asks the same question repeatedly in my ear. I fall asleep wondering, what does he mean? Thoughts of the guys fill my mind. Charlie's face materialises, and I fall asleep staring into his brown eyes.

WHAT FEELS LIKE SECONDS LATER, I wake in absolute agony. I try to move but can't. A heavy weight presses me into the floor and dust in the air catches in my throat. I cough, trying to clear my airway only to find myself unable to stop. My lungs burn and my throat's raw.

What the fuck? It's too dark to see. I slowly and painfully bring my arm up, pulling my device from under my head. I press the button, so the screen lights up, the music is still playing when I point it around trying to find out why I hurt. My other arm's stuck, I can't pull it free.

Turning the device away from me, I assess my situation. Panic rolls through me. Shit. The roof's collapsed on top of me! As the singer asks if we can be friends, I realise I'm trapped under the heavy boards on top of me. I can't move my left leg at all, it's pinned under something so heavy, I no longer feel my foot, the circulation's cut off. A large piece of wood across my stomach digs deep into my body. I see no blood, but it hurts like a mother fucker. Barely able to get a good breath through the pressure and dust, my head swims. How am I going to get out of this? With my free arm, I try to push the debris off me, but it doesn't budge an inch. It's then the panic sets in.

I'm going to die here.

I know better than to call out, but as I lay here, dizzy, thirsty and hungry, the basic instinct of survival kicks in. I scream. "Help! Oh, please." Coughing, I twist my head to the side and spit bits of god knows what from my mouth. With barely enough saliva there to clear it, I gag. "Help me!" I can't make my voice loud enough. Even if there were people around, they wouldn't hear me. My throat's raw. I hurt everywhere. Tears leak from my eyes as I realise it's useless to shout for help; nobody's coming for me. This is how I die. My grave; a small room in a building abandoned long ago.

Darkness rolls over my vision as my sight is slowly taken over by unconsciousness. My breathing's becoming slower, shallower. The end's near, I feel it. The cold from the floor seeps into my skin, making me shiver. Connor, Crowley and Charlie. Shit. I realize. I like them. All three of them. A connection I can't describe or put a name to sparked from the second I laid eyes on each of them.

Connor and his whiny personality morphed into a strong, fun one.

Crowley with his grumpiness, but he's sweet and caring. I stuffed the book he gave me into my bag, safe.

Charlie, my broken Charlie. His sweet heart calls to me like I wouldn't have thought possible. The scars on his chest left him with more than just the visible ones.

I want to be with them all, like... romantically. A relationship. Shit. I left them because I didn't want to go to

Tri-City. I tried to fool myself into thinking it was because I didn't like them when really... I do. Why am I so broken? I want to fight the darkness rolling over me. Instead, I finally let my eyes close and darkness takes me.

***

BLAZE

AMELIA K'OLIVER

K ayla

The pressure on my stomach eases; drawing a deep breath in I open my eyes. Someone's here? A shoe scuffs the floor beside my head. The weight's lifted from my stomach completely. Too dark to make out the features of my rescuer, I attempt to thank them. But all that comes out is a wheeze. Pain explodes behind my eyes, forcing me to shut them. A grunt echoes in the space, and with it, my arm's pulled free. I bring both my hands up to my head, the pain there unbearable. My fingers come away wet. The pounding in my head tells me my skull's cracked open, the blood confirms it is bad. My vision swims as more pain spreads through my body.

"Still," a gravelly masculine voice whispers into my ear. A finger touches my scalp, another grunt sounds. Oh shit, that isn't one of my guys. Too dizzy to panic, I just lay here.

"Bleeding. Stay," the voice tells me. Yeah, bleeding, no shit. It leaks from several places, the viscous liquid having gone cold beneath me, leaching the warmth from my skin. I'm dead, it's too late. It's just a matter of time.

My mum told me stories of heaven as a child. A place you go where you no longer have to struggle to survive, where everyone's safe. I couldn't wait to get there; darkness once again covers my vision.

"DRINK." Whoever helped relieve the pressure is back. Something cool splashes over my lips and I lap at it greedily. Liquid pours down my throat, causing me to choke on it as it slips past my cracked lips.

"Ah, shit." The pain in my body rages on; something's broken. Maybe several somethings.

"Can you stand?"

"No," my croaky voice barely audible. "Leg!" a gasp escapes me as I try to pull it free. "Trapped."

A groan escapes me as the man attempts to lift the beam pinning my leg to the floor. The bone's broken. I can feel it move when he lifts the wood a little, snapping into place when he lets it go again.

"Heavy. Push. I pull." His stunted words stir a memory, but I can't grasp hold of it through the pain. Doing as he says, I brace my hands against the beam and push with all my might.

"Yes!" It moves. Slowly but surely, together we move the wood from my leg. The pain eases enough for me to clear my eyes with the back of my hands. "Can't see the damage. Help me get to the hall?" Whoever this man is, if he'd wanted me dead or to hurt me, he could've already. Arms laced under mine; he drags me across the floor. I scream out.

"Shh. Panda." Odd jerky speech pattern. Perhaps he isn't a native? Pushing with my good leg, I slowly rise. The man's hands never letting me go as I hop into the hall. The faint moonlight from the window allows me to see that my leg is indeed broken. Shit.

I glide slowly to the floor, a small pool of blood at my feet. The skin's broken, revealing bone. An infection will set in and I'll die slowly. What a shitty end to a badass life. "I feel sick," I say out loud. Pretty sure I'm about to pass out, I lean back against a hard body. He smells faintly of rotten flesh, which reminds me of something. I'm forgetting what that smell means, but before I can figure it out, darkness takes me again.

Panda Alpha

LOOKING down the side of the vast yellow metal thing, I can't recall the name of, my brethren amble around on the ground below me. Memories surface in bursts. My name was Chris. I had a female; her name eludes me. Two smaller versions of me, their names whisper too quietly. I can't capture them as they whizz through my mind.

I recall being hunted, hemmed in by white. I had to get away from something. Then... nothing but utter frenzy. I'd woken in the dust, my face in something foul-smelling, anger rolling through my veins. I had shoved off the ground and assaulted the closest person. That female now stood below me, milky eyes hazy, blood streaks across her face. I don't know what her name is, but now she accompanies me wherever I go. They all do.

The others, they're strange. Or am I unique? All I know is I have this overpowering yearning to protect those beneath me. I have to find peace for us all. I know precisely how to accomplish that; I think. My mind's distorted. I struggle against fits of madness, the need to feed stronger than everything. But I strive against it, even though it's painful. I'm no longer human. That much is clear from the craving inside of me.

I don't know when, because time no longer bears any significance, but I met a woman. It wasn't long ago; I know that much. Her essence is still vivid in my mind. The one and only time I haven't wanted to tear into a human. Her long bright hair had drawn me from afar. Watching her from the edge of an expanse between the trees, something about her called to the human in me. I craved to make her mine. Unfortunately, she had three comrades with her, three males.

I instructed the Panda below me to close in on two of them when they severed from her. I'd been working to get the others to follow basic orders. Some did better than others. The milkier their eyes were, the harder I had to work to subdue them. I let them go when she stood in front of her men.

She put herself in peril from my people and I didn't want to harm her so; we left. As I peered into her eyes, my own became clear, the fog rising. She was mine; I just knew it. I sought her essence with the others trailing after me. She wandered around a lot, so identifying the place she lingered for any period was tough.

When we arrived at the place where my female's scent had been the richest, I'd taken the opportunity to look at myself in some glass inside this thing. I was alarmed and amazed at the same time.

The skin around my eyes and lips is black, not in refined circles but as if paint were sprinkled there. The edges are irregular, like a veil across my face. The rest of my skin is pale white. Not as much as the others, but paler than the humans we'd run across. I wanted to shield them all, but my clan had to feed. The only ones I had preserved up to now were my female and her companions. But I had a plan. She would be mine once I got rid of the others.

The sky gets dark. My followers are growing unsettled. Dropping from the roof I pull open the... I forget what it's called, letting them all enter the metal box. They'll lay on the floor, clustered together. We don't need to sleep, so they'll remain there, unmoving. I have yet to slumber since I woke up like this. I feel peculiar, not how I recall feeling, but familiar. Slower maybe. Hungry.

Locking the thing behind me, my head jerks up at the sound of a faint shriek. It sounded like... my female? My feet are running quicker than ever before as I run towards the building across from the yellow box. Her scent's all over this area, stumbling through the dark, trying to detect her feels insurmountable. Must find her. As I enter the building, my eyes adjust as I go. I detect a fresh bouquet. Blood. The monster in me roars to the ceiling.

***

MY FEMALE WAS TRAPPED. Blood pooled on the ground under her and the beast in me clawed to be set free. The need to feed on her flesh is so strong inside me...but I resisted. The need to make her mine was far more powerful. Now, she sits between my legs on the floor. Her leg's snapped. The skin there is broken and bleeding. Images flit through my mind. I can't remember why, but I know how to fix it.

I shuffle backwards, laying her head down. My clothing is what I have always worn. Dark shirt with a bright round shape in the middle. A smiling face. My bottoms are two colours. Lifting the hem, I take off my top. Scrunching it up into a ball, I place it under her head.

Then I return to my people.

WE'D BEEN HERE for some time. How long I don't know. But when I arrived, I had pushed my way into this place. The colourful rags on the sides fascinate me. A picture in my mind tells me I have what I need to help my female. I just need to find it. Turning over boxes, the contents spilling out, anger wells inside of me. It's here, I know it. Placing a hand under the sitting thing in the middle I flip it. Nothing. I search until I litter the space with things, scattered over my people until I find what I'm looking for. None of the people here moved or looked up at me as I tore the place apart looking for the things I now hold in my blood-stained hand. Several sniffs the air as I pass but they don't open their eyes. I rush back to my woman, grabbing a length of wood on the way.

Kneeling next to her pale form, I close my eyes. If I breathe through my mouth it isn't so bad. The scent of her blood torments my hunger. I will my mind to open, to remember what I need to do to save my woman. Images fly at speed through my mind's eye. I set to work as if on autopilot. Pouring the liquid in a brown bottle over the wound makes her gasp but she doesn't wake. I rip off what's left of the material on her legs, leaving her bare to me, but I don't look. Not yet.

I want to be better for her, no longer a monster. She makes me feel, want, need. All the things I never thought I'd feel again after I died. For her... I would beat back this monster clawing from the inside. For her, I would not fail.

Hands working on muscle memory, I stitch up the wound. They don't work like I want them to, but the gash is closed and the bleeding's stopped. My mind feels clearer as I wash her exposed skin clean with the water I found in the room she was trapped in. Full of scars, bruises and cuts, I can tell she's lived a rough life. Her hair's coated in mud, its golden tones peeking through. Using the sharp edge of her sword, I remove the rest of the clothes from her body. I wrap a cloth around the wood and then around her leg, binding it.

Feelings stir inside my chest along with something between my legs as I look at her face. Memories surface of a female in my arms, naked and alive. As I clean my woman, I'm reminded of my hunger as her scent permeates the air around me. Forcing my eyes to not look at certain places, I finish washing her.

Beautiful. She's the epitome of beauty.

Leaving her in just a covering between her legs, I move to the window. Not a sound comes from what I now remember is called a bus. I let out a pent-up breath. If I hadn't gotten here in time, if I'd been out in the wastelands, she would've perished.

Kayla

The copper tang in my mouth makes my stomach roll. Sticking my tongue out to lick my dry lips only serves to crack them further. "Water." I croak. A hand tilts my chin and liquid pours into my mouth.

"Chris," the croaking male voice says.

"Huh?" I ask, confused.

"Name."

Oooh, ok. "You saved me, Chris. Thank you." I crack my eyes open a little. The sun streaming through the glassless window burns them. I hurt everywhere. Memories assault me. The roof, the pain. My body stiffens as I realise my head's resting on the lap of a complete stranger. One who smells of death. I try to sit up, but he stops me with rough hands on my shoulders.

"Head hurt. Stay," he grunts. Shit. I'm naked. Fuck. I do a mental scan of my private area. Feels fine. He didn't hurt me. Something solid presses into my leg, a splint?

"Why?" I clear my throat. "You could've just let me die. Why'd you do it?" The man at my back grunts, something stirs in my belly. Sitting up, I slowly look behind me. "Argh!" He's a fucking Panda! Shuffling across the floor on my arse, pain rolls across my entire body as I try to get away from it. Battered and bruised, I push my back up against the wall with the window. I'll throw myself out if he bites me, I'd rather die than be one of those things.

"Won't hurt. Mine," it says, head cocked to one side.

Mine? Mine?! Is he shitting me? Blue eyes stare at me past the black area around his eyes. I can see that he was once handsome. Square jawline, a light smattering of stubble across it. His nose leans slightly to the left. The area around his lips is black, but not as dark as the other Panda I've encountered.

"How can you talk? You're infected!" I'm trying not to panic, the fact he's made no move to eat me is helping. He shrugs his shoulders, the movement drawing my eye. I'm distracted by his bare torso and the lion's head gracing one peck, the other displaying an eagle. His toned abs lead down to very dirty green and brown pants. Army?

Lifting a pile of black cloth off the floor, he unfolds it and slips it back over his head. I didn't see any bite marks and his bottoms are intact from what I can see. Where was he bitten?

"Cleaned you," he motions towards my undressed state. "Didn't look. Name?" My hair covers my breasts and my legs are crossed. He sees nothing he shouldn't, but perhaps it's already too late.

"Kayla. My head hurts." Lifting a hand to my head, a large bump and dried blood greet me.

"Not broken. Leg is." I'll be damned if I'm sitting here, almost naked, talking to a brain-dead zombie. I've either lost my shit or the world has. Could be both.

"How?" He shrugs again, seemingly lost for words. His t-shirt has a big yellow smiley face on it, a huge contrast to the sad look on his. "Chris, you're a Panda, do you know what that means?"

Nodding, he looks out the window behind me. "Not like them. They listen, I tell."

They listen to him? Like, he can train them? "Will they eat me if I go out there? I need some things."

"No!" I jump, despite being on high alert, the shouted word from the Panda, Chris, sets my nerves on edge.

"They... they're in there," he clarifies. That's the longest sentence he's uttered. We both freeze at the unmistakable sound of paws running down the hall. Turning a corner, Baby crouches low, a snarl on his lips.

"Baby down. No! He's a ... a friend?" Turning my eyes back to Chris's bright blue ones, I ask the question with them. He nods then turns back to Baby.

"Down," he commands. The timbre of his voice

screams dominance, so much so Baby actually dips his massive head, laying on the floor, his golden eyes never leaving mine. Well shit.

"Fuck, I'm hungry," I whisper to myself as I try to drag my t-shirt back on while Chris pushes from the floor. The muscles in my arms ache with cold, making it hard to get dressed.

"Food. How?" he asks, his eyes searching mine. His handsome yet scary as shit face looks confused. I suppose Panda have a different diet than me. Is he even a Panda?

"Um... I have some in my pack, in there." I jerk my chin towards the room that almost became my grave. When my head pops out from my shirt he's gone. The shirt's ruined, so I tie it around me to hide my chest. Picking up my skin, I drain the last drops of water from it. How am I going to get it with a broken leg? Grunts and groans come from the other room as dust plumes out of the doorway.

"Chris?" Did more of the roof collapse?

"What?"

"You ok?"

"No." A giggle escapes me as he emerges covered in dust and bits of plaster. Luckily, his head is bald, so he'll just be able to pour some water over it to get clean. Realising that's not possible, I hold back a sob. If I can't get water, I'll die slowly. Walking over to me, Chris hands me a plastic tub. I rip the lid off to reveal moulding food. Shit.

"Baby?" He lifts his head to look at me, "Food, boy. Please." My stomach growls and twists. Wrapping an arm around my belly, I groan. I've never felt so hungry in all my life. I've known hunger in intimate ways. Baby stands and slowly pads over to where I sit and licks my face. His long rough tongue feels like needles against my sore skin. "Thanks, boy. Fast as you can. Please." Turning, he runs down the hall, the sound of his paws pounding down the steps the only noise in the building.

"So-so-sorry." I turn my head so fast to look at Chris, I go dizzy. Did he just say sorry?

"Why?"

"Hunger bad. No food to give." Damn. This Panda feels bad because he can't feed me?

"Not your fault, um, Chris."

"Kayla! Kayla!" My name being screamed sends shivers down my spine. I recognize that voice. Crowley.

"My friends. Chris, the Panda! Please, don't let them eat my friends." Nodding, he rushes past me, jumping out of the window. Shitting hell. Grabbing the windowsill, I heave myself up off the floor. "Argh!" Agony lances through my leg. "Crowley! Fuck, turn back, man!" I scream from above as he enters the area where Old Yella is.

Kayla!" he yells.

"Stop shouting, you fucking idiot! You're about to be eaten by a bloody group of Panda!" Pointing to my bus, I notice the first Panda emerge from my home. Oh, fuck me. Shit's about to hit the fan, because Charlie and Connor run up behind Crowley shouting my name too. As they skid to a stop, they all stare at the Panda filing out of the bus just a short distance from them, then look back up to me. Shock and disbelief clear on their faces. "No!" I scream when Chris appears from the street at the side of the building I'm standing in.

"He's a friend. They are not! Get into the building. Now!" I shout down while cupping my hands around my mouth to make my voice louder. They must hear me because all three of them race forward, cutting around the corner, feet sliding on the rubble littered ground.

I don't know how much control Chris has over the

other Panda. I hope the guys make it inside without anyone being hurt. Leaning my ass against the wall, I wait. My leg throbs, my head's pounding and the pain in my stomach spikes again. Dizzy, I sink to the floor. Once again darkness overtakes my vision.

BLAZE

AMELIA K'OLIVER

"What the fuck? Kayla! Kay?" Charlie all but sobs.

Crowley growls, "Shit, look at her. She's been beaten."

"Do you think it was the Z?" Connor sounds pissed.

"Nah. I don't see any bites. Unless they're under this wrap," Charlie answers. I can feel his hands on my body. "Fuck! We should've gotten here sooner! But no, you just had to wait for the drop, didn't you? I knew I should've just gone after her."

"Charlie, you would've been killed, brother. Kayla will be fine, just," Crowley tries to calm the situation. My eyelids flutter open to the sounds of Crowley and Charlie at war with one another.

"Char?" I croak, barely able to speak, the thirst in my throat burning.

"I'm here, doll. Shit. I'm here." Charlie's voice wraps around me. He's here! Something cool touches my lips. My arms snap up and I wrap my hands around a skin, then greedily suck the liquid down my parched throat.

"Oh. Oh, my God," I gasp out.

"Kay, what happened to you?" Crowley asks. Charlie's by my side and Crowley's close, but I can't see Connor or Chris.

"I'm here love. I'm here." Humour laces Charlie's voice. His chuckle almost makes me smile, but the pain I'm in overshadows the joy I feel seeing them in one piece.

"She's in pain, Char." Crowley's face looks stricken as he looks from me to Charlie. Without a word, Charlie bends and lifting my good leg to the side, he spreads my legs. Kneeling between them, he takes my face in his hands.

"This will hurt, doll. I'm so fucking sorry." He looks like he wants to cry. Before I have time to react or ask questions, his lips crash against mine. My body spasms, muscles contracting painfully. Charlie swallows my screams as raw agony explodes through me. Stars burst behind my eyes. I'm mildly aware of shouting, the scrape of feet against the floor. A roar, human, not animal, more shouting as our lips press together.

Charlie pulls back just as the pain fades, his face scrunched up in agony. "What the hell?" I gasp out. I feel... bloody amazeballs. Not a single inch of my body hurts, even the old injuries are gone. Charlie's panting, sweat on his brow. "Are you ok?" Reaching out a hand, I place it on his cheek. He's burning up.

"Yeah. Just... need - a - minute," he replies between panting breaths. Looking to Connor than to Crowley, I wait for an explanation as Charlie lays his head down on the floor between my legs. My hand goes to his hair, playing with the golden locks.

"How?" I look into Crowley's green eyes.

"Charlie's a healer. He can heal himself, and others. But... there must be a bond, otherwise, it'll kill him," Crowley replies, sadness in his tone. All the air leaves my body at once, leaving me lightheaded.

"Is he dying?" Panic makes my voice higher than usual. Never have I been more scared to lose someone. Not even my mother. But that's because I thought she was well protected. Three husbands should've been enough to keep her alive, but they failed. I now understand. These last few months I'd blamed myself for not being there. For being cold-hearted. But it wasn't my job to protect her. It was theirs.

"No." Charlie pushes himself up so only a breath separates us, our eyes lock, blue meeting brown. The world fades, then disappears.

"I've never felt more alive, Kayla." His forehead meets mine and a hand slips into the base of my mud-caked hair. Our lips touch and sparks of electricity jolt through my body as he tenderly kisses me.

"I really like you, Kayla," Charlie whispers. A wide smile spreads across his face. He looks down at the small patch of floor between us, his cheeks turning red. An emotion swirls inside me, it's been there since I first set eyes on Charlie, growing without me acknowledging it.

"I like you too, Charlie." His face beams as he jerks his face back to mine. Even to someone like me, it's clear Charlie is absolutely fucking happy with my declaration. Smiling back at him, my eyes flick to Connor's odd coloured ones as he enters the hall. He squirms a little under my gaze. I wonder what he sees there? Looking into Crowley's eyes, I'm disappointed to see they're blank of any emotions.

"What the fuck was that Panda doing, Kayla?" he asks, clearly furious. The fuck?

Huh? Oh shit. Chris!

"Guys," Charlie moves back so I can pick myself up off the floor.

"Chris," I begin. But Crowley cuts me off. Bitch.

"Chris? First name basis with a zombie. What the fuck?"

"If you'd..." I try again.

"He talked to us, Kayla. Told us to go to HIS woman," Crowley practically yells at me.

"Well, he..." Anger heats my blood, this mother fucker will not let me explain. I'm about to kick his arse.

"He do this to you? Huh? Break your bones? Did he rape you, too?" His eyes flick to the discarded torn knickers on the floor. Anger wells inside me.

Without thinking, I spring forward, grabbing Crowley by the collar of his black t-shirt; the damn splint on my leg making me trip and fall into him.

"If you'd let me talk," nose to nose I shout and jerk my knee, breaking the splint in two, "I'd tell you what fucking happened! I nearly died! That," I point to the empty window. "Panda saved my life. I was buried, trapped, injured and dying. While you what?" My grip loosens, letting him go with a shove. "Waited for backup? A vehicle? Doesn't matter." Unable to process my hurt feelings, I walk away from them while unwrapping the material holding two pieces of wood to my leg. Not even looking back when Charlie calls my name, I let them drop to the floor.

"MOTHERFUCKER!" I seethe as I leave the building and head towards my bus. I need to thank Chris, get the Panda out of my home, and then ghost. I've got shit to do. Just as I reach up to open the door on Old Yella, Chris appears in the small window. The black around his eyes and mouth momentarily make me panic. But then I remember he saved my life and protected the guys, kind of. "Come out? Or shall I come in?" Slowly, the door opens, the stench of death hits my nose and I have to suppress a gag. There's only five Panda on my bus as I board her, six including Chris. Three are sitting on the floor, their legs spread out in front of them, chins on their chests. One's standing near where the driver's seat used to be. Like a sentinel. The other's crouched next to the old settee in the middle. None of them do anything or even look at me as I enter. Fucking weird. It's also a mess in here, my things strewn all over the place. Heathens.

"Sit?" Chris swings his arm out, indicating the sofa. My fucking sofa. Arseholes took my shit and I want it back.

"Sure." Moving further into the bus, I sit down on the opposite end to where the Panda is. Chris sits next to me, his arm flung over the back. "Thank you for saving me, Chris," I say before I freak out too much to talk.

"Leave," Chris barks. Confused, I scrunch up my face. I'm about to remind him this is my damn home, not his, when all the Panda suddenly move. One by one, they leave, the last one out closes the door behind her.

"You're... welcome," Chris says, his brows drawn low over his eyes. Letting out a breath, I lean back against the dusty sofa. Fingers stroke the back of my neck making me jump. "Never hurt, Kayla. You're... mine," he rumbles, his voice deep and smoky.

"Huh? No. No. No. I'm not yours, Chris. I'm no ones. Listen," I shuffle forward in my seat and his hand drops off the back. His palm now rests against the curve of my arse.

Our eyes meet and the blue in his burns brighter. Ok. That's freaky. "Chris..."

He leans forward, our lips only inches apart. It's then I notice the black around his lips has gone, so has that slight rotten smell. Pink, plump bow-shaped lips draw my eyes. They break into a smile, revealing straight white teeth.

"Beautiful, woman," he mumbles. He closes the distance between us, and our mouths crash together in unbridled passion. My arms snake around his neck, pulling him closer to me. Something I have no name for takes over as I push off the ground with one foot while the other swings out. My knee lands next to his hip and suddenly, I'm in his lap. Both of his hands grab my arse and he squeezes as our tongues massage each other. My mind goes blank as I let my body take over. The tips of his fingers tickle my belly as his hand slips under my t-shirt, grabbing my breast then tugging gently on my nipple. Gasping I break the kiss, what the ....

"Fuck!" Crowley shouts.

Connor growls, "Shit!" I push off Chris with both hands as Connor and Crowley burst into Old Yella.

"Kayla? Is this... Chris?" Charlie says as he enters behind them. As usual, Charlie's the only calm one as he moves from behind the two angry-looking guys to stand to the side of Chris, his hand held out. Chris stands and grasps Charlie's hand. They shake hands as Charlie says, "Thank you, you saved Kayla when we couldn't. Thank you."

My mouth pops open in shock, my mind finally kicking in. "Bloody hell." Wiping my mouth with the back of my hand, I meet Connor's mismatched eyes.

"So...the zombie and Charlie get kisses, where's mine?"

he asks, his eyebrows raised in question. I giggle a little, I'm not really sure what's come over me.

"Are you crazy, Connor?" Crowley turns his furious gaze to Connor, his arms flung out to the side. "He's a fucking Z!" Turning his blazing eyes on me, he continues, "You could be infected now, Kayla. We don't know how PV works."

"Sure we do! Bite or scratch and you're dead." I shrug because I'm not fully coherent right now.

I kissed a Panda and I liked it.

"What do you think is exchanged during a kiss, Kayla?" he scowls at me like he's talking to an infant, I bristle.

"Sex?" Connor says, his face serious.

"Love?" I turn to Charlie. I don't know what that is, not romantic love anyway. I find myself wanting to have a taste of it. Could these men give me love? More importantly, do I want them to? Connor's intake of breath tells me he heard my thoughts and his next words confirm it.

"Yes. Absolutely yes Kayla. We want to, we can give you love," pointing to Crowley then to Charlie he continues. "If you'd let us."

"You don't want to love me, Connor, I'm too broken," I fire back honestly. Charlie moves then, wrapping his hand around mine, the other turns my head to look into his eyes.

"Doll, we're all broken, together we can be a whole."

"None of this matters!" Crowley's booming voice startles us all, a Panda screeches outside at that moment and everyone's head whips in that direction. Chris swivels on his heel, bolting out of the door.

"Shit. What was that?" I ask, my eyes searching out a weapon.

"Sounded close. Kayla, have you got your katana?"

Charlie presses his lips to the side of mine then turns to the others.

"Sure do, Charlie." I pull one from a holster against the wall and swing it to puncture my words.

"Excellent, let's go," he says, pulling me with him. Crowley's hand shoots out as Charlie and I try to pass him, blocking our way.

"What are you doing? We don't need to take care of that." He jabs a thumb over his shoulder. "We need to take care of her." Jerking his chin towards me, he continues, "Kayla we all... I mean..."

"Listen, I'm attracted to you all. Even you grumpy pants." I rest my hand on Crowley's chest. Turning to Connor I say, "You too." Then I cup Charlie's cheek with my hand. "And you. But we need to discuss this later. The Panda with Chris? They're different." Pushing against Crowley's arm, he drops it. I wiggle past, my arse rubbing against his crotch, drawing a quiet growl from him. "I need to find Baby and warn him."

Jumping out of the door, I take off running in the direction Chris went. If any of Chris' Panda are out here, I don't want to accidentally kill one of them. Their eyes aren't as milky as the other Panda I've seen. But if one tried to attack me? They'd be Baby chow. As I run, I whistle through my fingers, calling my lion to my side.

Turning the corner of the building next to where I almost died, I pull back a little to let the guys catch up. It'll take some getting used to, not being on my own. Having Baby as backup is completely different than having actual people. Baby lets me kick ass, only jumping in when I call him. I'd never really fought with someone by my side. I'm kinda looking forward to trying it out.

Charlie, Crowley and Connor come around the

building behind me. Turning to watch them, I come to the realisation I really do like them. Almost dying in that room, the air being crushed from my lungs, death impending, my mind decided it without involving me in the choice. But I agree with it. I don't know how it'll go, or what happens next, but I want to let them into my cold, dead heart. It scares the shit out of me, but my life could end any day. The Wastes are harsh, deadly. I don't want to spend another second without them.

Then there's Chris.

That kiss. Fuck, that kiss. Bloody hell, why choose, right?

"Where is he?" Crowley's face isn't angry now. In fact, as he tilts his head to the ground, I realise I recognise the emotion on his face; embarrassment. They stop in front of me and I close the distance between Crowley and I. Resting my hand on his hard shoulder, I press a soft kiss to his lips. Then I move across to Connor, the smile on his face making me want to throat punch him.

"Was just a matter of time sweet face. I knew you couldn't resist..." I cover his mouth with mine, ending his cocky comment.

Pulling back, I tell the three of them, "Eyes sharp guys, I smell Panda. A lot of them."

BLAZE
AMELIA K'OLIVER

Letting our noses lead the way, we jog through the streets. As we move farther out of the town, the smell gets stronger. Rotten meat with a dash of excrement permeates our senses as we break from between the buildings into a large bare area. The ground is blackened like a fire had spread through the entire area. In the centre stands a large grey metal container. Surrounding it are at least forty Panda, all with their arms raised as they attempt to reach the figure on top.

Chris.

He's staring down at the gaggle of Panda. From this distance, we can't hear what he's saying but his arms wave around as he gestures wildly. The Panda don't seem to listen, though, they climb over each other to reach him.

"Shit." Turning to my three men, my face conveys my panic and worry. "Those Panda aren't like the ones who follow Chris," I say. Crowley clears his throat.

"He isn't human, Kay. It would be suicide to try and get

to him." Breaking eye contact, I turn to Connor. I beg him with my eyes and try to talk to him in my mind. Help me.

"I'm in," he says confidently which warms my heart. I turn to Charlie.

"I'd lay my life down for you, Kayla." He takes my hand in his and moves to my side until our hips press together. We both look out at the huge gathering of flesh-eating monsters. "That's a lot of Panda." We turn towards each other and our eyes meet. Just as I think he's about to tell me I'm crazy and that he won't be helping me rescue Chris, he says, "I'd follow you into the depths of hell, Kay." His hands cup my face as he leans his forehead against mine. "Let's go rescue the talking zombie." The chuckle in his voice makes me laugh, too.

"Fucking crazy, the lot of you. But fuck it, if I'm going to die... you better believe it'll be with the three of you." Crowley's words make me laugh harder. The four of us stand on the edge of a burnt patch of earth, laughing like crazy people, a horde of Panda at our backs. Looks like we will be entering the depths of hell.

"Con, Char, you got your blades?" The guys nod. Connor pulls out a smaller version of my katana from the holster on his hip. Charlie grabs two blades from his belt and twists them in the palms of his hands. Huh, cool. He clearly knows what he's doing with them.

"Kay?" With a lopsided smile, I pull my katana from my back. I swing her around a little, showing off.

"Sexy as fuck." I laugh at Connor; his cocky attitude stirs what I believe to be desire in my belly. My cheeks flame. I could get used to this flirting, couldn't I? Hell yes.

"Right. We form a cube. Two at the back, two at the front. Protect each other from all sides. Do not break formation. Connor, can you hear what Chris is thinking?"

Crowley barks out orders. My head swings to Connor's face so fast I get dizzy. I never even thought of that.

"Kind of. It's fuzzy, I can't make out any of the words," Connor answers with a frown.

"No bond," I say absently.

Connor replies. "Yes, that's what it is. I can't hear clear thoughts of people I don't know very well. It's why I didn't know who you were when we first met." He runs a finger down my cheek. "I couldn't hear you properly, so I tuned you out. It wasn't until your wig came off that I broke down the wall."

Huh, that explains why he kept calling me 'kid' and 'boy'. Pushing to my toes, I place a kiss on each of their cheeks. "Be safe lads," I say shyly, not sure how to express the feelings growing inside of me.

Charlie takes my face in his hands. "You too, doll." His lips linger on mine, causing tingles to dance across my skin.

"Right love birds, let's get this shit show over with. Kayla, grab your - boy - get out. Stick to the plan. Do not deviate. Understand?" By the time Crowley's finished giving me his instructions his face is right in front of mine. I'm so fucking tempted to throw my head forward and break his nose. Instead, I kiss the tip, turn and walk towards what's sure to be our deaths.

CROWLEY INSISTS he and Charlie take the front as we approach the horde, Connor and I follow with our backs to theirs. As we hit the first line of Panda, blood splatters the back of my hair as Charlie slashes into Panda with his small swords. Giving him room to swing, I let him get a couple of paces in front of me as bodies surround the four of us. I close my eyes and clear my mind.

When I open them again, all I see are dead bodies; they just haven't hit the ground yet. Holding my katana with both hands, I swipe left and right, heads drop to the floor and roll. Blood, guts and pieces of flesh fly through the air as the four of us decimate the crowd around Chris. A particularly fresh Panda lunges at me, his teeth filled with blood and bits of skin. He snaps at my face as I take one hand off my blade to push his chest, making him fall back into the bodies behind him.

I swing my weapon in an arc, taking down several other Panda on the way, I remove his head from his body. Something hard hits my ribs. Turning, I come face to face with a Panda who's clearly several months old, the skin on his face peeling away. Leaning forward to bite me, his foul breath fans my face as his jaws snap. I force myself not to puke as I reach out to push him back when something hits me from behind, sending me falling forward. I land on top of a gross Panda. My hand crunches through his ribs, my fist hitting the ground beneath him. Stabbing my blade beside his hip, I pull my hand back and thrust it into his face, palm out. It ploughs through his skull and into his brain, ending his life. Someone shouts my name, but I can't see who through the cluster closing in on me. Grabbing my weapon, I yank it out of the earth and stand. Connor, Crowley and Charlie have disappeared into the masses. That's fine, I got this. With a battle cry, I spin on the spot, my sword held in both hands as I slice limbs from bodies, cleave open throats and remove jaws from faces. A masculine voice rings out again just as my legs are taken from under me, a heavy weight lands on my back, taking the breath from my lungs.

"Fuck!" My blade drops to the ground as my wrist hits the dirt; pain shoots up my arm and I cry out. The weight shifts and the stench of death wraps around me. Suddenly, it's gone. Twisting my head, my eyes lock on a slightly milky pair. One of Chris's people has the head of a Panda in his hand, blood pouring from its stumpy neck. Hells yeah! Pushing off the ground, I stand still, surrounded by Panda, my katana nowhere in sight. I panic for just a second. Ending my little freak-out, the odd Panda thrusts its hand towards me, a small knife rests there. Hands grab my shoulders as I snatch up the blade and turn, jamming it into the skull of a bad Panda.

Fuck sake, we need to come up with new names for normal Panda and Chris' people. This is getting confusing.

Punching faces with one hand and stabbing with the other, Panda Beta? and I, make headway into the troop of old Panda. Hmm, PB for short? The grey of the container comes into view as more bodies litter the floor. Careful not to trip, I start to use their fallen bodies to climb further into the dwindling posse. Not moving towards the structure, but deeper into the Panda. Determined to clear the area, I continue to use blade and hand to crush, punch, rip and tear through bodies. I lose myself in the heat of the battle.

I love this.

"Kayla? What the fuck!" Crowley's voice can hardly be heard over the sounds of crunching bone, the shiver-inducing sound of my blade sinking into soft gooey flesh and my grunts of exertion. With so many carcasses around me, I have to climb over the top of a pile so more can reach me and their final deaths. I see a flash of the black t-shirt Connor's wearing, then a glimpse of the one Charlie's wearing as another Panda swings its arm out, hitting me in the face. Grunting, I shake it off until something hard hits the back of my head, making me bite my lip. Wiping the back of my hand across my mouth, it comes away wet. I don't need to look to know its blood, I can taste it. The world spins for the millionth time in a few short days. I feel myself falling.

Shaking my head to clear it, I push my hands against the Panda in front of me to stop myself from falling. Turning around, I come face to face with a massive Panda. Its milky eyes bore into mine as it reaches out, wrapping both hands around my throat, squeezing. Struggling to get air past the digits around my neck, I slam my fists into the creases of his arms, but he doesn't break his vice-like grip. Shit.

As it becomes harder to breathe, memories assault me; me lying helpless under a pile of rubble in a dark room. My blood cooling against the dirty wooden floor beneath me. Wishing with every ounce of my soul I wasn't a broken bitch, and I could just allow myself to love. And be loved. My mother's face looking concerned as I refused to get to know any of the boys who visited Kaleidoscope farm.

Have I wasted my life?

Hands grab my body in all directions and teeth sink into my flesh as four distinct male voices scream my name.

"Argh, fuuuuck." The words burst from my lips as fire erupts from my body, pouring out like water from a broken skin. The hands around my throat melt away, the skin dripping down the front of my body as my clothes fall. Pain unlike anything I've ever felt leaches energy from me. I sink to the ground, my legs no longer able to hold me up. Guess I'm not a muggle after all. Darkness covers my vision as the ground races up to meet my face. I am so sick of passing out!

. . .

***

"Kayla. Oh, my God. Shit! She's bleeding out," Charlie cries out. Warmth touches my cheek as the cold seeps into my bones.

"Heal her already, Charlie!" Crowley yells, the sound of skin hitting skin penetrates the darkness. Someone just got slapped. "Heal her!"

Soft, plump lips gently press against mine. I wait for the rush to start, he's healed me before so now I know what to expect, I brace myself. Only, nothing happens. He pulls away, taking his heat and sweet scent with him. No!

"It's not working," Poor Charlie sounds so confused. As I drift away, a sob makes me pull back. Charlie! No. Please don't cry for me. Did we save Chris?

"Try. Again," Crowley growls, he sounds so pissed, I'd hate to be Charlie right now. It's not Charlie's fault, you grumpy sod! Charlie's lips once again meet mine, this time they're wet with salty tears. The darkness closes in again. I hear Charlie scream my name and Connor's crying big sobs. Crowley curses everything under the Godforsaken sun and I take my last breath.

***

The ground beneath me is shaking. Or is that me? Opening my eyes, I'm surrounded by pure white light. Whoah, where am I?

"Kayla, my daughter."

My entire body freezes, snakes slither inside my stomach. "Mum?" Turning without even moving, I come face to face with my dead mother.

"Sweetie. Oh." Her hand goes to her mouth, "What happened?" I look down at my body because that is where her eyes are staring in horror, to find I'm on fire.

"Shit!" I bat at the flames consuming my body with my hands. Only, they aren't burning me, their gentle caress tickles like feathers across my skin. Ok, this is some weird shit right here. I'm on fire, but not. I'm burning but feel cool to the touch. I stop slapping at my skin.

I look around, spinning in a circle, my feet not moving because I'm fucking floating, seeing nothing but white. I face my mother once again. "Who are you? What is this? Why's it so white? And why. The. Fuck. Am. I. On. Fire?" My head spins from the onslaught of thoughts running through my head. I'm dead-dead. Not just dead, but really fucking dead. That's me, just floating around in white hell, my not-mother before me. I'm completely naked too, fire dancing across my bare skin. Because... why not? The dead walking, mind readers, healers, talking fucking zombies. Why not the crazy bitch on fire?

"Be calm, child. This," she spreads her arms wide, indicating nothing because we're surrounded by bloody white. "Is limbo. It's my domain now."

Hold up. Limbo? "Um... what's limbo?" Don't freak out Kayla. You're dead, but you could still give yourself a heart attack.

"The edge of Infernum," the woman wearing my mum's face says like I should know what that is.

Ookay. Not-mum has lost her mind. I blink and when

my eyes reopen, a ginormous tree has appeared. Shitting hell.

"Not hell, dear. Just right next door. This," Not-mum places her hand on the mammoth tree, its trunk so wide I can't see where it ends, a kaleidoscope of colours dances within its surface. "Is the world tree. It connects all of the Celestial planes."

The branches I see are all different shapes, sizes and colours. It's beautiful. My mouth pops open audibly as a limb moves closer, revealing what seems to be a water planet dangling from a leaf. So being dead made me lose my shit. Because this is beyond belief. The branch snatches away just as my finger is about to touch the water world.

"Ok. Could you point me to the exit, please? Because this," I spread my arms wide. "Is batshit. I need to leave. Ya know, got stuff to do." Are my four guys still alive? Wait... four? Is Chris one of my guys?

"Hmm yes, the undead one." Not-mum and I dove headfirst into crazy land. "Your undead choice was a surprise, daughter. You know," not-mum floats closer to me. As she approaches the flames on my skin pull in, leaving me completely butt naked. Oh great, just great. Not-mum snaps her fingers. I jolt as material wraps around my body. Dark blue cargo pants that feel soft yet sturdy, a strappy top, chains wrap around my neck, twisting around my belly. A simple glove appears on my hand as a leather jacket hugs me.

Wow, I look... badass.

"There you go, daughter. Green was always your favourite colour," she says.

I whip my eyes to look at not-mother. "Mum?"

"Yes, dear, it is I. We don't have much time now I've robed you." She looks around like she's expecting someone to attack. I glance around too; except for us, the giant tree and all the white, I see nothing. She's really my mum? I float closer to her, wanting to wrap my arms around her and never let go. "Kayla focus!" she bellows, the sound loud in this place.

I swallow audibly. Yup, this is my mum.

"The Earth realm needs you. You must find the answers, quickly now," her voice breaks in fear. "Go save them. And Kayla." Her hand touches my arm, her fingers ice cold.

Earth needs me? What the bloody hell could I do?

She continues, "The fate of everything depends on your return!"

"But, mum?....."

"Go!" she booms. "Henceforth thou shalt be set free!"

Darkness consumes me. Again.

For fucks sake!

* * *

"No! Try your hands, Charlie. Now!" Crowley growls. Something wet hits my face, pat, pat, pat, in quick succession.

"Not dead. Not dead. Not dead," Connor chants.

"She set me free. Mine," Chris' gravelly voice whispers. The pain in my body recedes slowly with each wet droplet that hits my skin.

Charlie's tears.

"Ughh," I manage to groan out. Every sound around me just stops, a blanket of silence that is almost deafening drapes over the world. Cracking open an eye, the light greeting me is blinding so I snap it shut again.

"Did you see that?" Connor gasps.

"Brother, she's gone. Let her corpse be," Crowley's tone is as dead as a doornail.

"Fuck off, Crowley. I ain't dead yet," I grind between clenched teeth. Mother fucker can't even shed a tear for my death?

"Holy shit!" Lips crash against mine; Charlie. Throwing my arms around his neck, he pulls us both to a standing position. "Oh my god! You're alive!"

"Yup. Can't get rid of me that easily." Not a single point of pain remains, healed again by Charlie. I feel more alive than I've ever felt in my whole life. My heart lighter, freer. "Charlie, I think your tears healed me." Huge rough hands clamp around my face and I look up into Crowley's green eyes.

"Never. Do. That. Again." He thrusts his body against mine, our lips smushing together so hard, I taste blood. When he pulls away, my body hums with need. The giant has a heart, huh? Chris steps forward as Crowley pulls away. His eyes glistening with tears.

"Mine?" His black surrounded blue eyes shine with unshed tears. Well shit, zombies can cry.

"Kinda. Come here," I order. He comes to me without hesitation. I wrap my arms around his waist and squeeze. Sure, I might have a soft spot for my zombie. Why not?

His arms are so tight around my waist I can hardly breathe, but that's ok. I like it. Letting go, Chris moves so Connor can throw himself at me, nearly knocking us both to the ground. "Ugh. Easy big guy, just died over here." The men surrounding me laugh, the tension broken.

"Knew you wouldn't be dead, Kay Kay." Connor's voice

doesn't hold the cocky timber I'm used to. I cock my head at him in question. "I think I shit my pants." He says it so seriously, we all burst into laughter again. I drag myself to my feet, Connor stays close. Crowley's breath tickles my ear as he pushes his body against mine from behind. Something hard and huge presses against my arse. Oh shit. Another hand reaches out and snatches me from Crowley's arms, I find myself face to face with Connor, his lips crash against mine as he kisses me.

"Beautiful. I can't wait to taste you," Connor says.

Huh? Like... is he a cannibal?

Laughing, he answers my unspoken question. "Nah sweet face, I'll explain it another time." He grins widely. I'm missing something, I just know it. Next, I feel a smaller hand take hold of my elbow, Charlie doesn't pull me roughly to him nor does he press his dick against me like Crowley and Connor did. Instead, he waits until I throw myself into his arms.

"I'm not like them, Kayla." He moves his chin to indicate Crowley and Connor, "I'm not...they're..." He struggles to say what's worrying him, so I softly press my lips to his. His arms snake around my waist as I push myself against him. The height difference between us is smaller than it is with Crowley and Connor. I don't have to stand on my tiptoes to kiss him. Lacing my arms around his neck, we kiss slowly, lovingly, with a tenderness I've never known. I break the kiss to hug him close to me. Even though he doesn't do it purpose-fully as the other two had done, I still feel his hardness against my belly. Oh boy. He feels bigger than the others. I can't believe this is happening right now, but it is. The beginning of something very special with Charlie and me.

The guys form a semicircle around me, their eyes on me. I squirm a little.

"We should go back to your bus, regroup," Charlie begins, but I cut him off. Louder than I intended.

"Shit!" Everyone jumps a little, my voice loud in the now completely silent field. Looking around, I see the ground is covered in black ash. Did I do that?

"Sure did, you bad bitch. Flames shot from your skin and burnt these fuckers to a crisp," Connor provides.

Shit. I'm a...

Charlie says, "Fire elemental."

My eyes flick to Charlie, fire what now?

"Fire elemental. You control fire, can produce it from deep within it seems." His eyes scan the area, the ground was black when we got here. Now it's definitely charred. Pieces are still glowing red with heat and steam rises from a spot or two. The side of the grey metal container Chris was standing on is now burnt black.

Don't freak out Kayla.

"How'd you guys manage to survive the fire?" I ask as it occurs to me my flames had reached them.

Crowley answers me. "We saw you getting bitten, the Brute-like Panda had you by the neck, your feet dangling in the air. We were going to come for you when you burst into flames." He runs his hand over the back of his neck, looking down with a smile on his face. Huh, Mr Grumpy Pants is smiling. "We hightailed it over to the other side." Turning his body, he reveals a scorched patch of material on his back. "Only just made it."

Crap. I almost burned them to death.

"Sorry. I didn't know that was going to happen but," I start to walk backwards slowly. "We need to move, back to my home. I'll tell you on the way." Turning, I break into a run. The sound of pounding feet behind me tells me the guys are following.

As we run back to Old Yella, I fill the guys in on what happened when I died.

"Are you sure it was your mum? I mean... not-mum could've been anything?" Connor asks, disbelief easily heard.

Yeah, I understand that. I didn't believe it at first. "It was her. I felt it," I reply, not even out of breath. I push my legs faster. The guys try to keep up but can't. I reach my home before they do.

Standing in front of my bus I lean back against the rough metal and watch as four hot as fuck men run towards me. White-hot fire pools between my legs at the sight. It's hot out here, huh? Too many t-shirts around here.

I say the words in my head loud enough so I know Connor can hear me. I watch his face go from "I'm running" to " Talking in my head." Then, one by one, the guys remove their t-shirts while still running. It's a sight to behold. Even Chris removes his shirt. Which means Connor feels a bond towards him if he can talk to him inside their minds. This gives me an idea. As Charlie passes me, I lay a hand over the scars on his chest, "Hey." With a wink, I let him know I find his body attractive; scars and all. His smile melts my heart further.

As they approach, minus t-shirts, down girl, I ask Charlie, "Charlie, do you think you could heal Chris?" We all turn to look at him. "Um... where were you bitten, Chris?"

"I wasn't." A series of pops fill the air, all of our mouths drop open at the same time. "I was created." He shakes his head like he's trying to clear it. "All white. Humans in white. Doctors."

Shit.

"A lab." We turn to Crowley. A lab? What's that? The question must be on my face because Crowley continues, "Where scientists and doctors work. They're the ones who created the Panda virus."

"How old are you, Chris?" Charlie asks, his face a picture of confusion. I try to concentrate, I really do. But so much skin is on display for my eyes it's hard. Really hard.

"I do not know." Chris shrugs. As Charlie approaches him, his body visibly stiffens but he doesn't move away.

"Maybe it is possible?" Charlie places his hands on either side of Chris's face and stares at him for long moments. Nothing happens. "Guess not." Charlie steps to my side, taking hold of my hand. A small smile plays on my lips as I look up at him.

"Thank you for trying," Chris says with his head down. Well... it was worth a try.

BLAZE
AMELIA K'OLIVER

"Let's get inside. I'm starving. Oh, shit!" I scream as I open the door to my home and Baby pounces on me. His massive body sends me flying back and I land on the ground with an oomph. The breath leaves my lungs and I cough repeatedly as his rough tongue licks my face, making the skin sting. "Easy boy! I'm fine," I say once I'm able to draw a breath again.

"Look at the door!" Connor yells. I peer around Baby to look at what Connor's pointing out. Huge, deep claw marks on the inside. Charlie climbs into Old Yella and shouts out to us.

"This place is torn apart. Looks like Baby was trapped in here."

"Oh shit! I'm so sorry, boy. Oh." I wrap my arms around his neck. I can't get them around fully because he's so huge. "I'm fine. Ugh, you're squishing me." Removing himself from my body, Baby crouches and growls loudly at the guys. "Hey boy, no! Friends. They saved me, well, not really, but they're friends." Standing, I run my hand over his giant head and walk onto the bus.

Baby stops growling, but his lip remains curled as we all pile in. The settee isn't big enough for all of us, so Charlie and I sit on the floor. Chris crouches next to me. I sweep debris out of my way with my leg. Crowley and Connor sit in front of us. I'm surrounded by half-naked men. It's a distraction. But a good one. I feel comfortable-ish with them, and none of them is trying to make a move, which helps. But it also leaves me feeling a little hollow.

Baby stays outside. The bus isn't big enough for us all. "Once we've got supplies, we need to go to the city." All eyes are on me, making my whole body tingle. I'm well aware things went from "Don't come near me" to "I need everyone's hands on me" faster than I can run, but two near-death experiences in as many days kinda put things into perspective for a girl. I want them to be close to me. Maybe even touch me? I'm a mess.

"Agreed. Kayla," Crowley concurs, always the boss. "You know this area better than us. Know anywhere we can find food and water?" He leans back, his hands balled into fists on his thighs. His go-to stance. It's as relaxed as this man gets.

"Nope. This area's picked clean. No wildlife," I reply while crossing my legs. These new jeans sure are comfy. They're tough, but still allow me full freedom of movement.

"I know where." We all look at Chris; his language is improving quickly. He no longer slurs his words. He almost sounds normal now, but still misses words here and there. It's a huge improvement from his one-word conversations. "Travelled a lot. Not far from here is a... a lot of trees. Inside - food."

The forest is a couple of hours away. I'd never attempted to hunt in there because it's filled with Panda. I tell the guys as much. Crowley sits forward, lost in thought, as Charlie laces his hand in mine. Turning so we're face to face, I smile at him. His answering one tells me he's thinking the same thing.

"So, we hunt. Little fire Queen over here can just flame on and toast them," Charlie announces proudly. Warmth spreads through my chest. What is that?

"No. A few are my people." Chris shakes his head. His people are in the forest too? Well, that complicates things, doesn't it?

"Ok, so gather them, Chris. Actually, that reminds me of a problem." I turn away from Charlie's umber eyes reluctantly. The spark between us is growing quickly, making it hard to not crush my lips to his.

"What?" Connor asks.

I jerk my chin towards Chris, his eyes dart around us all. Probably wondering why we're now all staring at him with confused looks on our faces.

"Can we get Chris into the city?" Leaning to one side, I grab a piece of wire off the floor and use it to tie my hair back. The heat is stifling inside Old Yella and taking my hair off my neck brings a little relief. "How are we getting me into the city?" I ask Crowley. But it's Connor who answers me.

"Me," he says simply.

"Huh? You? Um..." I no longer think Connor's an inept idiot, but how could he get us into the city?

He chuckles and continues. "I'll plant the thought in the guard's minds that they're expecting us to arrive with a female." He thinks for a second, rubbing his now prickly chin. "If we could hide the black across his eyes and nose, I could get them to believe there will be an extra male in the group."

"Huh, great idea! Will it work, though?" I ask, a little too loudly, excited at the prospect of a plan forming. I don't want to go to Tri-City, but apparently, I need to... so I'll go. Masters could be there; two birds with one arrow.

"I'm confident it will. How can we hide what he is?" Connor rubs a hand across his forehead and then massages his temple. Stressed?

Turning my eyes to look at Chris' handsome face, the black around his eyes has spread across the bridge of his nose, making it look like he's wearing a mask. An idea pops into my head.

I fill the guys in on my plan as we all begin to pick up things from Old Yella we can take with us.

"I'll be back in a second," I tell the guys as they attach blades to holsters, strapping them to their bodies. I have a good collection of them around my bus, picking them up whenever I found them. Even some I'd made from bits of metal, adding bone handles I'd collected from the Wastes. I strap my Katana to my back, the holsters on my thighs filled with my old friend, cold, hard steel. I jump out of the door and make my way inside the building across from Old Yella.

The hallway floor is stained with my blood, which makes memories assault me. Being almost crushed to death makes things weird for a girl. Even amazing things. Suppressing a shudder, I continue. Careful not to trip over chunks of the roof, I enter the room where I almost lost my life. Digging through the rubble carefully, I search ι device.

"Please be here." As well as the music I love so much, ιτ also contains photos of my mum. Seeing her in limbo, talking to her, made me miss her even more. Searching around one last time, I stand. "Fuck! It's gone," I say aloud. Wrapping my arms around myself, I close my eyes, bringing my mother's face to mind.

Things were hard for mum when I was small. I didn't know it then, but losing my brother must've changed her, made her cold and unable to bond with me. We may not have been close, but I loved her very much. I give up on finding it and head back outside.

THE GUYS ARE WAITING outside Old Yella armed and looking hot as fuck when I get back. They've put their t-shirts back on. I let my bottom lip slip forward, pouting a little.

"Sweet face, put your lip away before I bite it." Connor's words and the look in his eyes make me gasp. The sexual tension between the five of us is so heated that if I couldn't already set myself on fire, the heat between us would do it.

"Come on. We have to go to Tri-City to see if my mother was correct." How I could help the world was a mystery to me, but I hope the city would give me the answers I need.

The journey from Old Yella to the city will take three days. There's no time to waste.

***

. . .

Baby and I take point. His golden fur shining in my line of sight. Crowley takes the rear with Chris. I know the way to the forest where he told us there was food. As it appears on the horizon, he moves through the group to stand next to me. I squint at the trees. Overgrown, dark and wild, the area looks foreboding. But not to me, and probably not to the four men surrounding me.

"I feel them; my people. Twenty, perhaps. Distance makes it harder." Chris says, his voice is gravelly, sexy as fuck.

I turn to look into Chris's eyes as he speaks. The blue gets brighter when he looks at me, almost like there is light behind them.

"You know how many others there are?" I ask quietly.

Looking back towards the forest, he's silent for a moment before answering. "Hundreds."

Well shit, that's not good. Charlie takes my hand as he stands beside me, grounding me. Chris peers around my body to look at our joined hands. He frowns. He copies the move, lacing his fingers with mine, a small smile twitches on the corners of his lips. Between the two of them, I feel at peace, safe, liked, maybe even loved. Resting my head on Charlie's shoulder, I let out a breath. After so long without human touch, it's made me kinda needy.

Chris no longer carries the faint scent of rotting flesh. Now he smells like man; yummy. Thank God. The more they touch me, the more I want it. Remembering at the last second Connor can hear me, I'm not surprised when his hand snakes around my stomach, resting on the patch of exposed skin between my top and my low hanging jeans. Their hands on me send goosebumps across my skin. Fire flows through my veins.

"Here's the plan, we..." Crowley says, but Chris interrupts Crowley's plan making.

"No. I go. Before this," he lifts a hand to touch the black around his eyes, "I was hunter. I will bring you food, my Kayla. And for my new brothers." He tries to remove his hand from mine, but I squeeze tighter.

"Nope. We go together. Or never." Now I have them, I'm damn sure not going to lose them.

"Ok," Crowley claps his hands together. "Let's fuck shit up, shall we?"

A chorus of "Fuck yes!" answers him, Baby growls his affirmative.

Crowley, Connor, me, Chris and then Charlie walk in a line as we approach the grove. Baby goes ahead of us. He'll be fine on his own. This is what he does, hunt. Weapons raised, eyes roaming the darkness between trees, we silently search for prey. As we delve deeper, I signal the guys to stop, then climb the tree next to me. Making it look easy, I reach the top smoothly. It's dark under the canopy of leaves, but luckily for me, all remaining wildlife mutated many years ago to have glow in the dark eyes. My dads told me rabbits are now twice the size they were when they were kids. They also weren't bald and once had long floppy ears. Now they're gruesome. It's possible all the bombs somehow changed them.

Squinting my eyes, I scan the area for glowing orbs in the dark.

Crowley signals to Charlie to go with him while Connor and Chris wait at the bottom of the tree I sit in. Their eyes never stop moving. In the distance, I see four eyes bobbing up and down, low to the ground. Gotcha! Snapping off a stick from the branch between my legs, I let it drop onto Connor's head. He spins to look up at me. I jab my finger in the direction of the glowing eyes and then point to my mouth. **That way, food.**

Nodding in understanding, he turns, whispers something into Chris's ear, then stalks off into the trees. **No! Take Chris with you!** I scream inwardly.

Sweet face, it's fine. He needs to stay and protect you. Besides, Connor says in my mind, almost making me slide off my branch. It's the first time he's ever spoken to me inside my head. **I got this. And our bond has strengthened.**

Yeah, you got this, Con! Bring me back some rabbit. And... It sure has, Connor. The connection between us all is growing exponentially. I have to say, I fucking love it. Even if it's scary. The silly smile on my face makes me giggle silently. Working with others, having bonds with them, it's kinda cool.

Below me, Chris shifts foot to foot as he walks around the base of my tree while Connor stalks the rabbit. As the guys hunt, I allow myself to rest against the trunk and reflect a little. It's been mere hours since I came back from... limbo. Already, I feel less broken. Not-mum had said something about setting me free? The words were so oddly spoken it was hard to understand what she meant. Free to what, exactly? I get my answer when Charlie appears through the thicket below me.

His long golden hair fans out behind him as he races through the trees, two rabbits hanging from a rope in his hand. Our eyes meet as he runs towards me.

Free to love.

After I was raped at fifteen, I'd closed my heart. It had blackened, withering away more each day. When Connor waltzed into my life, I had fought my attraction to him tooth and nail.

Days later, when I'd met Charlie and Crowley, my feelings for the three of them began to bubble over. By the time I met Chris, I'd already accepted I wanted the three of them. In every way possible. Chris, well, I have feelings for him too, although somewhat different from the others. That could be because I've known him for a shorter time.

They each have their flaws as do I. In our own ways, we're all a little broken, but they each now own a piece of me. I couldn't be happier about it. Which is bad, really bad. Because this is the year 2200, the world has been torn apart by bombs, war, Panda threaten to kill you should you so much as let your guard drop for a second. Oh, and my body sets on fire. So many things could go wrong. I could lose them all in the blink of an eye. Then what? I'll be lost for sure. I couldn't survive losing them. Not even one of them. Having a mild panic attack in a tree isn't wise, so I calm my breathing before I fall.

Could I love these men? I want to. Could they love me? God, please let them just like me; I'd be happy with that. Time will tell. If we survive, that is.

"Come down, doll, we've got food. Let's leave this Godforsaken place."

Charlie's right, we need to leave. Several Panda roar from deep within the forest, meaning more will come. I scamper down the tree. As my feet land on mushy earth, Baby crashes through the bushes. "Let's go," I call over my shoulder. Together, we rush towards daylight. The sound of our footfalls is drowned out by the screeches behind us. Sprinting faster, we burst from the woodland and keep running until the trees are specks in the distance.

. . .

"Fuck." Crowley bends over, his hands on his knees, panting.

"What's up, Crow? Not enough stamina?" I tease with a half-smile. Pushing himself upright, he strides towards me, a heated look in his eyes. He grabs my waist, slamming his body against mine. A little squeal leaves my lips.

"I'll show you how much stamina I have, little badass." Grabbing an arse cheek in each of his hands, he lifts me. I automatically wrap my legs around his waist. The chain across my body clangs with the movement. Crowley's eyes look down at it only to be greeted with a view of my little tits. "I haven't had sex for a whole year in anticipation of finding you," he grinds his hips into mine, pressing the length of his dick against me, drawing a moan from a place inside me I didn't know existed, "and here you are, kicking ass, climbing trees. Fuck Kayla," his lips so close to mine, they brush mine as he speaks. "I'm a goner already." Our lips collide in a furious passion. My hands roam his head as he squeezes my butt.

A hand touches the curve of my neck, interrupting us. Connor reminds me we're not alone.

Charlie says, "Kayla, look."

Breaking the kiss with a gasp, I drop to my feet and turn to where Charlie's pointing. Twenty or so Panda walk slowly over the hill we're standing on.

"No." We all turn to Chris as he throws his arm out, halting us as we reach for our weapons. "Mine people. Safe." Well, shit. I'll never get used to safe Panda. Tilting my face to the sky, I realise it's getting dark.

"We need to find shelter. Follow me, it will take an hour to get there." Turning on my heel, I take off running, but not before shooting Crowley a wink. Yeah, I just winked at someone. Go, Kayla!

. . .

KEEPING my pace slow so the guys can keep up with me, we reach one of my hidey spots. On the edge of another small town that only just escaped the bombs is a little place I call "The Middle," because it's halfway between home and Tricity. Two more days and we'll be there.

The building we file into is in decent shape. Of course, there are no windows or doors to the entrance, but the stairs are blocked strategically so Panda can't get to the next level. "Up." I point towards the steps, then turn to Baby. "Protect me? Someone will switch with you in two hours." Of course, Baby can't answer me, so he turns and pads out the door, his nails scraping the tile floor.

Turning back, I see the guys are still navigating their way up. "Coming through. I'll show you how it's done." Moving to the sides, the guys allow me space to climb up and over the debris I'd placed around the base. They copy my moves, treading carefully so they move anything. I stand at the top with my hands on my hips. When everyone's standing in front of me, I head to the main room. "This is like the main living space. There are five bedrooms, which are handy." I look around at my four guys, aiming for a wicked glint in my eyes. It works because every one of them smiles back at me. "Pick your rooms, oh." I make my way through the middle of the four of them. "The biggest is mine." I exit the main area and go into the room I always stay in when I'm here.

The room isn't big, but the pile of rags on the floor covers almost the whole space. The last time I stayed here it was winter, and the temperature was way below freezing. I'd gathered every piece of fabric I could from the surrounding area and piled them here. The other rooms have what I now know are called mattresses on the floors. They're old, dirty and have bits of metal poking through, but the guys won't mind as long as they get some sleep. Chris stands in the doorway as I peel off my jacket and lay on the pile, moaning at the feel of getting off my feet. These boots protect my feet really well, but they make them ache.

"Comfortable?" he asks, his gravelly voice pulling at my insides.

"Hmm, come, join me for a minute." Chris's eyes widen. The black surrounding them makes the blue pop, like staring into a well with the bluest water at the bottom. Moving cautiously, Chris lays his head next to mine, his hands resting on his chest. Turning my head to look at him, I smile. He's come a long way in such a short space of time. I can't help but wonder what the future holds for him. "You ok, Chris?" He smiles then and beautiful white teeth greet me.

"I am. The more... time?... I'm with you," I nod, encouraging him to continue. "The better it gets. You're so pretty, mine."

"Kayla." I remind him. I secretly love the nickname Mine, though.

"Yes." His smile spreads like he knows I like him calling me Mine.

"My name. It's not mine. It's Kayla." He still gets his words confused, but by correcting him, I can at least help him a little.

"No, mine. You're mine and I'm yours. You," he blinks slowly, looking like he's having trouble opening them again. When he does, I'm almost blinded by the light shining from them. "Saved me. I am better, more, you fixed me."

Oh boy. He thinks I fixed him? I don't know what's happening to Chris, but it has nothing to do with me. Does it?

Chris closes his eyes again, only this time he doesn't open them. The poor man must be exhausted. I don't even think he's slept yet. Carefully pushing myself off the rags, I make my way back into the main room. I'll let him sleep for as long as possible. We're relatively safe here, so why not. In the living space, Charlie knocks things out of his way as he moves around.

Looking at the floor, he doesn't see me enter, so I lean against the doorframe and watch him. He's completely different from the others, not just bodily, but also in his mind. He didn't say as much, but I know he's a virgin. He'd hinted pretty hard at it. He's sweet, so much so I find myself gravitating towards him constantly. When I'm near him, he'll take my hand or touch me in some way. I find I've come to really enjoy it.

BLAZE
AMELIA K'OLIVER

"Charlie?" Interrupting his wanderings, I make my way across the room to him and take his hand in mine. When he turns to face me, I gasp at the tears rolling down his face. "What's wrong?" The panic in my voice is clear.

"Nothing. No Kayla," bringing his other hand up, he cups my cheek. "These are happy tears."

Oh, thank fuck! Wrapping my arms around his neck, I pull him to me. Tears land on my bare shoulder. "Charlie," pulling away just enough so he sees my face, I whisper, "Which room did you choose?" Softly chuckling, he drags me into the room across from the stairs. In the middle, he's laid out rags from the walls of my bus. "Oh, Charlie." Spinning on my heel, I kiss him with all the feelings inside of me. Love? I'm not sure. But it's the closest I've ever gotten.

As one, we lower ourselves to the floor. Pressing his weight against me, a groan escapes him. This is the only room with a door. Breaking the kiss, I peek over his shoulder to see he closed it on the way in. "Charlie?" I ask as he lays soft kisses on my neck. "Oh." My back arcs off the rags as he nibbles a sweet spot just above my collar bone.

"I want you, Kayla." He pulls back, looking deep into my eyes. "Do you want me?" Heat pools low in my stomach. My muscles contract in a way that makes me feel a little scared.

"Yes, Charlie, I want you, this. I want it all from you." His answering smile tells me he wants all of me too. I can give him my body. I'm safe with Charlie, I know, but can I give him my heart too?

Together, we push to our knees so we're face to face. His hands drop from my face to the circular piece of metal holding my chains together; a question in his eyes. Nodding, I move my hands to the hem of his t-shirt as he unlaces the metal from around my torso. I lift his shirt. He pulls down the straps of my top, kissing along the top of my breasts as he removes the material from my body. Our bare chests meet as he kisses me again, our tongues intertwining as we move together, taking off our boots with one hand, the other roams the other's body.

Dropping my hand from his shoulder, I hook my fingers into the hem of his pants. Held up by elastic, they'll be easy to push down. I hesitate and he stops the slow descent of his hands as they make their way down to my breasts.

"Connor told us, he didn't mean to do it... Connor and Crowley were talking and the subject of being with you came up." He lets his hands drop. I almost cry out from the loss of his touch. "I understand if this..."

I don't let him finish because I am so ready for this. I fucking own all the power; I won't let my past shape my future for one more second. I push his pants down to his knees, he lifts them one by one so I can tug them off. I work my jeans down and throw them behind the door.

"I want this, Charlie." I need this, him. Charlie. My sweet Charlie, to chase away the past, to rewrite what sex means to me. Only Charlie could thaw the coldness in my dead heart.

Completely naked, more than a little frightened, I take Charlie's shoulders and lay us down on the rags behind us. Charlie hovers above me. Looking into my eyes. He reaches between our bodies and lines himself with my entrance. On their own, my hips thrust up to meet him. The tip of him nudges my wet core. A moan bursts free from me without my permission. I'm so wet, he slides up over my clit as he leans down to take my mouth with his. Softly, our lips meld together as he slips over my clit, between my folds and enters. Inch by inch, he pushes his cock into me. The full feeling is both delicious and painful. His mouth swallows my moans as he seats himself fully inside me.

"Charlie, oh God." I'm barely aware of the words coming from my mouth or the moans interrupting them as he pulls back just as slowly, leaving the tip inside me. Doing this several times, Charlie's body begins to tremble, as does mine. Nerves and pleasure flow through me. Needing more, I use the heel of my foot to draw him back in. We both gasp as he thrusts forward, slamming into me. I cry out from the jolt of pain/pleasure. "Yes, Charlie!"

My words spur him on; he moves faster, harder, deeper until my eyes roll back in my head and my toes curl.

"Unh, Kayla, fuck...so beautiful, oh, god," he moans, his eyes locked with mine. "My love,"

Something deep inside me unfurls and spreads through my body. A warmth starts in the bottom of my belly as Charlie pumps into me over and over, hitting something inside making me want to lose my mind. His lips crash down onto mine as he presses further down onto me. With our whole bodies touching from ankle to lips, that feeling bursts through me, sending sparks of light dancing behind my eyes. His trembling hands roam my body before settling on the sides of my face. He stares into my eyes as he claims me as his. I've never felt this close to a person in my whole life. Never felt my feelings wrap around my heart and squeeze. I'm his and he's mine; irrevocably, wholly and completely.

It was always going to be Charlie.

"Charlie!" As I call out his name he groans while he pours himself into me. Spurts of hot wetness coat my insides as he moans my name over and over.

"Kayla, my Kayla." Our eyes lock together as we bathe in pleasure. Charlie stills as the last sparks of electricity tingle across my body. Resting his forehead on mine, Charlie whispers, "I love you, Kayla, you're the most incredible woman I've ever known." Something inside my chest hurts. I wish I could love him, too, but maybe letting him love me is enough?

He rolls over and takes me with him, my head on his chest. The pounding of his heart is loud in my ear as we both calm our breathing. We just made love, sweet, passionate, fulfilling sex. I can hardly believe how amazing that was, quick yes, but beautiful. As my eyes close, Charlie kisses my head one last time, we fall asleep wrapped in each other's arms.

Free.

* * *

. . .

"KAYLA, sweet girl, it's time to eat." Connor's husky voice wakes me from the most peaceful sleep I've had in, well, forever.

"Huh?" Sitting up, I rub the heel of my hands over my eyes.

"We prepared those rabbits; they're ready to eat. Come." He reaches out a hand. Taking it, he pulls me gently to my feet. Charlie must've wrapped material around me because my boobs and lower half are covered with a dark red cloth. "Before Crowley eats it all." He looks down at the material with a smile on his face. "That's a good look for you."

I giggle as we walk hand in hand into the bigger room. Crowley sits on the floor, Baby at his side, eating what looks to be rabbit innards from a piece of metal.

"Chris is making a sweep of the area. Charlie's up next so I'll let him sleep one more hour then wake him," Crowley, bossyboots barks.

"Where am I on the sweep team?" I ask him. Suddenly, Connor leaves the room, shaking his head. Huh? "What?"

"You're not," Crowley answers with a nod.

"Um... Yes. I am. I'll go after Charlie," I say firmly. I'm not weak, I can and will contribute to my group's safety.

"Not happening, badass. You need sleep." Crossing my arms over my chest, I stare open-mouthed at Crowley. How dare he?

"Yeah, not happening, big guy. I go after Char. You can suck my lady dick if you think I'm backing down." It's his turn to stare in shock. I back down to no one. Not even my promised. Sitting down next to Baby, I give him a pat on his head and shovel food in my mouth. Crowley remains stock-still as I eat, his mouth still hanging open. "Might wanna close that, unless you want flies with your rabbit."

A laugh behind me tells me that Connor is in the room. Without turning, I say, "Sit, Connor, better have yours before I eat it, too." Shaking his head, Connor walks across the room and sits next to me. Turning to me with a mouth full of rabbit meat, he laughs.

"He did nickname you badass, yet he thinks he can boss you around." He turns to Crowley. "Can't make her do anything, brother, didn't you learn that yet?" Letting out a huff, Crowley carries on eating.

That's right boys, Kayla's her own boss. The power is mine, always.

* * *

"So, Charlie, huh?" Connor asks as we stand outside the building watching Chris talk to a group of Panda. It's dark now, the moon is big in the sky, casting just enough light to see by. Looking up into his mismatched eyes, a silly smile on my face, I reply.

"Yes." Kicking the rubble at my feet, I avoid eye contact. I'm not ashamed, nervous perhaps? I don't know how the others will react.

"Great choice, sweet face. He's-"

"Special," I say, interrupting him.

"Yeah, he is." Chuckling, he walks towards Chris and his people. Following him with a smile that makes my face ache, I take my time.

"What do you mean?" Connor gestures wildly with his hands as he speaks. When I approach them, Connor and Chris turn to me.

"What the fuck?" Chris's face has been slashed down

one side. In the last few hours since I've seen him, he's clearly been in a fight and... has he grown some hair? Reaching up, I touch it; soft black locks cover his once bald head. "Um... I'm in love with your hair, Chris." I giggle like a schoolgirl as he dips his head so that I can reach better. "The fuck happened to your face?"

"City men attacked my people, over there." He jerks his chin towards the middle of town. City men? "They left but killed some of mine." He sounds so broken, sad. I cup his face in my palms as sadness fills my heart. Will we ever convince the world not all Panda are flesh-eating monsters?

"Ok. Go back and tell Crowley, he's chomping at the bit to get out here. Connor," I tell them all as Chris murmurs something to the Panda at his side. Still freaky having them so close. Chris is so different I barely see the black-ness around his eyes anymore. "Wake Charlie."

Nodding, Connor walks back into The Middle. Turning back to me, Chris strokes a finger down my cheek.

"I smell him on you." Well shit. Right to the point huh. "Did he... take care of you?" The small smile on his plump lips gives me chills. He's sexy - for a ... you know... a dead guy.

"Chris." I look down at my feet, the holes in the toes of my boots seem very interesting. "Charlie and I, we have... a bond like nothing I've felt before. We're connect-ed." He wraps both hands around my face, tilting it toward his.

"Mine, I have that for you. Bond." Softly he presses his lips to mine. His hands move to thread through my hair. Removing the piece of wire there, he lets my hair loose, running his fingers through the golden locks. "Kay-La." My name slurs on his lips as he pulls away, our eyes meet. His hands slide down my back to cup my arse so he can pull us closer.

"Chris." Letting my arms drop from around his neck, I drag them down the front of his body. His hard abs flex under the thin material of his shirt as I reach the hem of his pants. Desire shoots through my stomach. His hips thrust forward as the tips of my fingers connect with his skin. I bite my lip and stare into his eyes as if we are the only people on the planet. Fire burns through my veins. Jeez, he's so freaking hot. His sexuality rolls off him in waves.

"Kayla!" I don't even jump as Crowley's voice rings out behind me. Moving my eyes from Chris', I look around to see his Panda have formed a circle around us.

I gulp.

"Protect you always, Mine." Placing one softer kiss on my lips, Chris lets me go. Together with his people, he walks away as Crowley comes to a stop next to me. I take a moment to watch Chris leave, his butt a sight to behold.

"Charlie's asking for you. Connor told me about the attack on Chris'... people." Spinning on my heel, I face Crowley. As sexy as this guy is, his broad shoulders muscles upon muscles, tattoos and a badass attitude... he sure lacks in the smoothness department.

"Ok, it's my turn to take watch so you guys plan tomorrow's journey. Whoever's up can tell me the plan in two hours," I demand. He won't talk me out of this. I'm not the weak link here. Lifting my hand, I place it on his chest. Immediately, he covers it with his own.

"Kay I..." Shaking his head, he runs his other hand through his hair roughly. "I've never been so affected by a woman before. I'm not ashamed to admit I'm a little lost when it comes to you." He blows out a breath, frustrated with himself.

"Crow, you're doing better than I am!" I laugh. I seem to be doing that a whole lot lately. That and being constantly hot for these guys. "Listen, things are in that weird starting out stage my mum told me she hated so much. She and my dads fumbled around for months trying to work it all out. Things like this," I raise my hand to indicate The Middle, then to him and myself, "Takes time. It won't happen overnight." Slipping my hand from his, I hold his face. "Be patient with me big guy," Crowley growls low in his chest.

Just as I think he's about to fuck me right here and now, he picks me up and throws me through the air towards The Middle, and I crash to the earth in bone-breaking fashion. The breath leaves my lungs in a rush and I'm left panting on the ground as the world around me burns.

BLAZE
AMELIA K'OLIVER

All I can see are flames when I open my eyes. The ground around me is on fire but none of my clothes or skin is burnt. Lifting my hand, I check my hair, still there. Pushing off the ground, I try to find Crowley through the smoke. "Crowley!" I scream at the top of my lungs as I search, but I don't hear myself. All I can hear is the ringing in my ears. I nearly jump out of my skin when a hand clamps down on my shoulder. Spinning, I throw my fist out and it collides with a face I know well. I pull back before I whip the legs from under Charlie.

His mouth is moving, gesturing wildly while looking at the carnage around us. "Find Crowley!" I shout so loud, my throat burns from the effort. Squinting through the darkness and smoke, I see a body lying prone on the ground. I rush to it and drop to my knees. Using both hands, I turn him over. Tears spring to my eyes as Crowley's burnt face is exposed to the sky. "Crowley! Oh, shit." I turn and scream for Charlie. "Help! Come here, Charlie, Crowley's hurt!"

Turning back to Crow, I check for a pulse. Finding none, I press my lips to his and blow air into his lungs. His chest rises then falls, but he doesn't take the next breath. I repeat the process as Charlie skids to a stop next to us, the ringing in my ears quiets a little. "He's not breathing. Please, heal him." Without hesitation, Charlie places his hands on Crowley's chest, grunting with concentration. Connor rushes over as I lean down to blow into Crowley's mouth again.

"The fuck?" He shouts over his shoulder, "Chris come here!" then to me, "Kayla, you're bleeding." Connor tries to touch my head, but I bat his hand away. My focus is on bringing Crowley back to life. His face is almost fully burned down one side, black and red streaks across the skin, making him barely recognisable.

"Charlie?" I ask, tears rolling down both our faces as our eyes meet.

"It's not working..." Shaking his head, Charlie looks down at Crowley. Leaning down further, he plants his lips to Crowley's, attempting to heal him with a kiss as he had me. Moments later, he comes up for air with a gasp, I watch as realisation dawns on Charlie's face and that's when I lose my shit. Pushing off the ground, I stand as red and gold flames spread across my skin. The earth beneath me crackles and burns.

"Who did this? I will fucking burn them to ashes!" My gaze lands on the buildings in front of us, shadows play tricks with my mind as the flames on my body blaze brighter.

Men from the city. They did this. They killed my Crowley and now they will fucking burn.

Rage, pure and unadulterated, runs through my veins as I walk away from Crowley's body.

Vengeance. I will avenge Crowley's murder. The person who killed him will beg for my mercy, but I will give him no quarter.

"Kayla! No!" Charlie's voice rings out, echoing off the walls of buildings. Faces appear in front of me, but I cannot see them. The world blurs through the heat of my flames.

Connor's voice rings loud and true in my mind. **Baby girl, turn around. Look!**

Turning my body to face the fool who dared to interrupt my wrath, my mouth is poised to scream at him. My whole body freezes. Because standing on his own two feet, his face no longer black and red is Crowley.

The fuck? Our eyes meet across the distance as my flames disappear completely.

He's alive sweet face. Healed. Come. Connor's voice vibrates through my head.

Digging my heels into the ground, I sprint back to Crow in seconds and throw my arms around him. My face buried in his neck, my lips against his smoky skin, I sob.

"You were dead! Oh my God, Crowley." Between sobs, I look up at his face. It's then I see the scar. The spiderweb across his cheek and forehead on the left side. The other side of his face is mark free. Dropping kisses over the marks, I show him how happy I am he's alive. "Who did this? What happened?"

"A grenade. Thrown by a lone city dweller. Chris and his people dispatched him. But not before he told them his troop had been killed by Panda. They're all dead or Panda now," Charlie mumbles while he lays on his back in the dirt, panting. He must've given everything he had to heal Crowley.

"I checked the area, none are left. We're safe again," Chris tells us all. Thank fuck.

"Crowley, don't ever fucking do that to me again!" I smack him on his chest then pull him close once again.

He chuckles. "Sorry, Darlin. Are you ok?" He wraps his enormous hands around my face, using it to move me this way and that, inspecting me for injuries.

"No. I mean yes." My mind is still in a state of confusion. I almost went full-on fuck shit up for a minute there. I wanted to burn the world down to avenge his murder.

"It's ok, Darlin. I'm fine, see?" Grabbing my hands, he rests them over his heart so I feel it beating. "I'm fine."

"Your face... I..."

"Don't worry about it, it's just a face, besides," he grins down at me, a cheeky glint in his green eyes. "Isn't it my sexy body you love most?" Confusion rolls through me.

"No." My brows pull down in a frown. I shake my head at him.

His expression matches the look on mine. "Oh?" He looks a little sad at that as the corners of his mouth pull down.

"No, Crow," his eyebrows raise at my use of his nickname. "It's what's in here I really like." I tap my fingers above his heart. He blinks, long and slow like he's trying to make sense of what I'm saying. "Your heart, Crowley. You may think you've got everyone fooled, but I see you." Turning away from him, I look at the other three men surrounding us. To Chris, Connor and Charlie. "I see you all."

Reaching out a hand, Charlie takes it. Connor holds his other and he grabs Chris' who joins hands with Crowley. Standing in a circle, our hands joined, I realise then I'm falling for these men. Faster than a lightning strike, they've entered my heart and broken down my walls. It's not love yet, because I'm not sure I'm capable of that, but I really like them all.

"I'm in like with all of you." My version of "I'm in love with you" makes me cringe. I look around at them, hoping no one freaks out at my admission. Chris speaks first, and I almost cry at his words.

"Kayla, you saved me. I'm in like with you too." He leans forward and kisses me softly, his eyes glowing as our lips meet. When we move back from each other, Connor clears his throat.

"Kay I... I like you too, sweet face. Although," he chuckles, "that should be obvious." He looks down and my eyes follow his to the large bulge in his pants.

Oh, bloody hell.

"She means something deeper than your dick, Con," Crowley admonishes him while shaking his head.

"What? My heart's in my cock, big guy." That cheeky grin is back on his face as Crowley takes my hand in his.

"Darlin, I'd move the earth for you." He lays a sweet kiss on the back of my hand and steps away. Connor moves forward.

Looking into my eyes Connor tells me, "I really do like you, Kay. But I also find you sexy as fuck. The two things are connected for me."

Shrugging my shoulders, I let a quiet laugh out. "I know Connor. And it's Ok."

"Kayla?" The uncertainty of Charlie's voice makes my head whip around to meet his brown eyes.

"Charlie?" Is all I can think of to say because the emotion I see there floors me.

"My heart tells me I'm in love with you." Drawing in a lungful of air, I sway on my feet. "My body tells me I want you." Slowly, he walks towards me. "My soul says your mine." Reaching me, one of his hands cups my face, the other snakes into the base of my hair until our foreheads rest against each other. "Kayla, I'm yours. Wholly, irrevocably. For eternity. I love you, Kayla." Silence surrounds us as we kiss with a punishing passion.

"Fucking Charlie, way to outdo us all," Connor comments with a chuckle. Everyone bursts into laughter. Charlie moves back and laughs along with us. This is the first time I've seen Chris and Crowley laugh. It's a beautiful sight. Once we've all regained control of ourselves, we walk back into The Middle. Holding Crowley's hand, we enter the living space as a group.

"I don't know about anyone else," stretching my arms above my head, I yawn. "But I'm exhausted. Time for sleep. It's almost light out, no watch needed."

"Yes, I agree. To bed everyone. In three hours, we restart our journey to the city." Crowley orders. I find myself being turned on when he's bossy like this, I like it. Connor drops a kiss on my forehead and walks off to the room he chose.

"I... I actually do feel the need to sleep," Chris says looking and sounding surprised. "I haven't slept since I was," he indicates the black over his eyes. "Until earlier. Sleep well, angel," he says as he kisses me. He disappears into the room next to Connor's.

Turning to Charlie and Crowley I wonder aloud, "If he hadn't slept, I wonder if all the Panda don't need sleep?"

"That's interesting. So... where are you sleeping, Kay?" Crowley edges.

Hmm, is he asking me to sleep with him? Am I ready for that? Charlie and I had sex just hours ago, it wouldn't feel right to do it with Crow right after. He must see my thoughts on my face because he says, "I am exhausted, too.

But I'd... well, I'd like the opportunity to hold you." Turning to Charlie he asks, "If that's ok?"

A smile on his face Charlie responds, "That's up to, Kay. Not me, brother."

I take a minute to answer, mostly to keep Crowley guessing. He squirms. "Of course you can sleep in my room, Crow." I turn to meet Charlie's earthy brown eyes. "There's room for both of you, you know?" Smiling shyly at them, I twist my hair around my finger. Without saying another word, Crow and Char each take one of my hands and pull me towards the room where all my rags are.

I take off my boots and place them next to my chains and lay down. I watch in rapt fascination as Crowley and Charlie strip off their t-shirts. Admiring Crow's tattoos as they both pull off their pants I ask, "Do those things hurt?" Indicating the ink across his chest.

Looking down at them, he replies, "Nah. It's more of an annoying sensation than pain." Charlie's body is ink-free but just as sexy. Once their pants are off, I cock my head at the material covering their crotches.

"What are those?" I ask.

"Boxer shorts," Charlie replies as he lowers to the floor next to me. "Males in the city wear them. Like the male version of knickers."

"Oh. I like them," I reply as Crowley lays at my other side. Sandwiched between two of the hottest males I've ever set eyes on, I wiggle down until I'm face to face with Crow. The fresh scars on his face look gnarly, but I barely see them as I stare sleepily into his eyes.

"You're so beautiful Kayla." He signs deeply. "Could you ever love me now?" He touched the marks left by the explosion.

"I'm not sure I could ever love anyone, Crow. I'm sorry.

But you're still just as handsome to me." Sadness laces my voice. If only I wasn't so broken, I could see myself loving these four men. But I am broken. Charlie's arm snakes around my waist as he snuggles into my back just as Crowley's hand rests on my hip. I fall asleep almost instantly.

***

I COME AWAKE in my usual fashion, immediately, and I jolt upright. I'm alone, cold and refreshed. Which isn't usually how I feel. Voices float down the hall to me. Attempting to speak in quiet tones, the guys talk about how today's trip will be handled. But the walls are thin, and I can hear everything they say.

"We need to get there by morning. It's Tuesday and my contact will be on guard duty Wednesday morning." Crowley, in charge as always. What's Tuesday and Wednesday? Are they his contacts?

"Are you sure we can trust him, Crowley? I mean... I know you trained him but it's Kayla's life we're putting at risk with this move," Charlie counters. They've totally lost me now, so I stop listening. Climbing over the rags, I pick up my chains quietly as I stand, wrapping them around my body once more. The cold metal feels good against my heated skin.

Sprinkling a little water from my canteen into my hand, I wash my face and essentials. Using a smaller spare rag, I dry myself. A small piece of looking glass remains in a frame in the room. I stand in front of it and look at myself. Trying to see me through their eyes. My long golden hair sticks out at all angles, blood and dirt streaks across my pale skin. I look tired but there's a smile on my lips. I can't remember the last time I smiled so much.

Things went from Baby and me to a full house quicker than a speeding arrow. When I was trapped in that shack with Connor, more scared than I'd ever admit, I would never have guessed that in just a few short days, I would have four boyfriends. Running my fingers through my hair, getting caught up and pulling apart the tangles, I wonder if they're actually my boyfriends. Maybe Charlie is. We've had sex after all. But what about the others?

Do kisses stolen here and there constitute a relationship? They've all made it pretty clear they like me. But how do they all feel about me being with the others too? While almost every woman left has multiple partners, it doesn't mean it always works out. I've seen the way Crowley looks at Chris as if he'd like nothing more than to part his head from his body with his bare hands. Connor's still frightened of Baby, but we're a package deal, he and I.

While I'd like to think that given time, we could all work it out, that doesn't mean it's possible. Can I allow myself to get attached to the four of them knowing that one or more might reject me, or the others? Pushing away from the broken bowl I'm leaning against, I join the guys in the large space. No one sees me yet, Crowley's on the floor rubbing Baby's belly. His paws are in the air, one of the back ones kicking at nothing. Connor and Charlie are busy preparing what appears to be last night's leftovers. Their heads are bent in conversation; perhaps those two are closer than I first thought judging by how little space is between their faces. Hmm, possibilities? Chris sits on the couch, my device in his hand.

Oh shit!

"Chris!" All eyes focus on me standing in the doorway,

but I pay them no mind. Instead, I rush over to Chris and grab my most prized possession in the whole world from his hands. "Where'd you get this?" Clutching the sleek black screen to my chest, even bringing it to my lips, kissing it, I sigh in relief.

"After you were trapped. I found it looking for water for you. I couldn't remember what it was," he replies, his face breaking out in a smile.

"Oh my God, thank you! Oh, I thought I'd lost it." I can barely believe it. I thought it was gone forever.

"What is it, Darlin?" Crowley pushes off the ground to hover over my shoulder, looking down at what I hold in my hands.

"I found it years ago. I don't know what it's called," I tell him. Reaching out he takes it from my grip.

"It's an ancient communication device." He turns it over in his hands. "I've only seen one that worked."

"It works," I say, taking it back from him. "It's got my things on it. It needs a charge though." I turn back to Chris and ask, "Did you get the charger, too?" The look of confusion tells me he does not know what I'm talking about. "Black wire with a block on the end?"

"No, sorry, angel," Chris replies.

Shit. It's too far to travel back for it. The city is one day away. If we dash into the night, we should be there tomorrow. "Never mind." I plant a kiss on his forehead on the way back to my room where I put it into the bottom of my bag.

Back in the living space, we all sit on the floor and eat our small meals.

"Crow?" I look up from my empty piece of scrap metal, nudging his arm to get his attention.

"Yeah?" He must have been lost in thought because his eyes grow wide and he looks around the room.

"What happened to the Campo? And how did you call for backup?" I've been meaning to ask him, but I hadn't had the time.

"We left it. Charlie wouldn't wait, so we hightailed it to you." He looks down at his hands. "I'm sorry 'bout that. It was a stupid move."

I reach over and lift his chin with my forefinger. Looking into his eyes I say, "Don't be silly. You all came for me, that's what counts. And besides," letting his face go, I turn to Chris. "Aside from nearly dying... it ended well." He smiles back at me, his hands empty because he doesn't eat our food. Huh, what does he eat? I ask him.

"Animals, mostly." He runs a hand through his now chin-length hair. "Actually, that smells good." He jerks his head towards the scraps on the piece of wood in Charlie's hands.

Offering Chris the food Charlie says, "Try it?"

"Thanks." Chris takes a small piece of Tate and puts it in his mouth. Chewing, his face speculative, Chris hums and ahhs as he swallows.

"Good. Next time I will eat with you guys." Chris's speech has come a long way, he no longer speaks in short clipped sentences. His hair's growing as I watch, his skin's less pale, but the black across his eyes and nose remains the same.

"Let's get going, guys. We've got a long way to go today," I say as I stand. The guys all rise too. We each move around packing up our things for the journey. I watch out of the corner of my eye, unable to stop myself. A tiny, but loud part of me wishes I had slept with them all last night in one big puppy pile.

Once my bag's packed, I wander outside for some fresh air.

I can't help but wonder what sort of reception we'll get once we arrive at Tri-City. Obviously, Chris will be harder to sneak in than me. Baby even more so. Connor believes he'll be able to convince a guard to let us in. But then what? Where will we be sleeping? Looking out at the wastelands I've called home all of my life, a lump forms in my throat. Will I ever return here? Or will they will kill me before I even have time to know true happiness? So many questions, and not a single answer.

BLAZE

AMELIA K'OLIVER

We've been walking through the abandoned streets of outer London for hours now. My feet hurt. My stomach's rumbling. Baby went to look for food but hasn't returned yet. Crowley keeps his distance from me as I walk with Chris. Connor and Charlie are checking buildings up ahead for Panda and any supplies we might use.

"How do you feel, Chris?" I ask as we climb over the debris left behind by a building. Sharp edges and metal bars threaten to cause injury, but we navigate our way over them.

"I'm... good. The fog over my eyes has lifted." He jumps down a large piece of wall and holds his hands out as if to catch me. I jump into them. Catching me, he lets me slide down his body.

"Chris," I breathlessly mumble as his hardness glides down my stomach, the heat in his eyes makes my legs tremble a little. My feet touch the ground and he takes my hand in his, together we continue down the street. I smile from ear to ear. Never having a boyfriend, I'm not sure how to play this. So of course, I grin like an idiot and even whistle as we walk. Charlie and Connor emerge from a building to our left as we pass. "Hey guys," I say cheerfully.

Both of them look at me with open confusion. Charlie reaches out and takes hold of my other hand and my smile widens to impossible proportions. "So cute," I remark to no one in particular.

"Damn, if I knew all it would take is some hand-holding to get a smile like that on your face, girl, I'd've never let it go." Connor walks backwards in front of us, his cheeky smile lighting up the world. He ducks into a building, searching for supplies. I look down at my hands. It feels kinda intimate with our fingers laced together. The heat from their palms soaking into mine sends a tingling sensation travelling up my arms. Looking sideways at Charlie, images of us together flit through my mind. His hands on me, caressing, pinching, rubbing. My hands on him, exploring.

Electricity shoots to between my thighs. I bite my lip to prevent a moan crawling its way out of me from making it out. The sweetness in his kiss as he drove in and out of me, the way he felt inside of me. Suddenly, I'm pulled to a standstill from behind. Arms wrap around my waist, but Char and Chris don't let go of my hands.

"It won't be like that with me, sweet face. Keep thinking those thoughts and I'll take you on the rubble under our feet." Connor's husky words let loose that moan I'd suppressed.

"Fucks sake, Connor, let her breathe." Connor, Charlie and I all whip our heads towards Chris as he lets go of my hand and glares at Connor. The fuck? "You're always all over her without her permission. Making lewd comments and rubbing against her, it's... I don't have the word. But it's beginning to piss me off."

"Whoa Chris, it's fine..." He doesn't let me finish.

"No, it isn't! He's fucking perverted!" Shit. What the fuck is happening? Chris' face turns an odd shade of red as he stares at Connor like he wants to punch him or eat him, I'm not sure which.

"Chris-" I hold my hands out in front of me to calm him down. "It's fine, I swear. Connor's handsy, that's all."

"He should have your permission! He shouldn't... should..." His face goes blank. Free of all expression, Chris falls to the floor. His body crumples in on itself and he lands face first in the dirt.

"Chris!" My feet slide over rocks as I dash to his side in less time than it takes to blink. "Chris? Oh god." His body convulses. Arms and legs thrashing. So I lay my body across his to stop him from hurting himself. I look up just as Connor, Crowley and Charlie kneel next to us. "What's happening?"

"I don't know. I sense nothing wrong inside of him." Charlie runs his hands over Chris' body. His face is a mask of concentration as panic snaps and pops inside my stomach, threatening to spill its contents on the ground. Pushing off Chris, I look down at his face, my mind conjures up all kinds of scenarios.

Poison? No, that doesn't make sense if his body's dead, right? No, it seems to me his body's coming back to life. I study his contorting form below me. His hair grows, and his skin's no longer paler than the moon. He's getting better. Changing. Another wave of nausea hits me as Baby pads over to us, leaning down, he licks Chris' face. As suddenly as it started, it stops. Chris stops convulsing and just lays there, limp.

"Chris?" I shake his shoulders a little but get no reaction. Mechanically, I stroke his face for what seems like hours but in reality is only a few moments. "Should we move him?" Looking up at the darkening sky, I wipe away a single drop of rain. Rain means storms and with them, swirling clouds of debris and carnage. It's too dangerous to stay out here.

"Yes. Connor, take his legs," Crowley orders, his face conveys nothing. Unable to get a read on his feelings, I concentrate on the now. "Charlie, take her inside." His tone is a little too... I don't know the word. But I don't like how he says her.

"I'm completely capable of getting inside, Crow. And just so you know," in a move so fast, the guys don't see it until it's happened, I pull my sword from my back and stab it towards Crowley's shoulder. His eyes widen as he looks at the sharp steel in my hand then back up, confusion and horror clear to see. I jerk the blade back with a wet sound and a body hits the ground. "There's a fucking Panda behind you." Replacing the Katana on my back, I spin on my heels and walk into the closest building to us.

"Fuck me." I hear Crowley's words call behind me as I stomp my way into what appears to be some sort of sitting area. Chairs and empty frames dot the space in front of me. The smell is indescribable. When it hits me, my stomach rolls again but this time I tamp it down. Smells, like the one assaulting my senses right now, are nothing new to me. The world's dead, and it smells like it too. I'm used to the stench of rot and death. But this is beyond all of that.

My feet hit bits of wood and metal as I delve deeper into the darkness. If there's anyone in here, they'll come searching for whatever's making noise. Fucking Crowley, who does he think he is acting like I don't have a thought of my own? That huge mother fucker is going down, and soon. I gotta teach him I'm not a weak woman, he's met his match when it comes to being stubborn.

When the sounds of struggling reach my ears, I spin so fast my hair whips my face, the sting barely noticeable as I charge back outside to find Crowley and Chris throwing their fists at each other. Connor and Charlie are attempting and failing to pull them apart. Chris swings his leg out, which takes Crowley by surprise because he hits the ground with a thud.

"Bastard!" Crowley's bellow echoes off the structures around us, repeating as it reaches our ears.

"You dropped me on purpose! I'll fucking kill you!" Chris shouts so loud, my ears buzz in protest.

"In case you haven't noticed," Crow grunts and moans with effort as he pushes his gigantic frame off the muddy earth. "It's raining, you dickweed! You slipped outta my hands." He tries to bat off the mud now clinging to the back of his pants, but it only serves to spread it further. Clamping a hand over my mouth to hide the smile that creeps up on me, I listen to the two of them threaten to maim and kill each other. Chris lunges forward, his teeth bared and snapping. Crow lands a solid punch to his stomach. He goes down.

"What the fuck is your problem? Do not try to bite me again!" Crowley's brow draws down over his eyes as he glares at Chris who is bent at the waist, his hands out to the sides like he's about to jump on Crowley. But before Chris can pounce, Charlie speaks up,

"Hunger." Everyone except Chris flits their heads towards Char as he continues, "You're starving, aren't you, Chris?"

Fuck. The sky darkens, ominous clouds cover the sky.

Chris locks eyes with me when I turn back to him. His shining blue eyes are now filled with sadness as he nods his head.

"Oh!" My hand shoots to my mouth, the other to my stomach. It rolls back and forth like water in a skin as realisation dawns.

Chris has been acting strangely because he's starving. Was he about to take a chunk out of Crow? Holy shit balls.

"Yes," Chris answers, his voice laced with pain as he clutches his stomach. At that simple word, I bend over and heave until I see stars. A clap of thunder drowns the sound of the liquid inside me splattering on stones.

"We need to get inside. Now," Crowley growls at us then stalks off into the building I was in just moments ago.

"Go eat, Chris," Charlie says sadly as he passes Chris. "Come on, doll, let's get out of this rain." Charlie wraps an arm around my shoulders and guides me to the entrance just as fat drops of rain cleanse the world clean.

I stop and look back as I hear Chris tell Connor, "I don't want to be this monster anymore." His shoulders slump, head hanging, chin on his chest. He looks so defeated. "I cannot - I cannot do this anymore!"

Before I can do or say anything, Chris turns and runs down the street; back the way we came. A sob leaves me breathless as Charlie hurries me into the building, Crowley practically drags us both and deposits me on a chair. But the super-strong man doesn't let me go. Kneeling on the dirty floor between my legs he tells me, "He hasn't eaten since he met you, Kay. It was always going to end this way." The building shakes with another boom of lightning.

What? Why? Oh, God. Chris.

"He knows it makes him a monster," Connor explains as he enters the building. He wears a small smirk.

"Wait. How do you know this? I thought you couldn't hear him?" I demand. This can't be happening!

"I couldn't. But it's been happening in small spurts since yesterday. He..." Connor sits his arse on the floor next to Charlie. His hand squeezes my knee. "He thinks if he can appear to be more like us." He lifts a hand using it to indicate the four of us. "Then you could love him. He desperately wants that. But he thinks because he has the virus you couldn't ever love a Panda."

Oh, fuck me. Something inside me breaks, cracking open like an egg. It bursts forth and with it comes pain so deep I can barely breathe.

Love.

It swims through my veins like molten lava, burning, destroying the walls I'd built so long ago.

I love them all. So much so, my heart bleeds with it.

***

RUNNING headlong through the war-torn streets of London, my heart pounds against my chest bone. I search for the man I've given my heart to. He thinks he's unlovable. Thinks I could never fall for him. He's wrong. Because I already have. I've fallen for all of them and now my heart's torn into a thousand pieces. I run without direction for the man my heart bleeds for. For hours my feet dart me from street to street, in and out of buildings in search of him, but find nothing. Over and over I scream his name until my throat's raw from the effort. I can't find him anywhere.

Panda attack me at every turn, my blade making light work of dispatching them, severing heads from bodies as easily as human teeth cut through soft bread. He's gotta be around here somewhere. He can't have just vanished. But as day turns into night, I slow in my search. Having not been able to keep up with me, Connor, Crowley and Charlie returned to the building full of chairs as I tore up the streets with rain pounding on my head.

Finally, I stop. My hands gripping my knees. I fall to the ground in despair. He ran away from me because I'm a cold-hearted bitch. It's me who's unlovable, not he.

Who could ever love someone as broken as me? I couldn't even muster tears as my mother's broken body was lowered into the ground. Not when I was raped. Not when I took my rapests life, brutally. But now, crumpled on the dirty cold ground, my soul lets out an almighty sob as tears burst from my eyes. Big heaving sobs heave from my body as I mourn the loss of my Panda Alpha. He left me. Just upped and ran away. He starved himself to the point he wanted to eat Crowley. Now, I am one man down. One less person on this planet who cared about me. I feel the loss deep in my soul. It feels like he's dead.

BABY FINDS me some time later. He lays his body colossal body next to mine. I reach out and dig into his fur. His warmth and presence comfort me in a way nothing else can.

SOMETIME LATER, as I'm curled up in the mud, gentle hands lift me. Heat spreads over my skin as I'm pressed against a warm body and carried through the streets. Closing my eyes, I let the darkness take me.

· · ·

THE FEELING of being jostled wakes me. Cracking open an eyelid, I look up at Crowley's face. Stern, moody, take no shit from anyone, Crowley. He shifts me again so my head rests against his massive peck. I watch him for some time as he carries me God knows where, but from the ache in my body, I can tell I've been in his arms for a while. I reach up, gently caressing his cheek. He stutters to a stop and looks down at me.

"Darlin, you had us fucking worried." Grumpy Crowley growls down at me, his tone softening as we lock eyes. The unshed tears in mine make him pull to a stop. Lowering himself to the ground, Crowley rests my arse on his knee while cradling me like a baby. "Don't cry, Darlin. He'll come back; I know he will. Just... just give him time." he says the words with such surety, I'm half tempted to believe him.

I want to believe.

"He's gone, Crow. Because I couldn't love him." A sob burst from my chest, despite my efforts to keep it at bay. "I can't love anyone, Crowley, because I can't love myself. I can't be loved." Tears flow freely down my face now; I leave them unchecked. I don't have the strength to pull myself back together.

"No, doll. That's not true. You're loveable in a thousand different ways. But love doesn't come easily in the Wastes. You've never felt it, or received it, so you don't know what it feels like." Charlie appears over Crow's shoulder, tears in his beautiful, sweet, intense eyes.

"Trust me, Kayla, you are loved." Charlie bends down and kisses my head. My feelings either soar to the sky or plummet to the depths of hell, with no in-between. I've gotta get a handle on them before they destroy me.

Crowley sets me on my feet. I stretch my body and

several joints click and pop as I do. I must've been carried by Crow for a very long time because, as I turn toward where we were heading, I'm greeted by an iridescent dome.

"Tri-City," I whisper in awe and fear. I've avoided this place my whole life.

"We're here," Charlie says simply.

Shit.

"Baby, hide!" I give the command to my dog-lion and he charges off into the forest. He'll hide until I call for him. Hopefully, I'll be able to get him in soon. God, I'll miss that vicious fucker.

We all gather around Connor as he tells us the entry plan. I nod and act like I'm listening intently, but really, all I can focus on is the massive wall just a few steps away from us. I've only seen this place from afar. I never wanted to get this close, let alone go inside.

"Kay, are you ready?" Charlie digs in his pack and hands me the wig I'd worn every day for most of my life. "It's go time, beautiful. Remember, we're here and won't let anything happen to you, ok?"

"That's right, Kayla, we'll get through this together." Crowley wraps an arm around my shoulders and squeezes lightly. Despite their words, I can tell they're nervous about this. Entering the city's dangerous, to say the least. I'm not an Advanced, so I shouldn't be granted entry. If they realise that, I'm as good as dead and there won't be a thing Connor, Charlie, or Crowley can do about it. Taking a fortifying breath. I grasp Charlie's hand and walk towards the entrance. I hope we get this over with quickly, and we easily found Chris when we come back out, but right now, I must do this. With or without him by my side. It fucking sucks he's not here. I miss him already.

Four Brutes guard the gate to Tri-City, their massive bodies are shoulder to shoulder in front of a huge metal gate. Shit. These guys could squish me into nothing with one hit. Please let us all survive this.

"Craven," Crowley approaches one of the giant men, familiarity in his tone. "Is everything ready?" The Brute merely nods then looks over his shoulder to glance at me, lost for words as he stares into my eyes. Craven turns his body to the side and nods to the other Brute at the gate. Charlie pulls me forward as Connor and Crowley walk through first. As I pass Craven, I realise his eyes are oddly bright blue and haven't left mine since we arrived. He's at least seven feet tall, probably more. His head's bald and what skin I can see is covered in tattoos. He's handsome, in a scary kinda way. The guys told me not to talk, but I'm compelled to say something.

"Craven, find me later," I whisper as I'm rushed into the city. Something about the Brute called to me. It was clear that something about me did to him as well. I don't have time to think about it more though, because when I turn around, all of my senses are overwhelmed.

Advanced, lots of them, walk in every direction around me. Some in uniforms matching those of the guards at the gate, some look like they're extremely wealthy, their clothes impeccably clean and hole-free. Others; while clean and without holes, I can tell they're not as affluent as some. Smells of food being cooked assault me. My stomach grumbles, twisting into a painful knot. I'm pulled through the throng of people and down streets lined with foreign things. Tables cover either side of the street, filled to bursting with items I have no names for. People push and shove at me from all directions, almost all of them have clean faces and smell like flowers or something musky. I don't know the name. My already painful body quickly becomes bruised and sore as they push past, sensing we aren't meant to be here. Mud splashes my legs as a large Brute passes, his enormous feet empty puddles as he walks through them.

"Faster," Crowley commands through clenched teeth. I try to keep up, but Charlie practically has to drag me. I don't know where we're heading. All I know is my head itches and I want to eat everything I can smell. I want to touch all the shiny, clean things. I want to talk to the kids who run past us with smiles on their faces. All the while wanting to run and hide, to pull my jacket over my head and leave as quickly as possible. I shouldn't have come here. Mother was wrong. This isn't where I should be.

"In here, quickly." Connor stands half in a doorway ahead of us, his eyes flicking back and forth, checking for guards.

"I thought we were going to mine? This is... what is this place?" Charlie says as we explore our new surroundings. The walls are a reddish colour and the floor's packed dirt. Nothing's in the space, it's empty.

"I'm so sorry Kayla." Just as Connor says the words, huge men pour into the room. One grabs me from behind as Charlie shouts,

"What the fuck?" His face is the only thing I see as I'm roughly pulled backwards. A scratchy material is thrown over my head and the world becomes dark. Arms wrap around my waist as I hear Crowley and Charlie shouting and the unmistakable sounds of fighting.

BLAZE

AMELIA K'OLIVER

"**S**trap her hands, this one can produce fire." A deep masculine voice forces me awake. Leaving my eyes closed, pretending to still be out, I listen as the man talks to Connor.

"Be careful with her, for fucks sake! Dad!" Connor's angry tone matches how I feel inside. This mother fucker set me up! Now I'm stuck. They tied metal clasps around my wrists and ankles. Struggling will only bring more pain, so I don't bother. "You swore she wouldn't be hurt. She isn't like the others." The fucker he's talking to is none other than President Keeper. Connor's dad.

"Son, you're right, she isn't. No." An icy hand wraps around my knee. I just barely stop myself from flinching. By pretending to be unconscious, I'll be able to learn what these bastards have in store for me. And hopefully, where my men are. "She's much more. Quint! I want full diagnostic tests, ASAP, and get those results to me within the hour! And then," Keeper removes his death grip from my leg. "Testing begins."

Oh shit. Testing? What does that mean? Silence falls around me, but I wait a little longer before opening my eyes. When I do, they meet one blue eye and one brown.

"You traitorous bitch!" I twist and pull at my restraints, gaining nothing but bruises. "I'll fucking burn you until you're less than ashes!" My body breaks out in a cold sweat as Connor reaches out a hand to stroke my face. I turn my head, snapping my teeth to take a chunk out of this cock gobbler, but he avoids my teeth by pulling his hand away.

"Kay..."

"Don't fucking Kay me, you arsehole! Where are Charlie and Crowley?" My insides slither at the thought of them being harmed. If so much as one hair on their heads has been touched...

"They're in cells. I have not hurt them, Kayla." He smirks down at me as I struggle. "Dr Isaacs Junior has given you a shot. Your powers won't work."

Fuck! Shit!

"I'm so fucking sorry..." Connor begins, his voice changing tone. My anger bubbles over, cutting him off.

"Shove your sorry where the sun doesn't shine, you arse wipe. Get. Me. The. Fuck. Out. Of. Here." Anger burns and bubbles through my body. I need to get Char and Crow and then burn this mother to the ground.

"You'll see them soon enough. But Kay..." Connor stands and leans over me with his mouth just inches from mine. My eyes flick to his lips as I contemplate either throwing my head forward into his nose or just biting his lips clean off. Both. I want to do both. "You can't escape here. Because you're mine. I intend to keep you." He plants a quick kiss on my lips, just barely pulling away before my teeth sink into his flesh. Mother trucker! "By the way, Connor isn't home right now, but you'll see him real soon."

With that cryptic and fucked up statement, Connor turns and walks from the room.

What the actual fuck is happening? How can Connor say Connor isn't home? I'm so confused right now! As I lay here helpless on what feels like a metal table, my body cools until I'm shivering. Closing my eyes, I try to bring my fire to the surface, but nothing happens. Not even a wisp or spark. Fuck. Not now! I need to escape, and quickly, God only knows what they're doing to my guys. But my so-called power seems to have packed up her bags and left me. Just great, I fucking rock so hard right now.

Time moves slowly as I lay here, my body feeling like ice. Somewhere in the room, there's something ticking. I try to focus on that, trying in desperation to keep my eyes open. But eventually, exhaustion takes over and I fall asleep.

***

WHEN I OPEN my eyes again, a light blares in my face, burning my retinas. Snapping them shut again, I listen to the sounds of several people moving around. Calling out for help, I hoarsely say, "Please, help me, I need water." My pleas fall on deaf ears though, because no one helps me or brings me the water. Bitches.

"Prepping sample one." My eyes spring open as a tall man in a white coat appears on my left, his face blank of emotion as his bald head reflects the light into my eyes. Squinting, I look at his face as he wipes something cold against the crook of my arm and then he stabs me.

"Motherfucker!" Baldy doesn't even look up at me as

he continues to syphon blood from my vein. As it pours into the little tube at the other end of the stabby bit, I watch as vivid scarlet spurts out, filling it up. Speaking for the first time, the man at my side looks up, his fear-filled eyes on me, and utters the question I've been asking myself for days.

"What are you?" Standing abruptly, Stabby Mc'Stabberson pulls the metal thing from my skin, causing me to flinch at the slight pinch of pain, and then practically runs from the room.

"Jeeze, what a baby." If he can't stand the sight of blood, then he should pick a different job. A small spot of scarlet runs down my arm, trickling its way to the icy surface, distracting me momentarily. A loud bang and a hiss make my whole-body twitch in surprise. Then, like the harbingers of bad news, Connor and his father stand above me. This can't be good.

"Dad?" Connor turns his handsome face to his dad, my eyes flick to Mr Keeper's, confusion, awe, surprise, all war within the storm grey there.

What's going on? Why did that guy freak out so much?" So many questions flow through my mind at this point I can't keep up with them at all.

"What are you, Kayla?" Focussing my eyes on Connor, my anger flares.

"Screw you, Connor. You're a fine one to ask a question like that. What the fuck are you?" Something dark flits across his mismatched eyes so quick, I almost miss it. Evil.

"Why's your blood red, Kayla? I suggest you tell me." A sneer spreads across Keepers' face. "It could make the difference between life and death."

"Err... it's always red?" Now it's my turn to have a

confused look on my face. "Why.... What colour's yours?" My eyes flick between the two men, waiting for an answer, but none comes. Instead, Keeper walks away, leaving Connor to stare at the slight wound on my arm like it suddenly sprouted fur or tentacles.

Bending at the waist, Connor licks the now dried blood on my skin. When his hot, wet tongue makes contact, I can't help but be assaulted with memories of his lips on mine, his tongue massaging mine. The memories speed across my mind's eye as he licks, again and again, lapping my life force like it's the key to survival. That's when it suddenly hits me.

"You're not Connor, are you?" I ask shakily as he slips his now reddened tongue back into his mouth. Not-Connor straightens himself to his full height.

"Well observed, Princess." What. The. Fuck. The voice coming from Connor's mouth's not his own. "Connor's here, of course." The familiar stranger at my side licks his lips, a soft moan in his throat. "I let him out to play occasionally. I have to say, I like this body." Not-Connor presses a button near my head and the table tilts me until I'm upright. I dry heave as my perspective of the room changes, allowing me to see the horrors surrounding me.

Along the far sidewall is a row of clear tubes, inside them is a greenish liquid of some kind. With bodies. Human. Some are clearly dead. Others twitch, sending ripples through the sludge encasing them. Completely naked, I can see all of them are female. A throaty moan to my right makes my eyes flick to Connor. Standing before a large looking glass, he's stripped off his clothes. He holds his dick in his hand. Stroking it, he groans while looking at himself.

Ok, this just got fucking strange.

"Oh, Kayla, isn't Connor a fine specimen? Look at the size of this thing," Not-Connor says as our eyes meet in the glass. My mouth opens and closes, catching flies. Suddenly, he moves like he's made of fluid and slams himself against me. Both of us are naked, the sound of our skin slapping together echoes in the room.

"Mmm, he wants you, girl, ah..." The tip of his cock prods my clit, parting my lips. "So juicy, your body wants him too. Why didn't you take him out in the Wastes?" His hands travel my body roughly.

"Get your fucking cock off me, you absolute vile piece of shit!" I seethe between clenched teeth. My body stiffens and I'm about to call my flames until his face contorts in pure agony and he drops to the floor.

"Don't fight this, Connor! She could be ours this very second!" Not-Connor shouts, pushing himself off the floor.

"Get the fuck out!" Connor's true voice grinds out.

"Connor!" Oh, fuck me, this is crazy! "Fight it, Connor. You can do this," I encourage him. His knees give way sending him face-first into the floor. Ouch, that had to hurt. He jumps to his feet in one swift move, not even a second later and undoes the metal from around my body.

I stare dumbstruck as he works, not a single cohesive thought entering my mind. "Con?" What's even happening right now? His face is made of stone as he works. I feel like I could throw up any second.

The door bursts open just as our eyes meet. Men dressed in the same clothes as the guards at the gate rush into the room and wrap their hands around Connor's arms before he manages to unclasp my bonds. His father casually strolls in behind them as one of them checks I'm still locked up tight.

"You won't push him out, Connor. And you," he sets his evil eyes on me as the guards drag Connor kicking and screaming from the room. "It's time we showed you what we do with insolent bitches." Something hard hits the side of my head and in a flash of agony, I'm unconscious.

BLAZE
AMELIA K'OLIVER

When I next open my eyes, a throbbing in my head forces a groan from my dry lips. I'm thinking I'll end up with a damaged brain at this rate. How many times have I been knocked out now? Three? Four? Looking down, I see someone's wrapped a thin piece of material around me, but I'm still freezing cold. I can't believe I'm still trapped here; I need to get the fuck out. This time, I'm strapped into a seat instead of the table. Leaning to one side, I see it has enormous wheels.

Oh, this is cool! The possibilities...

"Let me out, you bastards!" Crowley? My eyes dart around, trying to pinpoint where his voice came from, but all I can see are two enormous brick walls with a corridor between them. My mouth's stuffed with material. Unable to call out, I try to push it out with my tongue.

"Crow, they ain't listening, brother. Shit!" Charlie's voice cracks with emotions as it echoes off the walls and filters over to me. They're so close!

"Muk!" The sound's muffled and barely recognisable, but Charlie calls out to me,

"Kayla?"

"Mumm um, me," I mumble around the cloth. Fuck, it hurts my tongue trying to push it out.

"No fucking way, that can't be her!" Crowley growls in disbelief.

"Um mee, mumm upp umh." I try to convey it is indeed me and I'm tied up, but of course, they can't tell what I'm saying. Thrashing my head from side to side while pushing out my tongue, I manage to get the material out. "Oh, thank fuck! Gah."

"Oh, my God, it's you! Kay, doll, are you ok?" Charlie's voice is the best sound I've heard in forever. I'm so glad he's ok. That they're both ok. Tears sting my eyes.

"Ah, yes, Charlie, I'm ok. Where are we?" My mouth's so dry, I can barely get the words out. Relief and terror flood me. Why would they leave me here alone with them? It makes no sense.

"Babe," Crowley begins, his voice cracking with emotion. One that until recently, I would have no name for, but now I know exactly what he's feeling. Because I'm feeling it too.

Relief.

"I'm ok, Crow, they took some blood, but other than that, they have done nothing. What about you guys?" The silence that follows answers my question. Fuck. Whoever laid their hands on my men is going to fucking burn.

Charlie asks, "Kay, can you get to us?"

"No, Charlie, I'm tethered to a chair." Despite my efforts, I hadn't been able to get the ropes around me to loosen. "What about you two?" If they can get to me, then they'll be able to loosen these things and together we can get out of here. But Crowley's answer leaves me crushed.

"We're behind metal bars Darlin, we can't get out." A small sob leaves me, bursting from my chest so thickly, I struggle to catch my breath. I'm desperate to see them. I need to ask if they knew Connor was a traitorous arsehole, but I need to see their eyes when I do. Otherwise, I won't know if they're lying. For now, I make do with just being glad they're not dead before I can find out the truth. But if they're behind bars, then it doesn't look like they knew about Connor. If they knew, then surely they would be by his side, not here in this corridor that smells like urine and blood.

"Have you seen him; Connor?" Crowley growls his name like it leaves a nasty taste on his tongue.

"Yes, he was acting... odd. Had a war with himself, it was freaky." I mean... I talk to myself often. Out in the Wastes, you could lose your mind if you spent so much time as I did alone, but what happened with Connor was way more than that.

"What?" Crowley asks, sounding frustrated.

I can imagine he hates being trapped. I feel the same. Drawing a deep breath, I explain to the guys how Connor changed on the flip of a knife. How even his voice had changed. Once I finish the tale of two Connors, Charlie and Crowley go completely silent. "What are you not telling me, guys?" My blood's turning to ice. The cold here permeates my soul, making me feel sluggish and tired. I force my words between trembling lips.

I will not cry!

"Tredici." That one word from Charlie's mouth is enough to make me gasp out loud.

Tre-di-see.

Thirteen.

My mother would tell me stories of the Tarot cards as a small child, making up stories for each one. Being that this is an apocalypse world and there's a severe lack of entertainment, stories were a great way to spend time when the work was done for the day. My favourites were about the thirteenth card. Death.

"What do tarot cards have to do with Connor?" Before anyone can answer me, the man himself pushes his way into the door to my left. He's changed his clothes and by the fresh smell lingering in the surrounding air. I'd say he's washed, too. Bitch. I would give my left tit to wash right now. Somewhere warm, preferably hot. His bubble butt glides past my face and I can't help but look. It's so perfect. Ugh, why'd he have to be all possessed and shit? He spins on his heel and looks down at me with a completely blank face.

"Kayla, still so taken by this body." Not-Connor runs his hands down the front of his black t-shirt, stopping at his crotch. Unbidden, my eyes follow. I've seen what's under those tight black jeans and as he squeezes the bulge there, my mind provides me with a mental picture. "Ah yes, you like how big and hard it is, don't you, Princess?" Snapping myself out of the heat, I flick my eyes up, meeting this arsehole's dead ones.

"The fuck you want, not-Connor? I've got places to be, men to kill." Once we escape, if Crowley and Charlie had nothing to do with this clusterfuck, I'll find out why my mum sent me here. Then, we'll leave and finally, I'll avenge my mother's murder. Maybe I'll come back for Connor. Whoop his ass, too.

"Clever girl, Kayla. You've worked out that I'm not who I look like, haven't you?" He runs a hand over his freshly washed hair. "But I can't let you harm Mr Masters. No, unfortunately for you, he's a valued employee of mine."

What. The. Fuck? Princess? Employee? What are these things? Frustration brings tears to my eyes, curse my lack of knowledge! Blinking, I refuse to let them fall and give this prick the satisfaction of seeing me fail to block my emotions.

Grunting fills the gap in his blabbering. My eyes flick down the hallway to where I know they trapped Crowley and Charlie. Are they hurting them?

"No little one, that is... well, it's a surprise. Allow me to show you why you should comply with everything I ask of you." Not-Connor stalks away from me. Arms come out of nowhere and attempt to grab him, but he avoids them by stepping out of reach.

"Come here, you fucking bitch. I'll show you why you should let us go!" Crowley seethes as not-Connor walks by.

"Oh, Crow, you do amuse me so." Not-Connor chuckles as he moves further away from where Crowley's arms reach out into the hall.

"Don't fucking call me Crow, you foul beast!" Crowley yells, but not-Connor simply ignores him.

Reaching his destination, not-Connor stops at the end of the corridor and presses something I can't see; the click echoes off the walls. I hold my breath.

"Bring him out," Not-Connor orders someone unseen to me, then moves to one side as two Brutes dressed all in grey emerge from a hole in the wall. "You motherfucker! I'll kill you!" I scream as I see who they're dragging between them. "I'll tear your god damned throat out for this!"

Bruised, bloody, his head lolling around as they drag him, he grunts as his feet are lifted off the ground roughly.

"Chris," I croak. The dam bursts inside me. I sob as tears slide down my face at the sight of him.

"Fuck!" Charlie shouts out.

Crowley seethes, "Motherfucker," as Chris is dragged past their cells. The black around his eyes blends in with the new marks covering his face. They drag him closer to me, throwing him on the ground face first with a sickening crunch. Turning his snake eyes on me, not-Connor smiles wickedly as he takes in the effect his surprise produced from me.

"Ah, Kayla, you care for the monster. That bodes well." Kneeling beside Chris, not-Connor grabs a fistful of his hair and jerks Chris' head off the floor. As his face is revealed to me, black blood pours from his nose, landing on the shiny white floor. My eyes watch the inky liquid. Why is his blood black? What is Chris? Is that because he's a Panda? Not-Connor's head flicks up from Chris. Our eyes lock.

"Kayla, his blood is the correct colour." Roughly pushing Chris back to the floor, not-Connor pulls a vial from his pocket, the crimson liquid there is familiar to me. "This is your blood." Twisting the tube, my blood sluggishly makes its way to the stopper at the other end. "This isn't the right colour, Kayla. Now tell me," faster than I can blink not-Connor's face is right in front of mine, "what are you?" Curiosity and more than a hint of madness light up his blue and brown eyes.

What am I? Kayla is my automatic answer. Because that's what I am. I'm human. An orphan of the Wastes. A product of radiation from bombs dropped way before my time. Just hours ago, I had four very new relationships. I had plans to kill the man who ordered his men to kill my mother. Days ago, I was just Kayla... but what if I'm not?

"You're not. But I'll find out what you are, little Princess, and soon. I'll discover why your blood cures not only the Panda virus but also the immortality I've granted to my minions. Otherwise, I will kill the four men that your heart desires," Not-Connor seethes, his handsome face contorted.

The jolt of terror that hits me is so powerful, I barely twist my head fast enough and I almost throw up all over myself. As my vomit flies through the air, not-Connor jumps back as liquid splatters his pristine clothes. Giggling mid-hurl, I try to aim the next heave in his direction. Not-Connor turns his furious gaze on me, as it just misses him. Spitting the last of the contents of my stomach from my mouth, I lock eyes with him again.

"You've got the wrong girl. But trust this, not-Connor," I lean my body as close to him as I can to make sure he sees the emotions in my eyes. "If you hurt Chris, Charlie, or Crowley, you will beg for mercy as I char the flesh from your bones." His chin tugs sharply to his chest and his eyes widen a fraction. **That's right not-Connor, you know I will melt you into a puddle of gore. Do not test me further. Let my men go. Now!**

Answering the words I projected into his head, not-Connor surprises me by saying, "Kayla, that coldness you feel? That isn't a temperature thing. It's perfectly warm in here." He touches my arm, making me squirm to get my hands around his neck. "That's a serum made by scientists created especially for you. It's suppressed your element. Your powers won't work, Princess." The smug look on his face turns my insides to jelly. My powers? Holy fuck, I can't feel them! I'm completely defenceless. I've been so distracted I didn't even notice the missing heat inside of me. It's not like I'm used to the feeling, either, having only just discovered I could set myself alight.

What the actual fuck? "That's right, you're in no position to demand anything from me. I will torture you and your men. Unh!" Suddenly not-Connor's face crumples, changing from one of victory to that of pure agony as he drops to his knees.

"Kayla! What's happening? Speak to us!" Crowley's voice brings me from my shock.

"Fight Connor! Fight, oh, please!" All I can do is watch as Connor fights against whatever or whoever has control over his body as he writhes on the floor. "He's fighting for control!"

"That's it, fight, brother!" Crowley roars.

"Come back to us, Con!" Charlie bellows.

"Connor, find me. Hear me, please." My whole body is shaking.

I need my Connor back.

All at once, Connor's body goes slack as he slumps to the floor, going completely still. "Connor!" No, no, no!

"What's happening, Kay?" My blurry eyes snap to watch as Crowley and Charlie's arms wave around in the air through the bars.

"I.... I don't know." Turning back to Connor, I watch as he pushes himself from the floor. I gulp in air as he turns his mismatched eyes on me. "Connor?" Could it be him?

"Kay, I... I can't fight him." The internal strife he battle is clear on his face. His teeth grind together, and his eyes scrunch tightly closed. "You need... ah, to leave!" Collapsing on the floor again, Connor grunts and moans in agony.

"Please fight it, Con, we need you." Wiggling in the seat, I try once again to get loose. Hot fingers wrap around mine, and I look down to watch as Connor unlaces one of my hands. "That's it, Connor!" He's doing it! Just as the rope is loose enough to pull my hand free, an invisible force throws Connor's body back. "Connor!" He lands with a thud as the guys who dragged Chris run back into the room and stick one of those stabby things in his neck. They drag his body out the door.

Fuck!

"Chris?" I jerk my hand back and forth and finally, it comes free, taking pieces of my skin with it. "Wake the fuck up, Panda!" I yell as Chris, who is still laying on the floor, not moving. "Ugh, guys." I work on my other hand, pulling at the rope, my short nails scrape at my skin. "I've got a hand free."

"Yes! Where's Connor?" Charlie asks just as the door crashes off its hinges.

"Shit!" A massive Brute looks from Chris to me, his wild eyes torn between doing his job or saving the girl tied to a chair before him. "Craven, help us. Please." Seeming to make a choice, Craven strides to me and grabs the ropes at my wrist. "Thank you." His strength makes light work of the restraints holding me down. "Get Charlie and Crowley out, I have Chris." I bend beside him on the floor and lightly slap his cheek as Craven stomps down the hall. "Rescue coming guys," I shout out so they don't think Craven's an enemy. The next slap I hit Chris with wakes him with a start. Moving sluggishly, he finally looks up at me. "Chris! Get up, quick." Any minute now, more guards will come through the opening left by the door and we'll be trapped.

Hooking my arm under Chris', I help him stand. Something screeches behind us and I know soon my other guys will be free. Thank fuck. "Can you walk?" Pushing his long, black hair out of his face, I make eye contact with Chris; his eyes no longer glow but are now dim. Normal. Not what I'm used to seeing.

"Yes," he croaks, as his eyes flit to the floor, refusing to meet mine. There's no time to think about why he won't look at me, because Charlie and Crowley storm towards us. Anger, relief and pain on their handsome faces. Chris leans against the arm of the chair I was in. Panting, I let him go. He doesn't fall. More tears pour down my cheeks as Charlie wraps his arms around my waist, lifting me off the floor as he buries his face in my neck.

"Oh, Kay!" Charlie squeezes me so tightly I can barely breathe. More hands wrap around my body as Crowley stands behind me and holds me just as hard.

"Guys." As much as I want to stand here and soak up the love from my guys, we have to get out of here. I tie the material wrapped around me to the side. It allows me to move but exposes more of my skin than I like. Charlie takes off his blood-stained t-shirt and pulls it over my head. It'll do for now.

"Thanks." He smiles a little, but it doesn't reach his eyes.

"Come on, we need to ghost." Pushing myself from between them, I move to the empty door frame. Their faces crease with confusion as I turn to the giant at their backs. "Find a way out. Craven, get these three out of here. Go with them, keep them safe, please." Turning towards the exit, I formulate a plan. As I move, three hands grab me in different places.

"No, we stay together," Crowley insists.

"Fuck no, you're not going anywhere without us," Charlie says, hurt clear in the way his pitch changes when he says 'us'. Shit.

"Let us protect you, Kayla." My eyes meet crystal blue

ones as Chris finally speaks. "They had me drugged, experimented on. I need to feed." His eyes flick to the floor again and frustration stabs my stomach.

Why won't he look at me?

"Guys, I don't need...." I start to say I don't need help, but Charlie interrupts me.

"We don't think for one second that you need our help, Kayla. We know what you're capable of. With or without your fire." Charlie steps up to me, our bodies touching from our knees to chest, his intense eyes holding mine hostage. "We protect you, not because you need it, not because we are arseholes with hero complexes, but because you're precious to us." His warm hands cup my face and I lean into his palm as his heat spreads through me. "We did not know Connor wasn't himself. Trust me, if we had, this wouldn't be happening right now. Let us help you find him." His eyes flick back and forth between mine, searching for something. "I love you, Kayla, don't split my soul in two by pushing me away now."

A soft gasp forces its way from my throat. He has such a way with words. My heart melts and heat spreads through my veins as he gently presses his lips to mine. I greedily kiss him back, savouring the passion and love that flows from him in waves.

"I'm not smooth with words like Char is," I turn my head but leave my lips barely touching Charlie's to look at Crow. "But we want to be by your side for all eternity, Kayla. If you'll have us?"

My eyes track to Chris's face as he says, "We are yours, even if we don't deserve you."

Can I give these guys my love? My forever? Do I even have it in me to truly love? Yeah, my mind, my heart say I love them. But I've spent a long time ignoring all feelings. What if I can't be... normal?

"I will protect you with my life, Miss Kayla." Craven nods.

Drawing a steadying breath. "Let's go get the fifth piece of my heart and cast out whatever's taken him from us." The three of them smile, nodding in agreement. Together, we exit our prison.

Crow takes point, Charlie behind him, then me, Craven and finally, Chris at our back. We slowly make our way through the halls, checking doors as we go. Connor has to be here somewhere. I don't know what will happen when we find him, but I know one thing for sure; when I get my hands on his dad, I'll fucking burn him to a crisp. Crowley's fist shoots up into the air and we stop and press ourselves against the shiny white wall. Everything here is white, it's freaky as fuck and it makes my eyes ache from the brightness. The sound of scuffling feet fades, and Crow signals us to keep moving. Charlie has yet to let go of my hand. His hot palm against mine continues to thaw my blood.

We can do this. We can escape, save Connor, and maybe. just maybe, move out of Ole Yella and make a home for the five of us.

BLAZE
AMELIA K'OLIVER

"This room's unlocked," Crowley whispers sometime later. His face made of stone, he looks at each of us, his neck craning up to meet Craven's eyes. "I go in first. You guys follow. Craven, close the door behind you. Ready?" At our nods, Crow pushes down the handle and rushes in with all of us filing in behind him.

"Shit." We pull to a stop as we're confronted with large tubes of green liquid like those in the room with me when I first woke up in this wretched place. Except, these contain males. In different stages of life, they range from a young boy to men around my age. They're all the same person.

Connor.

What the fuck? "Err, what the holy hell is this shit?" I ask no one, but Charlie answers.

"Clones. Looks like Keeper's been playing God with his son's genetics."

I do not know what any of that means, but it doesn't sound good at all. Walking further into the room, I realise all the bodies inside the tubes are dead. "They're dead, right? I mean, they can't be alive. None of them has moved since we entered." I turn to Charlie. The sight of Craven's immense body in front of the door allows me to relax a little. If anyone wants in this room, they'll have to get past that wall of a man first. Releasing my hand, Charlie moves to a wall of panels that look like bigger versions of my device.

"Yes, all dead." He presses his fingers to the screen, and it changes to a different picture with lots of writing on it. Scanning through it, Charlie continues, "Experimental genetics gone wrong. Shit!" He turns his brown eyes to mine. "According to this, the real Connor's not the one we've been talking to. The original died years ago." Shaking his head in confusion, Charlie turns to Crowley. "Connor was bitten. It says here that he was bitten as a child, turned into a Panda. The subject couldn't be saved. Luckily, DNA samples are kept of all the major players' kin."

"That's impossible. We would've noticed if he swapped Connor for a clone. Wouldn't we?" Crowley asks angrily. He's so tense, his hands shake and his neck muscles bulge.

I continue to search the room as they argue about whether they would've noticed their lifelong friend being replaced. I never knew that Connor. Well, maybe I did at one time, but I don't remember that. I need to focus on the here and now. The people I do know. There must be something we can use for when we come across guards. Moving further into the darkened room, I soon realise there's nothing here. Just boxes of papers and plastic things I have no name for.

"Kayla, it's time to move." Crowley's voice filters to me.

Rushing, I rejoin them back at the door. Charlie doesn't take my hand again but walks behind me, deep in thought. Exiting the death room, we continue our journey through the blinding corridors. Crowley checks doors as we go, and when one opens, we file in and look for weapons of any kind to help us fight our way out of here.

"Craven." Charlie halts and looks up at the giant. The rest of us stop and press ourselves against the wall. "You work here, big fella. Where can we find weapons?"

Huh, good fucking point. We all twist our heads to the side and up to look at the Brute. My neck aches.

"Yes, I show you, pretty girl." The bass of Craven's voice rumbles through my feet. My mouth pops open in shock because as he speaks, I'm thrown into my mind as images flit through it at speed.

"You cannot do that, Kayla! You mustn't ever choose a Brute. They'll crush you without meaning to." My mother stands before me, her face is flushed, patches of sweat under her arms. I have to crane my neck up to meet her eyes, so I must be tiny. All four of my dads stand behind her, their faces furious, shaking their heads while looking at me in disdain.

"Well then, I'll never choose, mummy. I want Crave! He's fun." I stick out my little lip and pout. Mummy doesn't understand me at all. Crave is twice my size, super strong, and he calls me pretty girl. I like him. I want him to be one of my guards. Princesses like me need guards; mummy tells me that all the time. So why can't I choose them?

. . .

THE HEAT of a palm against my cheek brings me back to reality. Shit a duck. I'm a princess? Of what, exactly? Did she just call me that as a nickname? The way Charlie calls me Doll or Crowley calls me Darlin? Or could I actually be a Princess, whatever that is?

"Kayla? Doll, we need to move." Opening my eyes, I see Charlie's sweet smile.

"Ok, let's go." Nodding, Charlie continues down the hall and this time he takes my hand in his. More heat slips into my soul, and I feel the first stirrings of my power. Oh, thank fuck, whatever they drugged me with is wearing off. Looking back towards Craven, I can't help but wonder if he remembers we knew each other as children. Once we're out of here, I'll make sure he and I have a conversation about the vision I just had, but right now we have to hurry and find Connor.

My face meets Charlie's shoulder as we skid to a stop. Ouch. Licking the blood from my lip, I realise why we suddenly halted. Blocking the hall in front of us are three Brutes, four guards and Connor.

"Where are you going, little Princess?" Not-Connor's lip pulls up in a snarl as he takes in the four of us. "Traitor! Craven, I should've known you recognised her at the gate." Shaking his head at the giant, he turns his evil gaze to me. "Stop this, immediately, and I will be generous. I'll allow one of them to live,"

"Fuck you, demon!" Crowley barks as he launches himself at the nearest guard. Charlie follows and tackles one to the ground. Craven pushes past me and takes one of his brethren in each of his massive hands. He's much bigger than the rest. As fighting breaks out all around us, not-Connor and I stare at each other. My eyes flicker between hazel and cerulean.

"Connor, please see me. I know what you are, and I don't care. Kick Thirteen's arse out of your body!" I yell over the cacophony of noise in the small space. An errant fist hits me in the ribs, but I don't even blink as I watch Connor switch between Death and the real him. Avoiding the brawling bodies between us, I make my way to him. A Brute wraps his arm around my waist and lifts me above his head. A shriek leaves my lips as I fly through the air towards Connor, only to be jerked to a painful stop as another set of arms plucks me from the air. The flimsy cloth covering my body slips, rips. Bollox. I bring my elbow down onto the hardest skull I have ever felt, sending shock waves up my arm as it connects.

"Kay," my name rumbles through my whole body as I look down into Craven's bright blue eyes.

"Shit, sorry Crave." My guys are kicking arse while I look down at them. Crowley stands atop one clearly dead Brute while he swings a large, red tube at another. The sickening thunk it makes as it connects with its skull brings a sense of pride to my heart. Crowley's a brutal fighter. I bloody love it. Twisting my head again, I find Charlie in a throng of people. He's light on his feet as he weaves between guards, taking out knees and knocking them out as he moves like lightning. Fuck yes! He takes out two guards at once while another watches, his mouth hanging open in shock. Abruptly, my feet meet the floor as Craven sets me down in front of Connor, who then pulls out a blade from the holster on his hip. Shit, I have nothing to fight him with. Wait! Closing my eyes briefly, I attempt to call on my fire, but the space inside me it usually sits is dark, just a small spark in the middle, not enough to set me afire.

Crap.

241

"You can't win this Kayla! I'll punish your men while you watch." I slide forward and wrap my hands around not-Connor's face.

Looking deep into his eyes, I say, "Connor, Death has no place on this earth anymore. Cast him out." Lifting on my toes, I let my lips hover over his. "Come back to me." I crush my mouth to his and pour every ounce of love I have within me into him. Our tongues intertwine as he kisses me back, his hands roam my body greedily. **Come back to me Connor, I need you.** Pulling back, I dare not open my eyes for fear of seeing not-Connor staring back at me. "I love you, Connor." The gasp that leaves him makes me snap open my eyes.

"I love you too, Kayla," Connor replies, then crumples to the floor as he screams in agony. I hardly breathe as I wait. Long moments pass until a black wisp of smoke pours from Connor's mouth and slithers across the floor, disappearing into the grate on the wall. Connor slumps, unconscious, his breathing laboured.

"Craven?" I can't carry Connor, but he can. I turn back towards the bodies littering the floor behind me, pride, awe and love flowing through me. "Come on guys, we gotta get out before Keeper sends more goons." I grab two pieces of the cloth covering me and tie them together the best I can. It covers my boobs and between my legs, but most everything else is on display.

"This way." Craven's gravelly voice wraps around me. He carries Connor over his shoulder, not even breaking a sweat at the extra weight. He stomps down yet another hallway towards an enormous set of doors.

"Wait." I barely hear Connor's hoarse voice over the noise Craven's gargantuan feet make as we run towards them. Connor struggles against the hold Crave has on his waist, and the big guy lowers him to the floor.

"Kayla, my dad... he plans to release another virus," he says, turning to me. Connor's haunted eyes roam the hall behind me, pleading with his brothers to listen to him. Turning his gaze back to me, he continues, "It will kill humans and Panda." Chris steps forward and takes my hand.

"Even my people?" he asks, fear clear in his tone. Nodding, Connor swallows thickly.

"Everything outside of Tri-City will perish. Kayla, I... it's made from your blood. I... I created it. I remember every-thing." Tears slip from Connor's eyes as his knees give way and he lands solidly on the concrete below his feet. He sobs into his hands as we all stand still, dumbstruck. How the fuck are we meant to stop that? Laying my hand on Connor's head, the most comfort I can offer him at this moment, my mind works overtime to formulate a plan. But it runs blank. There are thousands of Advanced here. We can't fight them all.

More guards appear from the doors we were just about to run through.

"Stand down and let the Prince go!" One of them shouts.

Prince? Princess? Those are connected, but how? Crow-ley, Craven, Chris and Charlie rush at the men holding swords. I dart around Connor and join the fight; the first tendrils of fire lick my palms as I throw my fists at the faces in the crowd. Drawing on the feeling, I allow it to take over my hands. My fists burst into flames as I drive one into the gut of a guy twice my size. His screams of pain and terror are music to my ears as he flies back into the men behind him and they fall to the floor.

Sending flames to my feet, I set fire to the skin there, kicking out at another guard. My fire flicks from me and onto his clothes. Spreading over the cloth covering his body, he goes up in flames. They jump from him to several others as he flails around. I watch, open-mouthed, as it spreads to every guard before us. I look down as something tickles my skin. Not only have my flames returned, but so have the clothes mum gave me. That is so bloody cool! Thank god I don't have to walk around naked anymore. I pull the leather jacket around me, revelling in the comforting warmth.

"Oh wow, that was cool!" I whisper as the guards fall one by one, their bodies ashes before they've touched the floor. Spinning around, I stride over to Connor and kneel in front of him. "Are you ok? Has Thirteen really gone?" I have so many questions for him, but I just don't have time to ask them all.

"Yes. He's gone, I'm sure of it. Shit Kay, the things I've done." Tears roll down his face and my heart breaks a little for him.

"No time. We gotta move. Now!" Crowley growls while he lifts me from my knees. The floor rumbles beneath us with what has to be thousands of Brutes coming our way. Together, we rush through the doors and out into a field I recognize. This is where Connor and I found ourselves after we'd been kidnapped! As we pass the small wooden shack, my mind answers my own questions. It wasn't Connor they trapped me with and it wasn't a coincidence it was him I woke up with. How long was I unconscious for before I came 'round to him in that room? Not-Connor set me up, and I let him worm his way into my life. Into my heart.

"Kay," Connor runs beside me with Crow and Charlie

taking the lead. Chris and Craven are behind us. I throw up the mental brick wall Connor taught me about, needing to keep my thoughts to myself in case he's not-Connor still. Just as we're about to cross over from the field to the woods, a huge black vehicle pulls up in front of us. We skid to a stop.

"Not now," I whisper, not having the capacity to help us escape and deal with the shit show that has been the last twenty-four hours. "What's that?" The panic in my voice makes the words come out as a squeak. Something huge rolls towards us.

"Get in!" A colossal head peers out the window and shouts down at us. Who the fuck is this? Before I've gotten the chance to say or do anything, I'm grabbed in a punishing grip around my waist, hauled into the air and thrown into the back. Just as the door closes behind me, a flurry of arrows thunks into the side of whatever this thing is.

"Argh!" As they hit, I scream out, thinking they'll come through and stab me. I never want to be stabbed again. I throw myself across the lap of a mammoth Brute. He looks down at me spread across him, but says nothing. My stomach rolls at the unfamiliar feeling of moving without meaning to. Oh shit. This thing is awesome! The time it would save me travelling across the wastes, not to mention the safety it would provide. Those arrows didn't even peek through the side.

"Thank you, Cell and Can. Let's make haste, they will follow." Craven's voice booms in the small space. Pushing off the Brute's lap, I press myself against the side of the vehicle.

"Err... who are you guys? And what is this thing?" I ask everyone and no one. Craven answers me.

"These are my brother's. Cell." He nods to the one whose lap I'd sprawled across moments ago. "He's Can." He indicates the man at the front.

"This is a truck, Kayla." Turning my narrowed eyes on Connor, he seems to remember himself. He continues. "Like a car, but bigger. This one's electric and armoured, so we're safe." Ok, that makes no sense, but I'll roll with it. The truck moves really fast through the trees, sliding me this way and that as we turn and jerk to avoid hitting anything.

Gotta get me a truck.

After spending what feels like way too long trying to figure out how to open the door, I finally manage to push it open a little. Sticking my head out, I scream for Baby. Hopefully, he heard and follows us. Please let him be ok. I slam it shut again. Several times I'm thrown into Cell's rock-like body as Can masterfully navigates the thicket, so I push my back against the truck's side and put my feet against his hip. This way, I can barely move when we turn sharply. He looks down at my feet but says nothing. He gives me no facial expressions in order to read what he might be thinking, either. I guess if he objected to me using him, he'd let me know. I sit back, letting the heat from his giant body warm up my frozen toes.

"Connor, how do I know it's you?" I ask as the familiar streets of London whizz past. I wince inside at the sad look on his face, but don't allow it to show. None of us had any idea he had Death inside him the whole time we were with him. He could be fooling us right now.

"Kay, I... I know you can't trust me right now and I've got to prove he's gone, but Kay..." He climbs over the seats behind me to sit between Cell and me. I move my legs so he can sit back, my toes freeze with the loss of contact with

Cell. Taking my hands in his, Connor continues. "I swear to you, I fought that bastard as hard as I could. He'd let me out at night, during the day I'd be able to wrestle control here and there." Looking down at our hands, he shakes his head as a sigh leaves him. Fuck, this is twisting my insides. "I kidnapped you, Kayla, I locked Baby in the bus, I did so many bad things..."

I snatch my hands away. Just for a second, he holds on tight, but then lets go when I tug harder. He tries to say more but just opens and closes his mouth several times.

Mother fucker!

"I'm so sorry. I wasn't in control!" He finally manages as rage builds inside of me. "Not at that point, later when we were in the bus, he gave me back control. I wanted to tell you, but how could I? Oh, by the way, a tarot card has taken over my body! But trust me?"

I wouldn't have believed him, maybe I might've even killed him because I would've assumed he'd lost his mind. Given him mercy.

"I don't know what to think, Connor. How much of it was you?" Inside my chest, my heart's bleeding. I was well on my way to falling in love with Connor. Or as close to it as I can. But now I feel like it was all a lie.

"I can't explain it because I don't understand it. It was like... he was there under the surface making suggestions in my mind." He taps a finger to his temple, his face haunted. "He knew you wouldn't want to be with him, given he's an evil arsehole. So, he let me out for most of the time we were together. He needed you to come with us. It was mostly me you fell in love with Kayla and I...."

"No! I'm not in love with you, Connor." Before he can say it, I interrupt him. I spread my hands out in front of me to hush him. "I said that to bring you back. I don't know who you are!" The hurt that spreads across his face pulls at my heart. I'm so fucking confused! Half of me wants to hold him, kiss him, maybe even fuck his brains out, the other half? Well, she wants to chop his dick off, shove it up his arse, then throw it in his mouth and sew it shut. "I'm sorry, I... that was..." I let out a pent-up breath. I'm not handling this well. "Listen, this is far too confusing right now. Let's just concentrate on stopping this new virus from killing the entire planet, shall we?" Connor nods and sits back against the seat. I do not know how to feel or what to say. How can I trust anything he says? Leaning back against the side of the vehicle, I let my eyes close. With my stomach painfully empty and all my energy drained, I fall asleep, tears still wet on my face.

***

THE VEHICLE SKIDS to a stop and I barely manage to keep myself from being thrown forward into the seat Can sits in. The rude awakening does nothing for the sick feeling inside of me.

"Bug out everyone. Grab the bags and enter this building," Craven orders. We all jump into action, opening doors and climbing out. When a Brute orders you to do something, you do it double-time or risk being smushed into a puddle of nothing.

Charlie takes my hand and gives me a small smile. One that tells me he is having a hard time with the whole Connor thing, too. I mean... they've known each other since they were children, possibly since they were born, and now he finds out this Connor is a... clone? This whole situation must be eating him up inside. Together, we walk around the massive black vehicle. The wheels it moves on are black and come up to my hip. It's bloody huge and impressive.

I want one.

Chris walks to my left and suddenly every single human in the area draws guns and knives from holsters and points them at Chris. Shit! That's the moment Baby chooses to make his appearance. His massive paws dig at the dirt as he prowls across the clearing in front of the building.

"Shit! A lion!" someone unseen screams.

"They've got a Panda with them!" another arsehole comments.

Oh crap, we're in so much trouble. As an arrow sinks into the ground next to Baby, flames burst from my skin. "Harm either the lion or the Panda and you're toast. You understand?" I seethe between clenched teeth. Apparently, my fire is emotional. I need to learn how to get it under control, lest I set someone on fire for eating the last chunk of bread.

"Calm brothers. The Panda is a friendly, as is the... lion." Craven doesn't raise his voice, simply because he doesn't have to. The moment he talks, everyone focuses their eyes on him. "As is decreed by Constantine, these new people will be treated like one of us." The heavily armed people surrounding us nod, put away their weapons and disperse.

I crane my neck up to look into Craven's eyes. "Thank you."

Simply nodding, he sweeps his tree-like arm out, inviting us to proceed into the house. Letting my fire go, I draw in a deep breath. Well, that could've been much worse. Charlie, Connor, and Crowley stand down and pull back.

Baby draws up beside me, rubbing his large body against me. "Good boy." I kneel so we're face to face. "I love you," I confess. I've never said it before. Not to anyone. Other than Connor and I didn't mean it. "Go hunt" I plant a kiss on his snout, and he licks my face. I'm so thankful he didn't get hurt today; I couldn't live without him.

The building we enter is small and surrounded by trees. I don't recognise this area at all. "Where are we?" I ask Craven as he passes us, his hands laden with bags.

"This is the headquarters of the rebellion." Craven shoots Charlie a confused look as he answers me. My head twists to look at Charlie, who simply shrugs in response. Fuck this shit. There's so much no one is telling me! I've had just about enough. I'm getting pretty pissed at not being told things. It makes me want to ghost. To just leave and not look back. No one would find me. And neither would that twat, Keeper. Tempting... if not for Charlie. And Crowley. And Chris. Shit.... even Connor. Looking up at Craven's face, I realise I wouldn't be able to leave any of them behind. Can't take them with me either, too many of them. Well, looks like I'm stuck, so they'd better start telling me things before I blow up on their arses.

"Craven, when we're settled in, I want answers. Understand?"

"Yes, Princess, of course." My whole body freezes, Princess. There it is again. Before I can ask what they mean, I'm pulled into the building by Charlie. As we enter, I realise this place is much bigger than it seemed on the outside. The living space is massive, packed with tables and seats. Things I have no names for litter the surfaces. It's clearly somewhere many people do important things.

At the very back of the room, one entire wall is taken over with a giant screen like that on my device. Someone pushes past me, nearly knocking me over, but firm hands grip my shoulders. Turning, I look up into Connor's eyes. Mine narrow.

"Careful, sweet face." He looks around us while I stare in wonder at the scene before me. "Want to see where Char, Crow and I have lived on and off for years?" There's hope in his voice, nervousness too. Like he's worried I'll say no. I kind of want to, but then again, I really want to see the place these guys call home. So, I nod, not trusting my words right now. I war against the part of me that wants to burn Connor into ash. The betrayal, although it's clear he wasn't in control of himself, still stings.

This house is bustling with people. As we make our way up the stairs, it's clear it's not often they see unfamiliar faces. Everyone stares at me as they pass, but then it occurs to me I don't have the wig I wore on my head as we entered Tri-City. I feel naked as one guy stops, staring open-mouthed. He has the nerve to look scared. So, like the mature woman I am... I jerk myself towards him, acting like I'll attack him.

"Shit!" he yelps as he jumps back so fast his head connects with the door frame behind him. A giggle snort escapes me. I lift a hand to stop it, but it's too late. Every set of eyes in the hall turn to look at the girl with the golden hair laughing like a menace. My anxiety hits me hard then. The feeling of snakes in a barrel kicks in and I almost throw up. Luckily, though, Connor pulls me past them all and into a room at the end of the hall, ending my misery at being stared at.

Charlie and Crowley are already here. They turn to greet us as Connor closes the door behind me. Charlie drops the pile of material in his hands and rushes to me, grabbing me around my waist and lifting me off my feet. He's so dramatic, I love it.

"We need to have that talk sooner rather than later, guys. I do not take kindly to being kept in the dark," I demand over his shoulder. Charlie pushes me back a little to look at me. Close to tears, his brown eyes are shadowed with emotion as he lowers me to the floor. Feeling guilty at ruining his joy, I say, "Ok, later. But I fucking mean it, no more keeping Kayla in the dark." Charlie smiles. It finally reaches his eyes. "Show me your home." Taking my hand, he guides me to the strip of material hanging from the roof and pulls it aside. Behind it is a bed, the cloth covering it a faded red. A small table next to it contains books that look like they've been rained on, the pages wavy and the covers barely readable. A small window to the left casts a soft glow across his personal space.

"This is mine. Wanna sit?" Charlie motions to the bed, a look of hope spreads across his face again. It pulls at my heart. I lower myself onto the hard bed and Charlie sits next to me, his hand on my bent knee.

"We've been a part of the rebellion for a long time, Kay. When we realised Keeper was evil, we joined up. We didn't know he was playing with magics though"

BLAZE

AMELIA K'OLIVER

Fucking hell, I'm way out of my depth here. Magic? Is that how he got that beast into Connor? With magic? Surely, he wouldn't've been able to push a thing like that out so easily. What if he's still not-Connor? Shit, he'll probably slit my throat in the night. Or worse... one of the guys! Did Connor tell them where this place was? Are we all in danger here?

Suddenly, the material is pushed back, revealing a determined-looking Connor. I let out a shriek as he comes towards me with his hands raised. On instinct, I call my flames to my hands and raise them, ready to fry this moth-erfucker.

"Wait." Charlie wraps his fingers around my wrist. In an instant, I let the flames go for fear of burning him. Shit. Connor takes my face in his hands and bends between my legs.

"Let me in, sweet face, please?" What's he asking of

me? I flick my eyes to Charlie, who just nods. Well, ok, but one wrong move and I will barbeque Connor.

"Trust him, Kayla, we're with you and he can't hurt you here." Charlie laces his fingers with mine as I let down the wall inside my head. The first sign of trouble and I'll burn him to ash.

Images and voices tear their way into my mind all at once. Gasping I try to pull back, but Connor just grips me harder.

"Oh, I got it now, doll face. Just relax. I promise it won't hurt again." Connor's eyes close tightly, so I close mine and concentrate on opening my mind to him.

"You will let him in son, and then... I will rule over this world with an iron fist."

The image of Connor's dad standing over me with a menacing look is frightening. Spittle flies from his mouth and hits my face as he screams. He's clearly mad, lost his mind and is a danger to not just me, but this entire country. But the feeling of being powerless to stop him weighs heavy on my chest.

The images switch again to me looking down at my hands. Only these aren't mine, they're masculine.

They're mine, Kayla. These are my memories, love. Let me show you all of it.

Connor's voice enters my mind, soothing and gentle. My soul recognises him as Connor, the real one. Relaxing further, I fully open myself to him, breaking down the wall inside me completely.

"No dad please, don't do this! I'll bring her back, she'll come. Then you can get her blood and we can just leave. You'll never have to see her or me again."

"NO! She must remain here. Safe. She cannot be allowed to be killed! Understand me, boy, I do this for you too. She is your promised, I will keep her safe. Now let go, do as Tredici commands, bring her to me."

Changing again, I see Connor's image reflected back at me. He screams at the copy of himself in the looking glass. "Don't hurt her or I will end this. I'll kill myself and then you won't be able to get her!" His own reflection answers him back;

"I will not hurt her, Prince; I want her safe too, but if you continue to fight me, I will kill your brothers with your own hands."

I WATCH as Connor's memories flow through me, seeing them through his eyes. I see my face staring, hard and cold whenever I looked at him, but slowly it becomes softer. A grunt echoes around me and feelings that aren't my own snake their way through my very being. Love. So much love my heart feels like it could burst in my chest. Fear. The fear of losing that love. My body trembles with it.

"Connor..." bursts from my lips, barely audible to my ears. Unable to open my eyes, the memories keep coming.

Connor screaming at himself in a looking glass, him watching me from afar, the ache inside his chest at not being able to hold me. Changing again, I find myself looking down at Connor's hand wrapped around his cock, pumping it hard as he pictures me in his mind.

My gasp breaks the connection. "Um..." He pleasured himself while thinking of me?

"Sorry." Connor's cheeks flame as he opens his eyes to look into mine. "I'm not filtering anything, Kayla; I want you to see it all."

I close my eyes again and Connor rests his forehead against mine as more memories burn themselves into my brain.

A large and ancient book clutched in Connor's hands the title; How to perform an exorcism. Over and over, he searches every single book in his dad's extensive collection of relics. Then I watch and feel as Connor hovers over a woman. Tears roll down her face as not-Connor fucks her brutally.

"Cover your face, wench. You look nothing like my bride." not-Connor's hand flies forward into the poor girl's face as she scrambles to pull the material over it.

He made me Kayla; I didn't want to. I couldn't control him at all. Death violated my body many times. I'm so sorry.

My whole body is shaking violently. So is Connor's. Strong, familiar arms wrap around my waist and I know Charlie has me in his arms.

A bright light flashes, and suddenly Connor is standing before a very short woman.

"Please help me, he... he's pure evil. You must help before all is lost."

The feeling of wetness on my face brings tears to my eyes. This tore Connor up inside, but he felt absolutely powerless against Thirteen and his father.

The small woman before him disappears in a puff of smoke. The despair inside Connor makes my stomach roll. When the smoke dissipates in the space where the little woman was now stands a taller figure. As her face comes into the light, shock waves roll through me.

Mum?

"I will help you, dear Connor. But first, you must tell me," her face hardens as she stares down at Connor, who is now on his knees at her feet. "Would you die for my daughter?"

"Yes!" Connor immediately answers, not even pausing for breath.

"Then I will free you, but only when the time is right. And there will be consequences. Are you prepared to pay them?"

"Yes. Anything."

The next scene Connor shows is me tied to a chair.

WHEN CONNOR LETS GO of my face and sits back, I leave my eyes closed. Unable to look into his mismatched eyes and see the pain that now coils around my heart reflected in them. That bastard Death can suck my metaphorical balls if he thinks I'll let him get away with the torture he forced Connor to endure for these last few months.

"You see, Kay? Do you understand I did everything I could do to be free of that... evil? I kept all this," he gestures to our surroundings. "To myself. He doesn't know I'm part of the rebellion. If he did... they'd be gone already." Connor's desperate voice breaks through my thoughts.

Opening my eyes slowly, my vision blurry with tears. I throw myself out of Charlie's grasp and wrap my arms around Connor's shoulders. Our lips crash together. I pour everything I have into the kiss. Our tongues sweep against the other, sending shivers down my spine. His hands move to my shoulders and I press myself against him. All at once, I'm lifted into the air. Instinct has me wrapping my legs around his thick waist. The feel of his hard body against mine draws a moan from my lips. Connor swallows it as his hands squeeze my arse.

Moving his mouth to the side, Connor breathlessly says, "Kayla, I am so, so sorry, I..."

"It wasn't you Con; it wasn't you." Pulling him to me again, my tongue swirls around his. I realise I have two options.

One; I kill Connor. His soul is tortured, torn, and broken. Not unlike mine was before he sauntered into my life just a short time ago.

Or two; I do what Connor, Charlie, Crowley and Chris did for me; show him that the challenges we faced in the past don't have to define us, but can show us the way into the light.

I think of Charlie as I kiss Connor. I picture the scars on his chest from the explosion. How they broke his soul. Changed him. Shaped him into someone less than what he should've been. How together he and I bonded enough to break through the barriers he built around himself.

I think of Crowley. Remembering how the grumpy sod jumps between being a dick one second, but the next he pushes through his issues and shows me the sweet side of him that I can't wait to explore more of. How his darkness calls to mine in ways I can't explain, but I know together we'll explore the dark.

I think of Chris. Of how he starved himself because he didn't think I could love him. How together we overcame that and all the other problems him being a Panda brought.

My heart fills with joy as memories fill my mind of my guys. That together, we can face anything. Do anything. Together, we can heal our brokenness. I was meant for these men, and they for me. Bad things happen in this fucked up world. Trials will be sent to test us. But so long as we're together, there's nothing we can't face. The things we've faced already, not just since we met, but before that, our pasts, all led us here; to this moment. To each other. I realise at this moment that I would do it all again if it meant I'd find my guys.

As his hands roam my body, his passion for me presses against the apex of my thighs. Long, thick and hot, it makes my pussy clench. Connor isn't a wicked man; They forced him to do a lot of terrible things. Sure, he should've told Crow and Char, they might've helped him. I don't know how, but they would've tried. He absolutely should've told me, but I also understand he didn't feel able to. He feared for their lives, too.

Decision made, I grind myself against him. A moan tears from him, vibrating through my chest. His hands snake around me and unclasp the chain around my body. Slowly, Connor undresses me, his hands gentle and soft against my heated skin. He doesn't take his lips from mine as he takes our clothes off.

He slowly lets my feet touch the floor. Confusion and heat war against each other on his features when he pulls back slightly. Cupping his face with one hand, I turn my head to look at Charlie. The fire in his brown eyes makes me press my arse against him. "Charlie..." Answering my non-question, he rubs against me and presses his face into my hair.

"Doll, I'm so turned on, you're going to have to tell us what you want because I can't think straight." Charlie's hot breath skims across my skin, a shiver runs down my spine. Turning back to Connor, my eyes lock with Crowley's over his shoulder. "Crow?" His arms come around Connor's body, his hands resting on Connor's bare stomach.

"Yes, Darlin, oh, fuck yes," Crowley replies, his voice husky with need.

Chris stands near the door, hands in his jeans pockets, looking confused and a little lost. Raising my hand, I beckon him to me. He comes willingly, if a little slow. "I want all of you right now. We could all be dead in the morning; I want to have no regrets."

"Kayla, I... I don't even know if... I can?" Chris crossed the room to stand next to Crowley. They're both so handsome my heart can barely take the sight of them so close together.

"I know you can." I drop my voice to a whisper, aiming for seduction and apparently nailing it because Chris slides in between Connor and me. Reluctantly, Connor moves back, allowing Chris to kneel before me. His eyes shine once again as he looks up at me. It does things to my body I can't explain.

"Mine, I want you more than I could ever explain," he whispers, his eyes locked with mine. I feel all of their eyes on my body as if their hands were on me instead. Completely naked before my four men, I feel not a single ounce of self-doubt. They're all hard, hot and ready. If I ever had any doubts the four of them would find me as attractive as I found them; the thought dies a death as I drag my eyes around the room.

"Fuck me, all of you." The words come from me before I can stop them. Not that I would. I absolutely mean what I say. I want them, wholly and for however much time we have left in this world. Moving away to give them room, I watch as Charlie, Crowley and Chris remove their clothes. Chris takes off his black bottoms, revealing that he can indeed get hard for me. I bite my lip at the sight. He's long, thick, it pulses. Then Charlie pulls the shirt from his back.

The soft ridges of his muscles make me want to lick them. My tongue darts out to wet my lips. Crowley's all muscle and when he's naked, I can't help but moan a little. He's truly a sight to see. Connor stands in the middle, his cock bouncing off his abs as he stares at me, enjoying the view of my naked body and no doubt listening to my naughty thoughts as all four of my men stand in a line, waiting for me to take this further. Their cocks are hard, visibly throbbing, dripping liquid from the ends, bouncing off their abs.

It feels like an eternity passes as I close the space between us. I stop before Charlie, letting my hands roam his soft skin. Cupping my face, he presses his lips to mine and kisses me with a soft passion. As with everything Charlie does, his hands and lips explore me with reverence and gentleness. His kind soul calls to the deepest parts of me. The fifteen-year-old Kayla inside me begs me to accept his love, his touch, his heart. I listen to her, soaking up everything Charlie has to give me. Ending the kiss on a gasp, I move to Chris.

The black around his eyes and nose reminding me that a short time ago, this man was a killer, a Panda. But the sparkling blue of his eyes also tells me he's no longer a monster, and that makes me lean forward and crash my lips to his. His hands grip my hips as he pulls me to him, his body alive and ready. Sparks of electricity sparks at every point of contact. By now I'm so wet, it coats my upper thighs.

Pulling away with a moan, I force my legs to move me to Connor. I can't help but feel a small stab of pain in my chest. We were all nearly killed, they turned my blood into something meant to kill two races. The Panda and the humans. But I also know it wasn't Connor. My soul knows he'll fight beside me to fix what they forced him to do.

Lightly, he presses his soft, full lips to mine. Licking the seam for access, his tongue swirls against mine. His hands grip my arse. He bends at the knees so his cock rubs my clit as he gently thrusts. Pulling away, I look down. His dick is shiny with my juices, the sight making me even wetter. Crowley impatiently clears his throat as I stand there looking at Connor's cock. With a small giggle, I move in front of the mountain of a man. The satisfied grin on his lips making me want to headbutt him. "Crow, always so bossy." Chuckles burst from the others as Crowley grunts and yanks me against him.

He's so tall, I have to stretch on my toes to kiss him. He doesn't lean down to make it easier for me as the others do. One of his huge hands snake to the base of my neck. He wraps it around my hair and pulls my head back so my neck is exposed.

"I'll show you bossy, Darlin." In a flash of movement, Crowley buries his face in the crook of my neck, and he bites down, hard.

"Oh, fuck!" bursts from me as the pleasure-pain causes me to cry out, the wetness between my legs now dripping down them. He obliterates the fine line between pain and pleasure as he drags his other hand between my boobs heading straight for my core. He inserts one large finger inside me.

"Crow! Oh!" I melt against him as his finger fucks me.

"Who's the boss, Darlin?" he huskily whispers, his gigantic cock rubbing against my belly.

"Huh?" My pleasure-filled brain can't comprehend what he's asking me.

"Tell me I'm your boss, call me Daddy!" Crowley growls as he thrusts his fingers faster and harder.

"Oh, fuck. Yes... Daddy!" I manage on a gasp. The heavy

feeling in my stomach becomes too much as he curls his finger inside me.

Heat envelops me as a body presses into me from behind and on each side of me. Caged in the arms of my four lovers I come apart at the seams. Moaning in abandon as mouths close in around my nipples, sucking and nibbling, fingers rub furiously at my bundle of nerves. The room spins as my orgasm rushes through me so fast, my legs collapse under me, but arms hold me upright. Light bursts into a million pieces behind my eyes. My moans turn into growls as my pussy clenches around Crowley's finger over and over. My juices rush out, coating both Crowley and Charlie's hands, who's rubbing my clit, and my legs as it squirts from my pussy in a way I never knew it could.

"That's it, Kayla, give me all you've got," Crow growls next to my ear as he continues to finger fuck my pussy. Barely aware I'm even alive at this point, the feeling of being weightless forces my eyes open. Connor's azure and chestnut eyes hold mine. My body feels weak, but my soul feels solid. Fulfilled. Happy. Loved. In love. The world around us disappears as his sultry voice soothes over my mind.

I love you, Kayla, more than I have words for. I will make this right, I promise.

I do not know what to say back to him. I'm not even sure that I know what love really is.

That's ok sweet face, for now, I'll settle for you being "In like" with me.

A slow, sexy smile spreads across his face as he lays me down on the bed. Crowley nudges him out of the way and kneels between my legs. I lift my head a little to look down at his dick. Oh shit. That's not fitting in here! The sight has me scrambling back up in an attempt to get away from the monstrous thing. He's far too big, nope. I quit. He'll split me in two! My vagina clamps shut and refuses to even entertain letting him near her.

"I'll make sure you're ready for me, Darlin," Crowley chuckles as his hands dip to between my legs. I squeeze my knees tighter.

Chris lays his hand on Crowley's huge shoulder. "Maybe we should... go first?"

Nodding, but snarling, Crow looks down at my bare pussy, a forlorn look in his eyes.

"Ok, but I warn you, Darlin," leaning down, he drags his tongue over my core, making me call out when he nibbles my clit "I won't be as gentle as these three." With that hot remark, Crowley's replaced with Connor.

Our eyes lock as I snake my hand between us and guide him inside of me. As the tip of him enters me, he hisses in a breath.

"Kayla, so fucking tight! Unh." His words, the timbre of his voice and the sheer size of him, all combines to make me moan loudly. Several gasps reach my ears as Connor slowly pushes his way inside me.

"This won't last long, I'm sorry," Connor forces between his teeth, his eyes squeezed tightly shut.

"Give me all you've got, Connor." I want it all, everything they have to give. A small whimper leaves my lips as Connor pulls back out, then slams into me with force. My hands fly to his shoulders as he bounces me off his hips. Over and over, he pounds into me with an urgency I feel in my soul. He needs this just as much as I do. He grips my hip with one hand, the other roughly kneading my breast. The stirrings of what I now know is an orgasm flits through my belly. The unbridled need in his movements and the passionate way he kisses me tells me he's close. Lifting my hips slightly, the next time he thrusts into me, he goes deeper. It's enough to make him throw his head back and let out a throaty groan as hot seed coats my insides, leaking out around him as he continues to move.

"Kayla!" He rests his forehead against mine, still slowly thrusting with jerk movements. His body shivers with each spurt, his mouth moaning against my lips. "I'm so sorry," he whispers once he stops moving.

"Why?" Completely confused, I look up into his beautiful contrasted eyes. I think having sex with him is a clear sign I know his actions weren't his fault; therefore, he has nothing to be sorry for. He looks so sad and disappointed. Is it me? Was I not... good?

"I wanted our first time to be better than this, I..."

Cupping his face in my hands, I force him to look into my eyes. "Con, it was beautiful. If we survive what Keeper has planned for us, then we'll get more chances to do this, because..." Casting my eyes down to where our bodies are still connected, I draw my bottom lip between my teeth and bite. "I want to do this again with you, like... a lot." A giggle works its way out of my parched throat.

"Fuck yes, I want that, too. You're so beautiful, Kay." His words stab at my heart as I look back into his eyes. Every so often, a memory flashes in my mind. He would tell me he thought I was pretty all the time when we were little.

It's fascinating to learn about things I did not know happened if a little worrying. With a last kiss, Connor moves off the bed. I stretch out my muscles, my arms above my head when Crowley runs a hand up my stomach, spreading it wide across the space between my breasts, the look of a starving man in his eyes.

His thumb rubs over one hardened nipple while his little finger flicks over the other.

"You're already filling out Kay, healthier than when we first met you, I like it," His palm is barely touching the middle of my chest but the warmth radiating from it sends shivers over my body. His vast hands can cover the distance between my hips easily, they're so big.

"Crow, I..." At that moment, my stomach makes a loud rumbling sound. Having not eaten for a long time, my body's protesting just as I was about to tell Crow to show me the darkness my own craves. Instead, he pulls back and Charlie hands me a cloth which I use to clean myself up, then pass it back to him. I thank him with a smile and throw Crowley an apologetic version. He just growls in response as he moves back to give me space.

"I'll go see if we can get some extra rations." Sitting up, I watch Connor redress, pulling clean clothes from a big box across the room. "Chris... What do you eat, mate? We won't have any raw meat or anything like that."

Looking decidedly uncomfortable with the question, Chris ducks his head and mumbles something none of us catch.

"What?" I ask. He lets out a deep breath as his bright blue eyes are on mine.

"They gave me animals to eat at that... lab? Yes, that's what they called it, lab. But I couldn't eat it. It made me sick. So, they gave me human food, and well... I wasn't sick."

A slow, serene smile spreads over his handsome face. Does Chris now eat human food? Does this mean he's... human? The black mask on his face tells me he isn't. But maybe he's in between the two?

A hybrid.

"What's a lab?" I ask myself for the millionth time. "And that's great Chris, at least you no longer have to starve yourself." The thought of him starving himself again to appear normal makes me want to vomit. He looks so happy right now I have to blink hard, so I don't cry.

"I'll be back shortly with food for everyone." Connor turns to Crowley. "I'll also reach out to Constantine, let him know we all arrived safely." Crow nods but says nothing. His hand grips my shoulder.

"You can let go, Crow," I say as I lay my hand over his. "I'm not going anywhere." Shock flashes in his eyes.

I hit the nail on the head then, huh? He loosens his grip but still doesn't let go. I allow it because he clearly needs the comfort of touching me.

"Sorry, just when we were separated from you, and each other." He shakes his large head back and forth. "I didn't like it. Emotions are still new to me."

"He pounded those bars for hours. Good thing his bones are unbreakable, otherwise he'd be in trouble," Charlie comments. Unbreakable, huh? That I'd like to test.

"It didn't work though, did it? They made those bars out of something that even I couldn't break. Fuck knows what, but I want to make a suit of it for Kayla," Crowley growls back. His hand slips down my arm, then lets go, leaving my body feeling cold. Gooseflesh spreads across me as I sit here naked, my head flicking back and forth between the two polar opposite guys.

"Like she needs that." Charlie laughs. "'Did you not see her ash those Brute guards? Fuuck," Charlie counters while moving to sit behind me. His arms snake around my waist as Chris walks out of sight.

"Yes, true. Remind me to never piss you off, Darlin." Crowley sits at the bottom of the bed, his gigantic frame taking up most of the room there. He takes my feet and rests them on his knees. Chris comes back with a wad of material in his hands. Draping it over my legs, he sits on the floor beside us. A brief break is just what I need. It's like they all know me so well they don't push me or rush this. It makes me love them even more.

***

THE THREE OF them discuss the merits of having fire as an element versus water while I relax against Charlie. Crow's hands massage the soles of my feet. The small window to my side is level with my eyes so I stare out of it, letting my mind wander. The sounds of my men talking animatedly about things I can't begin or have time to understand fade into the distance. I watch as the sun makes its slow descent below the horizon.

The naturalness of the situation I'm in at this moment isn't lost on me. The feel of Charlie's arms around me, his fingers grazing the patch of curls between my legs, Crowley's rough hands moving across my sensitive feet, making my eyes feel weighed down. Chris strokes my leg from his position on the floor. With their hands on me like this, I cad almost let myself believe we were just four normal people relaxing as day turns into night. Not that the world is about to experience its second apocalyptic event, a second coming.

But we're not normal people. Charlie heals himself and can heal others. Crowley's Brute-like with bones that can't break. Chris is a Panda who should be attempting to eat us right now, not lightly running the tips of his fingers across my skin. Connor can read minds and project his thoughts and memories into others' minds. Me... I'm a freak. My body sets itself on fire but doesn't burn me. There's nothing normal about my little family.

Huh. Family.

I guess that's what we are now. And I love each one of them. Even if it scares the shit out of me to do so.

A gasp brings me out of my inner thoughts, and the room goes silent. Turning my head, I see Connor standing at the open door, a large piece of wood in his hands laden with all kinds of food.

"Family?" His eyes are wide, and the colour has gone from his face as he stares at me in shock.

"Yes, family." Smiling, I look around at the guys surrounding me. "You're all mine, and I'm yours, if you'll have me?"

"Fuck yes," Connor answers.

"Damn right we are," Crowley says, squeezing my foot, drawing my attention. He leans over and kisses me hard and fast. Turning around a little to look into Charlie's eyes, I see they glitter with unshed tears. Turning fully, extracting my feet from Crowley's grasp, I place my legs over Charlie's. Chest to chest, he holds my face between his hands. Our foreheads meet. "Charlie?" Fear jolts through me.

What if he doesn't want this? Me? Because I'm broken!

"Kayla, I have something I want to give you if you... please?"

My brows draw down. Completely confused, I pull back from him as he moves my legs and climbs off the bed. He disappears behind the material hanging from the ceiling. I turn to look around at the guys, questions in my eyes. What could Charlie want to give me? No one's ever given me something before. The bow and arrows I lost when someone - I guess it was not-Connor - kidnapped me, I stole from a Brute when I was in my eleventh year. His back was turned, dealing with a group of Panda. I'd stolen the bag he dropped to defend himself. The bow, quiver, and several arrows were inside. Damn, I miss that bow. Everything else I owned was either stolen, made by my own hands, or scavenged from the Wastes.

"Don't ask us. We promised we wouldn't tell you," Connor says while passing me a metal bowl filled with meat, bread and Tates.

Oh shit. Food. Hells yes. Resting the cold steel against my crossed legs, I lift the bread to my nose and take a long sniff.

"Oh, fuck me." Biting into it, I tear a huge chunk off and chew. "Hmm." So bloody good. I need to find out who makes the bread here because he or she is about to become my new best friend.

"Jealous of a bread roll," Connor utters while shaking his head, a small smile on his lips.

Crowley chuckles as he watches me demolish the bread.

"I feel that, brother." They all burst into laughter as I pick my way through the meat and Tates. I do not know what they're talking about, but it's not worth stopping to concentrate or ask questions.

When my bowl's half empty, Charlie comes back into the room, an excited look on his face.

"Kayla," he frowns down at the food covering my fingers. I wipe them on a piece of material lying next to the window. "I have something I've wanted to give you for a long time." He holds a pouch in his hands. The material's dark blue and worn in places with small patches of white showing. He clutches it to his chest as he approaches us. His eyes are focused, and it makes me squirm a little. I've never seen this look on Charlie's face before. He looks so... sexy. Striding across the room, he kisses me softly on the lips, then kneels between my legs as he moves them to dangle over the edge of the bed.

"Kayla, this is.... it means so much to me. My grandparents, those are my parents-parents," he explains when he notices the look of bewilderment on my face. Ah ok so old-gen. "They discovered a special place as they journeyed across the Wastes in search of a legend." The corners of his lips rise in a half-smile. "They never found that, but they did find what they later called the Hissing Banks. Near the ocean, deep within a cave, the earth had cracked open, allowing scorching heat to escape. They settled there for a time, the heat seeing them through nuclear winters until my granny fell pregnant and they moved to the city. See, they were Advanced, Kayla, but not from the cure, from the effects of the gasses coming from the earth itself. My mother was special too. She controlled water. A water elemental, like you with your fire."

Holy fuck, there are more like us? His mum could control water? This is so cool!

"So anyway," he scolds lightly as he realises my mind ran away with me.

I wish I'd been able to meet his mum. I wonder if she and I would've been friends, given that we both had an affinity?

"They visited the Hissing Banks often, taking their children and those of their new neighbours. Your parents, Kayla, Connor's, Crowley's, I don't know about yours, sorry Chris." Charlie turns his piercing gaze to Chris, who simply nods. Everyone's full attention is on Charlie as he tells us the story of the past. "I think that's why we're all so different from humans. That gas changed their DNA, and they passed it on to us. But I'm no scientist, I can't be sure. So, when my granny passed away, my grandad took her body to that place." Pausing, he looks down at the bag in his hands. Untying the top, he tips it up, spilling its contents into his palm. He lifts his hand so I can see it. Something colourful catches my eye as he fiddles with a delicate chain, letting it extend. A chunk of the most colourful rock I've ever seen falls from the palm of his hand and dangles in front of my eyes.

"This is my grandmother Kayla." The stone glitters in the low light. Pink at the top, fading to green, then azure blue at the bottom. Intricate golden wire wraps around the gem, allowing it to attach to the chain. It's absolutely stunning. "My grandad, he, well, he gave her body back to the earth, and this is what the earth gave him back. From that day on, they would take anyone who passed away in our family to that same cave." Leaning towards me, Charlie laces his hands around my neck. When he pulls back, the stone hangs on my chest, the crystal warm against my skin. "Now I want you to have this." He looks down at his hands, then back up at me with enormous eyes. "I know marriage is obsolete now but I still... I want you to marry me, Kayla, if you'll have me?"

The whole time Charlie talks, my mouth hangs open, catching flies. And now I'm rendered speechless. I stare down at his beautiful face, completely lost for words. I clutch the stone in my hand, the other held tight within Charlie's. First, he bombards me with information, half of which I barely understand, then... then he asks me to - marry him? Never have I ever considered the prospect of marriage. No one gets married anymore because love in the Wastes is mostly fleeting; those who do manage to survive longer than average are those in harems. Safety in numbers.

But Charlie... he looks up at me with love shining in his fawn eyes... has been planning this since we were tiny.

Fuck me sideways.

No one moves a muscle or says a word as Charlie and I stare at each other. The air becomes thicker the longer I don't answer him. Heat tickles my palm where the stone's clutched. Flames lick their way up my fingers as my emotions spin. Marriage? Could I give myself so wholly to Charlie this way? To the others? Connor's voice enters my mind, stopping the runaway cart that is my thoughts.

Kayla, he's so in love with you. I can feel your love for him, too. Don't deny this for yourself, or him.

He's right, Charlie's become my lifeline. They all have. My flames die as I realise I love them all so much.

"Of course, things would remain as they are now. Just one minor change." Charlie pushes himself up so his lips are barely touching mine, his hands close in around my face. "You will know I love you, Kayla. I plan to spend the rest of my life not just telling you, but showing you I love you each and every day. You will never have a single doubt, I promise you."

God. Tears sting my eyes, then fall freely down my cheeks. He presses the sweetest kiss to my lips as I throw my arms around his neck and deepen the kiss.

"Yes!" I cry, breaking the kiss just long enough to say it, then crashing my lips to Charlie's again.

The room erupts in a series of whoops and yeses, but all I see is Charlie. He's still naked and I only have a scrap of material around me; that falls away when he lifts me from the bed. My heated skin meets his coolness and unashamedly, I wiggle against him. He moans into my mouth as his cock slides across my belly.

"Charlie, make love to me," I say against his lips. I'm so turned on right now. All I want is for him to touch me, to show me love, to give him love back. His hands are hot as they travel down my back. Taking my arse in his hands, he lifts me then lays us down on the bed. Hovering over me, he looks deep into my eyes.

"Kayla, I love you now, tomorrow, forever." My body trembles beneath him. Why deny it, Kay? You feel the same way.

"I love you too, Charlie." As soon as the words leave me, Charlie leans forward. His dick slips inside of me at the same time his lips crash into mine. The bed dips at either side of me and hands slide between our bodies. Rough skin glides down to my clit. Crowley rubs the little bundle of nerves as Connor tweaks a nipple. Charlie pulls back a little, so they have better access, but his lips don't leave mine as he thrusts into me. The onslaught of sensations drives me wild. I moan in my throat as Charlie fucks me just like I need him to. Hard and fast. He pulls back completely, just the tip of him inside of me, looking down at me. Love sets his eyes on fire as he says, "You're so beautiful, Kayla. Everything I dreamed of." He thrusts in shallow jabs, driving me crazy. "Oh, you feel so good around me." Tears prick behind my eyes. Not letting them fall, I concentrate on the feel of his cock inside me as it pulses in time with Charlie's heartbeat.

Chris appears over Charlie's shoulder; his bright blue eyes taking in the sight below him. He reaches a hand around Charlie's body to where we join. I feel his fingers caress Charlie's cock. Charlie, Connor, Crowley and Chris all moan, deep and rumbling. The combination sends me into overdrive. I thrust my hips up and forward so Charlie is pushed into me as Chris snakes his hand further down, cupping Charlie's balls.

I sit up to watch him roll them between his fingers. "Holy shit, that's sexy." Chris watches me the whole time as Charlie pulls almost out. Chris wraps his hand around him and strokes all the way up, then back to the base again. "Fuck, that is so hot." Charlie's eyes roll into the back of his head as he sinks into me once more.

"So wet, I can't..." Charlie groans as his thrusts become faster, erratic. On the brink of exploding. Chris moves to his side and Crowley takes my nipple in his mouth, sucking hard. Chris rubs my clit hard and fast, speeding me towards an explosion just as Charlie yells my name to the ceiling. Together, my four men bring me to an electrifying orgasm that makes my pussy clench Charlie's dick so hard, he can't pull out.

"Oh, God!" I scream as my body curls in on itself, my muscles contracting with every wave of pleasure. My eyes squeeze shut as Charlie presses a sweet kiss to my lips, and then cold hits my skin. Still panting from my release, I open my eyes to see that it's Chris who is gently skimming his fingertips down my thighs.

"You're so beautiful, Mine," he whispers as he lowers himself between my legs and flicks the tip of his tongue against me. The hot, wet touch feels like sparks of fire as he licks me over and over. Charlie moves to the base of the bed behind Connor and watches. A huge smile on his face.

I've never been licked down there before. It's glorious. As his tongue dips into my opening, I realise he's cleaning Charlie's spend from me. The thought sends desire shooting through me. My back arches off the bed and I reach down to lace my fingers through his long black hair and push his face into me greedily.

"Unh, so sweet," Chris utters as he settles back in. This time he sucks my clit into his mouth. Using his thumbs, he spreads my lips and flicks me over and over until stars collide behind my eyes and I scream my pleasure to the ceiling. Faster than lightning, Chris stands and thrusts himself to the hilt inside me.

"Ah! Fuck, yes!" bursts from my mouth.

"Fuck! Oh, Mine, you feel like hot, wet silk." Chris' eyes roll as he pounds into me furiously. Connor and Crowley tweek my nipples between their fingers. Crow pinches harder than Connor. My eyes flick to his grass green ones. I'm shocked to see he's grinning.

"I'm next, Darlin. I can't fucking wait to get my hands on you."

Crowley's dirty words send me over the edge. My pussy clamps down and pulls Chris over the edge with me.

By the time Chris pulls off me, I'm completely spent. The room spins a little and my throat's parched. I'm sore in places I never thought I could be sore, but it's a delicious feeling. One I want to roll over and savour, but the clearing of a throat has my eyes popping open.

"A drink for you, my love." Charlie hands me a skin. I push my body into a sitting position and gulp it as Chris rolls off me.

Sex is thirsty work; I could also eat two lots of food right now.

"We'll go make food. Chris, do you want to join us?" I look up into Connor's eyes, a question in mine.

"We all need to eat." He kisses my head before continuing, "Besides, Crowley wants us out." He winks at me, then his face changes expression. He's obviously telling the very

278

confused-looking Chris something in their minds, because he nods, drops a soft kiss to my lips, then leaves with Connor and Charlie.

Leaving Crowley and me alone. Swallowing thickly, I push myself back against the wall.

"Don't worry, Darlin, I won't hurt you. I swear. But I'm not like them, Kayla. I don't show love with soft touches and words." He wraps a cloth around his middle and sits on the bed next to me. "Kay, you have to know a few things first. I don't want to hurt you, but... I do like pain." Um, what the fuck? "I'm really turned on by slapping arses. Want me to demonstrate?"

Holy crap. He wants to slap my arse? Hmm, I didn't know you could get turned on by that. I nod cautiously, hoping I've not just made a huge mistake.

"Get on your hands and knees," he demands in his usual bossy tone. I can't help the little thrill that runs through me as I assume the position he's asked me to, or rather... told me to.

"Good girl. Now," his large hand caresses my exposed arse cheek, the tips of his fingers brush my wetness, sending shivers down my spine. "I'm going to spank you, Kayla. Only lightly this time. Do you trust me?" The heat of his palm disappears, and it's all I can do not to flinch.

Can I give this power I worked so hard for to Crow? Can I put myself at his mercy?

Turning my head so I can see his eyes, I remind myself this is Crowley. The guy who saved a book for years so he could give it to me. Crowley who's helped keep us all safe, who loves me, who I love.

"Yes, I trust you, Crow."

A slow, sexy smile spreads across his lips. "Are you ready?"

I try to nod, but Crowley barks, "Use your words, Kayla. This is about trust; without it, I can't proceed."

Shit. "Ok. Yes. I'm ready Crowley." I own the power. He will not hurt me.

His palm softly swats my butt.

Oh, that's nothing. I raise my brow at him, a challenge in my eyes.

"Do you want more, Kay?"

Do I?

"Yes, Crowley. I'm really ready," I say, then face the wall again. I relax my body, giving Crowley all control. I can do this. If this is what he wants, then I'll give it to him. His hand lifts then whistles through the air as he swipes it down, hitting my arse with an audible whack. As it makes contact, the sound combined with the sharp sting pulls a moan from me. Goosebumps pop all over my skin as he rubs the spot he just hit.

"Red looks fucking sexy on you." His voice is hoarse as he hits my other butt cheek a little harder.

"Ah!" This time I call out, the sting barely on the line between pain and pleasure. My juices run down my thighs as he hits me again.

"Once you've put on a little more weight, there'll be a jiggle. Oh," he leans over my back until his lips are next to my ear, grabbing my hair, he pulls it sharply. "I do so enjoy the jiggle. Can you feel how hard I am?" he asks while thrusting his thick cock between my cheeks. He feels as big as he looks; intimidating. He grabs my arse in his hands and jiggles them.

"Yes," I reply throatily. His actions, his words, all serve to make me wetter.

"I can't wait to be inside you, Darlin. You're almost ready for me." He laces one hand at the base of my hair.

Grabbing a handful, he tugs harder this time until my eyes meet the ceiling.

"Are you ready for me, Darlin?" His dick rubs back and forth over my pussy, coating it with my wetness. "You're so wet." The tips of his fingers travel down my spine, over my arsehole, where he lingers. "One day, I'll own this too. But for now, I want to fill you with my cum until I've got nothing left. "

"Oh," is all I manage. His dirty talk has me practically begging. Continuing their journey, his fingers rub over my hole then to my clit. Instead of rubbing, he slaps two of them against me, sending a jolt of pleasure and pain through me. "Oh, Crowley, fuck." By this point, I'm one giant sensation.

"That's right Kayla, you've never known pleasure like I'm about to give you. Let's get you ready," he rumbles into my ear as his finger seeks entrance inside me. Slowly, he pushes it in, then adds a second. He spreads them inside of me, stretching me.

"You're so tight, I don't know if I'll fit. What do you think, you dirty bitch?"

Oh, fuck me. He curls those fingers and hits something inside me. I feel pressure low in my belly.

"That's your magic spot. We'll discover the things I can do with that another time. Right now, I just want to bury myself deep inside this tight pussy. Lose myself," Crowley whispers in my ear as his fingers pump in and out of me, the whole time he thrusts against my arse.

"Crowley, please..." I don't know what I'm asking for. More of him? His cock? All I know is I need him right now.

"Yes, Darlin?" he drawls as he tugs my hair a little harder. "You want my cock? Yes, your pussy wants it."

Pushing to stand upright, Crowley lines the broad head of his cock up with my hole, my body tenses.

He's not going to fit!

"Relax, Darlin. I'll let you get used to the size first. But then," he pushes forward just a little, and he breaches me with just the tip, "I'll fuck you, hard and fast. It will hurt," slowly he gains entry, the size of him stretching me almost beyond what I can take. "It'll hurt so good Kayla, you'll be screaming my name before I'm done."

Just as I think he can't get any deeper, he continues to sink into me. The other guys are all big, different shapes and sizes, with Charlie being the longest. But Crowley's beyond thick.

"Ah! Oh god, Crowley," I call out, the pain-pleasure of being so full confusing my senses.

"That's it, Darlin, take all of me. Oh, oh yes. Fuck," I feel his legs shaking against the back of mine. When his abdomen meets my arse, he stills. "That's all of me. Oh, you beautiful little bitch. So sexy, so wet. Unh." The sting inside me lessens as he slaps my arse again. Hard, fast and delicious.

"Yes, you like that, don't you, Kayla?" he growls as he slaps the other cheek. I let out a whimper at the assault of his hits. On my hands and knees in front of Crowley, this way should scare me. His slapping my arse should enrage me. But in reality, it feels fucking amazing. So right. Like this is what I've always wanted, but never even knew.

"I've waited all my life for you, Kayla. Are you ready for me to show you what you mean to me?" Crowley's words vibrate against my back as he leans over me.

"Y-Y-Yes," I stammer, so many sensations roll over my body as his hands travel across my skin. Suddenly, his heat disappears. Confused, I look over my shoulder to find him standing stock still behind me. "Crow?" I shake my head to make sure I'm not losing my mind, because Crowley has his head dipped low, his hands laced together on his stomach. I push off the bed and face him. "What's happening?" Panic laces my voice. I've never seen Crowley so...

"I'm yours, Kayla. Do with me as you wish," he says while staring intently at my feet, then kneels before me. Shit. He's... submitting to me? Crowley bossy boots? No fucking way. I rub my chin with my hand, just looking at him for a moment.

"Crowley," I use my forefinger to tilt his face to mine. "Get on the bed." The second I finish the words, he stands, moves to the bed and lays down. He's completely surrendering, showing me the only way he knows how that he's mine completely. I'm not sure I can do this, but for him, I'm willing to try. Turning on my heel, I run my fingers up his thigh. His hands rest low on his belly. He's hard, huge and panting. My inner badass wars with the new Kay, the one Crowley, Connor, Charlie and Chris have awakened.

BLAZE
AMELIA K'OLIVER

As I reach the apex of his legs, I trail the very tips of my fingers over his length, over the tip where I allow my nails to scrape the end. "Don't touch me, Crow." I give the order; his eyes are on mine when he nods. Obviously, I've never done this. Dominated someone. But I'll go with it, do what feels right. Crowley trembles beneath my touch as I continue my journey up to his chest. Flicking lightly over his nipple, I bend and suck it into my mouth.

"Unh, oh, fuck," Crowley growls low in his throat. Moving back, I allow my breath to skim over it.

"You like that, Crow? Hmm, I knew you would." I look down at his mammoth body to see his hands clenched by his hips. Yes, I'm going to have fun with this, I think. Knowing I won't be able to take his girth into my mouth, I pepper his taut muscles with nips and kisses, all the way down to his tip. Then I flick my tongue out and gently lick across the head.

"Oh, Darlin, your tongue is so hot." His husky voice makes my pussy clench.

"Don't speak Crow. And don't touch." I continue to lick him, pinching with my teeth all the way down his enormous shaft. His moans tell me I'm not hurting him, but he likes what I'm doing. Wrapping my fingers around him, I realise I can't touch my fingers together. Oh, fuck me. Crowley grunts and my eyes flick to his. The smirk on his face tells me he realises I can't grip him. I push my tongue out of my mouth and lick in one long stroke from base to tip, loving the way his legs tremble as I do. I suck the tip into my mouth and suck, hard. His back arches off the bed and his hands fist the material beneath him as I suck more of him into my warm, wet mouth.

He screws his eyes shut as he hits the back of my throat. Can I go lower? Planting a foot on the metal of the bed, I heave myself over him. My bare pussy rests on his leg, my feet on either side of his. I lean forward and take him back into my mouth, pushing myself to take more of him. A choked sound leaves Crowley as I swallow him. My eyes are watering and my gag reflex kicks in as I reach halfway. I'm doing it! I can feel him throbbing against my tongue and it's driving me wild. Using the friction of his knee, I rub myself against it. Moans fill the room as I ride his leg while sucking on his dick.

"Oh, Kayla! Stop. Stop!" His whole body shudders as he lets out a loud moan, "Kayla!" I keep sucking and licking as he vibrates.

"Oh fuck! Unh. Yes!" He grinds out between his teeth. I pull back sharply, ending his pleasure. "What?" he barks out. His face is a mix of rage and pain.

"Tut tut, Crowley, you can't cum yet. Not until I say so. Got it?" I lower my voice to a fierce whisper, daring him to challenge me. The view of him warring with himself just serves to turn me on more. I want him to beg for it, to plead.

Throwing my other leg over his body, I position myself just behind his dick. Taking him in my hand, I pull his cock up to meet my stomach. He goes past my belly button. Fuck me. He feels like silk against my skin.

"So beautiful."

"Didn't I tell you not to speak, Crow? Naughty boy." Reaching out with my other hand, I flick his nipple.

"Unh, fuck!" I grind against him, my pussy wet against his shaft.

"Oh, Crowley, you've been so moody," I say as I lift myself and position the end of his dick to my entrance and slide it across my clit "So grumpy." The hole at the tip is large and leaks clear fluid, making it slide easily over me. Slowly I push myself down on him, the feeling of him stretching me almost enough to make me stop, but I keep going, just a little at a time. Crowley has his eyes squeezed tight, his lips forming a perfect O. As the tip slips in, I pause for a moment. "I think you should be punished."

"Please, Kayla. Move. Gods, so tight, ah!" Crowley barely seems able to control himself much longer, he's shaking and I can feel him pulse inside of me. Letting go of the sheet, he lifts a hand as if to grab my hip, then snatches it away just before he touches me.

"Want to touch me, Crowley?" I purr, the high of being in complete control of a man like Crowley making my head spin.

"God! Yes! Please, let me touch you," he replies enthusiastically while nodding. Opening his eyes, he begs me with them while his hands clench and unclench by his sides. I allow myself to sink a little further as I run my hands over my body.

"I'm so soft, Crowley," I say teasingly while playing with my nipples. His eyes watch my every move. The material beneath him rips as he fights against himself. Dropping lower, I bob up and down on him, his eyes roll into the back of his head and he sucks his lip between his teeth and bites. Lower still and he lets out a moan, his reactions making my juices flow from me, dripping onto his legs and balls. I reach back and cup them. He jerks and moans again. I reach down between us and feel I'm almost all the way down. Rubbing my clit, I roll my hips to take the last of him.

"Fuck, Kayla, you are glorious!" Crowley's words spur me on, and I move. He's huge, so thick I can feel every vein, every pulse. I lean forward, resting my hands on his chest as I let myself bounce off his hips.

"Fuck, Crow, you're so big. Oh, god yes!" Losing myself to the full sensation, I let myself go and fuck Crowley hard and fast. My small boobs bounce, and my hair tickles my arse.

A growl bursts from Crowley's chest as the sound of tearing rents the air. His hands come up filled with material and he takes my hips in a punishing grip. I stop moving.

"The fuck?" he says loudly as his brows draw down over his eyes.

"I said don't touch," I breathe. Growling again, he lets me go and runs a hand through his hair.

"Please, let me touch you, fuck!" he begs, his teeth clenched. I shake my head at him. Those are the rules. No touching. Now he's no longer touching me. I start to move again. His moans come thick and fast, barely a breath between them. I know he's about to cum, so I stop. Lifting myself off him, I plant my feet on the floor.

"You spoke when I told you not to Crowley. Stand," I demand. Not sure about what I'm doing, I move to the side to allow him room to move. Unsteadily, he pushes off the bed and stands in front of me. His cock glistens with my juices, an idea pops into my head.

Kneeling in front of him, I look up into his emerald eyes. I flick my tongue out and slowly lick from base to tip. His legs shake so I reach my hands out and press my palms against the muscles on his stomach to feel them tremble. "Umm, I taste good on you, Crowley." Slowly, I take his length into my mouth. I reach a hand up and cup his balls in my palm.

"Oh, fuck Kayla. I don't know how much more of this I can take. You'll ruin me." Crowley looks down at me with wide eyes. His lip between his teeth. I can see he's biting it hard by the colour of the skin beneath them. Just as I feel his cock jerk in my mouth, on the precipice of an explosion, the door crashes open and Connor barges in.

"Crow, Kay, shit sorry." Connor uses a hand to cover his eyes, but I can see him peeking through one finger. Naughty, naughty Connor.

"The fuck, Connor?" Crowley's whole demeanour changes. His muscles contract under my hands and he goes as rigid as steel. My mouth is still on the tip of his cock as Connor pretends to not look.

"Sorry! Constantine has demanded a meet! He wants to see her." he jerks his chin in my direction. "Now."

"Fuck! Can you buy us some time, Con?" Crowley asks, more politely than I imagined he could. My head whips to Connor, my breath held.

"I'll try to get you ten, but that's all. He's planning

something. The entire house is involved," Connor replies while running his hand over his neck.

"Ok, give us some time, Connor, and then I'll meet this guy," I tell him as I remove my lips from Crowley's dick. Seriously, this Constantine guy sure has shit timing. We've been here for hours, and yet now he wants a meeting?

Just before Connor turns to leave, he drops his hand and sends a wink my way. Then he swivels on his heel and leaves the room.

"Bad timing, huh?" I look up at Crowley through my lashes. While I'm enjoying this little role reversal game, we just don't have the time right now.

"Yup. So..." Crowley nudges his hips in my direction, the tip of him brushing against my cheek.

"Fuck me, Crowley," I say in answer. Seconds don't even pass when he bends down and scoops me up in his arms. I wrap my legs around his thick body. Seizing the opportunity, I lean my head forward and lick his nipple.

"Want me to fuck you, do you?" Crowley grunts as he takes my arse in his hands and moves me away from his body.

"Yes!" I moan, looking between us at his enormous dick. "Fuck me, Crow, show me what you've got." Suddenly, I'm on my back on the bed. Crowley kneels between my legs, his thick cock in one hand. The other he wraps around my throat, squeezing.

"Oh, Kayla, I've waited so fucking long for this. If it's too much, yell out the word orange. Ok?" he says the first half low and rumbling, the last part he speaks normally. Well shit.

"Yes, I will. Now fuck me." Pressing my heel against his arse, I try to move him forward.

"We don't have much time. But I'll be damned if you

don't enjoy this." With that delicious statement, Crowley thrusts forward so hard and fast, he buries his dick inside me to the hilt in that one move.

"Fuck!" I moan/scream. The very fine line between pain and pleasure becomes even thinner as his thick cock stretches me.

"Ready?" Crowley asks, his eyes never leaving mine as I nod. He fucks me senseless. Over and over, he drives into me, bouncing me off his hips. My moans come loud and fast, barely able to take a breath between them. The hand around my neck tightens, not enough to hurt or to stop me from breathing, but enough to let me know Crowley's in charge. He's taken the power back. But I am so fucking ok with it.

"Yes, Crowley! Yes!" My world explodes into a million pieces as my orgasm washes over me, breaking me from the inside out. Yelling his pleasure, Crowley leans down and kisses me passionately as his cum coats my insides. My whole body tingles, my head spins and my body tries to curl up on itself, but Crowley doesn't stop fucking me until I break the kiss and beg him to stop.

"Crow! Oh god, please!" I beg as I feel myself being pushed towards another mind-shattering experience.

"Cum for me Kayla, now!" Crowley demands as his thrusts speed up; his cock still hard as steel inside me. His dirty words send me over the edge for a second time and I clamp down on him again and again. "That's my girl, yes. Unh I feel you, Kayla."

What feels like hours later but is only seconds. I lay across Crowley's chest, listening to his racing heartbeat.

"Did you enjoy that, Darlin?"

"Umm." Is all I manage. I'd be perfectly happy to just fall asleep in his arms, but a knock on the door reminds me we have shit to do. "When this is over, if we survive this, I want to do that again." I push myself up so I can look into his eyes. "All of that," I say simply.

"I enjoyed that too, Darlin. Huh," he sits up and presses his plump lips to mine. "Didn't expect to. But I did, fuck you're so sexy when you're in charge." Wrapping his arms around me, Crow pulls us both back down on the bed and kisses me like I'm the air he needs to breathe.

"Sorry! I know, I know. But Constantine's getting antsy," Charlie shouts through the door.

Fuck! "Coming now!" I shout back, breaking the kiss. God, I could do that all day! The stubble on his face leaves my chin feeling a little raw as I rise and get dressed. With one last kiss, we leave the room to be greeted by pandemonium.

***

"BOUT TIME you came in here, Crowley. I'm your leader after all." The man in a strange chair barks as Charlie, Connor, Crowley, Chris and I all pile into a small room at the back of the building. Looking around, I'm shocked to see that it's really clean. Not a speck of dust or dirt is on any of the crazy-looking things packed into every available surface in this place. The walls are lined with shelves and all manner of things are squeezed onto them.

"Sorry, Const. We had some, um," Crowley begins, but the man in the chair cuts him off by raising his hand. Which makes me look back at him with a frown.

"Fucking. We were fucking," I blurt before I've even got my brain in gear. It just comes out; everyone turns to look

292

at me as I'm about to pick up a plastic cube with different colours on it. Snatching my fingers back, I clear my throat. "I'm Kayla, by the way. Listen, I don't know what I can do to help." I shrug my shoulders and look around at my guys. "But I'll do whatever is needed." I absolutely agree with the rebellion's agenda. Everyone on this planet deserves to have freedom, food, water and safety. I've often wondered if the lack of children is actually a choice. Who wants to bring a child into this fucked up world where it'll either have to fight for its life every single day, or it'll be turned into a fucking Panda! Nope. I absofuckinglutely won't be having any children. Like, ever.

"Yes, I know who you are, child. You look a lot like your mother," Constantine replies rather smugly. Trying not to wince, I focus on his face. His head is grotesquely shaped and out of proportion to the rest of his body. An Alpha, his brain must've grown to such proportions that he needed several metal plates inserted to give it room. I can see a few of them beneath his almost translucent skin.

"You knew my mum?" I already know the answer because if he says I look like her, then he must have.

"Yes. It was I who told her you were special, child. It was I who chose your promised," he announces. What the fuck. His head is so distracting. A large strap across it holds it against the odd chair he's sitting in.

"Really?" I once again look around the room at my guys. "Great choices," I say without really thinking. The guys chuckle and Charlie takes my hand and raises it to his lips, planting a soft kiss there.

"Enough!" Constantine yells, spittle flying from his mouth. "We go to war! Tomorrow we fight for what's right. Will you join us, Kayla?"

Fight for what's right? "I'm in. But, uh," I place my

hands on the desk in front of us and lean in closer to this would-be leader. "Don't think you can boss me around, pal. I'm not part of this. I'll help you win this war. But I won't be anyone's soldier."

"That's my girl." Crowley chuckles behind me. "If that's all, Const, we all need R and R. We'll report for duty in the morning." Taking my hand, Crowley leads us from the room. Looking back at Constantine, I see his mouth hanging open, catching flies. He stares dumbly at us as we leave. He's probably never been spoken to this way and can't quite comprehend what just happened, despite being super brainy.

Four sexy as fuck guys and I walk through the house in a large group like we own the place. We spend the rest of the night eating, fucking, getting to know each other. Lost in our own world. Connecting our family in ways none other could ever be.

BLAZE

AMELIA K'OLIVER

S tanding outside the rebellion headquarters with Connor, Crowley, Charlie, Chris, Craven, Can and Cell feels slightly surreal to me. The convoy set off towards Tri-City some time ago, leaving the eight of us behind. We're the first line of attack. As a group, we'll infiltrate the walls and sneak our way to Keeper, hopefully ending his tyranny swiftly. I let go of Charlie's hand and move to stand in front of these men who would put their lives on the line for strangers, for Panda.

"There's not much I can say, guys." I straighten my body to its full measly height. Each of them is so much taller than me yet I don't feel overshadowed by them. Instead, they make me feel stronger, powerful. "This could end with us all dead. Or worse, captured and tortured. Each of you means so much to me. Please don't die today." I hold my hand out in front of me, stopping several of them from speaking. I'm not done yet. "I may not be big on words. I might not be the best pep talker in the world. But shit," I shrug my shoulders and kick at the dirt beneath my feet, "I fucking love you guys." I don't know what I expect when I say the words, but it isn't that I'd be caged in by so many arms. I can't even tell who's who. Charlie grabs my face after everyone lets me go, his brown eyes shining with unshed tears, my own falling freely down my face.

"I love you Kay; we'll make it through this. I would lay my life down for you."

I break away from him with a gasp. "Please do not do that! No." I stand back once again and search their eyes; I know they're all thinking the same thing. That they would give their lives for me. "Protect yourselves first and foremost. Do not put your lives at risk for me. Understand? If any of you die, I will be really pissed."

Connor chuckles at my words, but I'm deadly serious. I would never forgive them if they were killed because of me. I couldn't live with myself. I shoot him a deadly look and his laughter dies away. "Do not fucking die," I say with finality, then turn and walk away from them. If we say goodbye to each other, we admit we could die today, and my fragile mind can't handle that. So, I pretend this is just a normal day and walk through the city streets with Baby at my side, my Katana and my small blades strapped to my body. Only this time, seven men who I care about walk behind me in a long line, ready to set this world free.

But at what cost?

***

No one says a word to each other on the way to the City. Our packs are filled with supplies, but we don't stop to eat or drink. The air's thick between us with things left unsaid.

Once Tri-City is within our sights, we stop and set up a small camp inside what Can tells me was a fuelling station for vehicles. The building is still fully standing, but I don't go inside. Instead, I climb on the roof. The guys try to talk to me several times, but I stalk off with Baby to make sure the area's safe from bad Panda. I can't be distracted right now. I need my head clear to do this. If I allowed them to speak to me, they might say goodbye.

I can't do goodbye.

It's not until the sun that sets I realise my mistake when Connor and Crowley start to yell at each other.

"What the fuck is this?" I scream at them, louder than their shouting, so they can hear me. As soon as they hear my voice, they stop arguing and turn to look at me. Wincing, Crowley throws his hands in the air.

"Connor's just decided to tell us he doesn't remember where the virus is being stored." He throws Connor a shitty look.

"Death would let me out. I was always present, but I can't remember where it is. Which means I either didn't hide it or my dad purposefully had me distracted in order to hide it," Connor explains, frustration making him gesture wildly. His hand accidentally hits me across my stomach, making me bend double. Suddenly, he's lifted into the air, his feet dangling.

"Touch the Princess again, worm, and I shall end you. Prince or not," Craven's booming voice echoes in the small space.

Fuck me.

"Put him down, Crave, please." I rest my hand on his massive arm. Connor immediately drops to his feet, gasping for breath. "Please explain this Princess and Prince thing," I ask, desperate for answers before it's too late. In a few short hours, one of Craven's rebel brethren will be on duty and will let us into the city. At least that's the plan. It could mean the end of us all.

He turns his gargantuan face to mine, confusion drawing his brows down. "You do not know?"

"Know what?" I ask while looking around at my men. Each of them shakes their heads and look at Craven, waiting for an explanation too.

"Your mother Connor and yours, Kayla, were royal heirs. They planned to take the throne after killing Keeper, but unfortunately, he killed them first," Craven explains. My legs almost give out when he finishes. My head whips to Connor.

Royals?

My mum would tell me stories when I was really little about princesses. But why didn't she tell me this? If I'd known that Keeper wanted to kill her, I would've.... I could've... my legs give way and my knees hit the ground. There aren't kings or queens anymore. What the fuck did it matter who our ancestors were?

Hands reach out to catch me, but I fall anyway. A sob breaks from my chest. Keeper killed my mother because of a fucking ancient title. "Did he kill my brother?" I ask no one in particular. Can answers me.

"Yes "

His simple word makes my body go numb. Everything falls into place in my head. Keeper took the guys because he didn't want me to have them by my side, making me stronger. He killed my brother because he could've protected me. He had my mother killed because she was an heir and knew of his plans. It wasn't Masters after all. He had Connor possessed by Death, not really sure why.

President Keeper is fucking evil. And I intend to rid this

world of him. But first, I have to get to him, then I will char his body to ash. My eyes flick to Connor for a second. A small piece of me wants to stab him in the neck.

Hands touch me then; it feels like a thousand people are closing in on me and my breathing picks up. "We've gotta move," I say loudly. I stalk away from my little group. Needing air. Needing something to kill. Taking off in a jog, I put distance between me and the answers I've always wanted, but now wish I didn't have. Everything about this situation is fucked up.

***

THE GUYS and I run until we're sweaty. It takes too long for me to realise we're exhausting ourselves. I pull to a stop and wait for them to catch up. Baby sits next to my leg. His weight against me is comforting. While the guys and I can enter the city quietly and under the cover of darkness, Baby can't, so I'll be forced to leave him behind, again, and it kills me.

"We need to rest up. The city isn't far from here. From this point, we walk." I say as they all approach me. Turning to Charlie, I realise he's struggling with something. "Charlie?" As he comes to a stop in front of me. His chin rests against his chest and he refuses to meet my eyes.

"He's broken, Princess. You refuse to talk to your men. They feel rejected," Craven announces in his booming voice. But somehow, he manages to say it softly. Charlie looks up at me through his thick, dark lashes and something squeezes inside me. I've been rejecting them on this journey. The fear of losing them is making me crazy. I loved my mum, I did, but I wasn't that close to her. Losing her was hard, and it still is. But if I lost one of my guys? Fuck. The world would go up in smoke.

"Fuck, guys. I'm so sorry. I..." Instead of facing my fear like the badass I pretend to be, I pushed them away.

Like a dick. Crowley interrupts me. "I get it, I do. But Kay-"

"We need you," Charlie cuts him off, the words said on a sob.

I swivel and throw my arms around his neck. Fuck, I'm such an idiot. "I need you all too," I say into his soft, sweet-smelling hair. "I couldn't bear to lose any of you. I thought it would be easier if..."

"I can't lose any of you either, but we gotta do this together." Connor says as he wraps his fingers around mine. Chris takes my other hand.

"Together or never," Crowley whispers in my ear. His cool breath tickles my neck and I shiver. Turning from them, I look at Tri-City in the distance. My hand wraps around the necklace Charlie gave me when he asked me to marry him. I don't want to do this, to go into that city and fight a war that could kill one or more of my guys. That forces me to leave behind my best friend. But if we don't, we all die anyway. This virus will kill us all, humans, Panda, whatever Charlie, Connor, Chris, Crowley and I are too. Probably. Do it or die trying, right? Save humanity, in all its forms.

They all look at me as I turn back to them, their eyes so full of love. Can, Cell and Craven loom over us like giants. In four hours, a new war begins, the eight of us are tasked with starting that war. I see the burden of that weight on each of their faces, in the thin lines of their mouths, in the soft, plump spots between their eyes. But I also see their determination, their commitment in the way they stand tall, their shoulders squared and their weapons ready.

"We can do this, we can win. This isn't the day we die, no. This is the day we set this world free." I scan each of their eyes. The fire I see there calls to the flames inside of me. "Let's Blaze this motherfucker!" Some of them chuckle. Charlie kisses my neck in a way that completely distracts me. I pull away a little to look into his soft brown eyes, a surprised look on my face. He grins at me and knocks the wind from my lungs.

"When we defeat this evil, I'm going to marry you, Kayla. I want you round with my babe, barefoot and kicking arse." He reaches up to smooth my golden hair from my face as I stand here open-mouthed.

Kids?

"Fuck, Char! I second that, minus the kid, though. I'm happy to wait." Connor chuckles, his eyes on the ground beneath him.

Crowley strides to me and pulls me from Charlie's arms. "I'm next. Twins. Two boys, ain't that right, Darlin?"

God, I love the way he calls me Darlin. I splutter as I try to come up with something to say, but then my mind clears and it's like I can see it.

Me with an enormous stomach, kids running around an open field chasing after Baby. Connor and Crowley building a house, Chris and Charlie cooking over a huge brick stove. Craven Can and Cell standing guard even though they really don't need to. The sun shining down on us all. A happily ever after, just like in my books.

I want it, all of it.

"Ok," I start, but I don't get to finish because Charlie rips me from Crowley and lifts me off the ground. His lips crash to mine with such passion, I taste blood. He kisses me like he's trying to take the air from my lungs, and I love it.

I showed him what you just saw, Kayla. I showed it to them all. Connor's voice enters my mind.

Tears spring to my eyes and I let them fall. My very first happy tears.

"Let's do this, everyone. The sooner it's over with, the sooner we can start our new lives together." By the tone of Chris' voice, I can tell he's excited. The heat of the battle calling him or the prospect of our lives starting, I don't know. But I feel him on both levels. Breaking the kiss with Charlie, I let myself slide down his body. Which is a mistake because I feel how hard he is and now I want to turn back, find somewhere soft to lie and fuck him. Them all. Except for Can, Craven and Cell.

"Let's do this," I yell, cheers ring out around me as I turn and sprint towards Tri-City. Eager to get this over with.

***

BY THE TIME we reach the gates, it's pitch black. Wildlife howls and skitters around in the fallen leaves as we flatten our bodies against the stone wall that holds in so much evil. With the love of my men still lighting up my veins, I check my flames are as ready as I am. Closing my eyes, I search for the heat. Finding it, I let out a steadying breath as Crowley breaks from us and approaches the entrance. Seconds later, he turns and silently motions for us to come to him. In a single line, we join with him as he stands in front of an open gate. With the guards are nowhere to be seen, we slip in unnoticed. I take one last look out into the forest and send up an internal prayer Baby remains safe while we're in the city.

Turning back to my guys, I follow as Crow leads us through darkened streets. Snakes churn in my stomach as we pass the buildings housing Advanced and move right to the immense building housing the Alphas and Keeper. Crowley opens a door I didn't see and disappears inside it. Here goes nothing. I follow behind him, my feet silent as we walk into the enemy's house. The feeling of being watched makes the back of my neck itch as we power walk down a million empty, white corridors. The place is eerily silent. We don't even pass a single person as we travel deeper into the building. As we turn yet another corner, Crowley thrusts up his fist, which he told me means to 'fucking stop'.

When he turns to face us, we soon realise something's very wrong. Crowley's a big powerful guy, he's a badass warrior and doesn't scare easy. But whatever he sees behind this wall makes him go paler than a Panda.

"Come out!" a masculine voice demands. Keeper. "Quickly now, I wouldn't want to have to kill this magnificent beast."

The shitty tone added with his words makes me break away from the guys and rush around the corner. The sight I'm met with makes my knees buckle. If it wasn't for Char, I'd have fallen to the floor. "Shit!"

At the back of the room, behind metal bars, is Baby. He roars and butts himself against the sides. "You utter slimeball!" I scream at Keeper, who is standing behind several rows of Brutes the size of trees. Each of them holds swords in their gigantic hands, their faces passive, waiting for the order to attack.

BLAZE

AMELIA K'OLIVER

T don't wait for Keeper to give the order. As soon as I feel the guys behind me, I rush forward with my Katana raised.

"Argh!" I slash out at the closest Brute. It slices his biceps as he reaches out, grabs my shoulders and lifts me. I hit his massive head with the butt of my sword, and he drops me. Before I hit the ground, I thrust my blade up into his neck, the tip breaking through the top of his skull. It takes all my strength to pull it out. Placing my foot on his chest, I yank and almost fall to the floor when it comes free.

"Kay!" Charlie screams my name as I fight my way through the horde of giant bodies. My target is Baby's cage, then... it's time to kill Keeper. Sidestepping mammoth Brutes, slashing as I go, I make my way further into the room. Being short is coming in handy right now. Huge and strong they may be, but Brute can't bend for shit. Using that to my advantage, I sever several shins from knees as I make my way to the bars holding Baby back.

From the corner of my eye, I see Connor on the back of a Brute while Crowley slashes his throat. Blood pours from the wound, soaking Crowley in brown blood. I'd always figured that all Advanced had brown blood, and mine was red because I'm human. Apparently not. A Brute grabs my hair as I slide through his legs, making me scream. I twirl my blade and cut off the hair he has in his grasp, then I shove it between his legs, straight into his boys. With both hands, I press it further, grimacing at the bloodcurdling scream he lets out.

My hair flutters to the floor as the big guy falls tree-like onto his back, his blank eyes staring at the ceiling. I plant my feet on his chest to get a better view of the room. Charlie and Crowley are working together to take down the beasts while Chris and Connor sever heads from bodies. Can, Cell and Craven each fight on their own, taking on two of their brethren at a time. They don't even need weapons; I watch as they tear limb from limb. It's beautiful, really. Baby's roar shakes me from the beauty of war.

"Do not come closer, witch. Or I will kill your beast," Keeper threatens, his face a mask of pure hatred as he stares me down.

"You know, when I get him free, he will tear you to shreds, and then I will dance on your innards as you watch," I yell while stalking closer to him. He has a small dagger in one hand, and a gun in the other. Just a few weeks ago, I wouldn't even blink at attacking him. But now... now, I have so much to live for. But I won't allow him to kill Baby. Baby paws at the metal bars in front of him, the growl coming from his chest vibrating in mine. Baby's my kin; I'd lay my life down for him.

"I know that look. Your mother wore the same one

when I told her that her precious daughter was no good for my boy," he spits at me. Motherfucker. "Kill me, Kayla, and you'll never get the answers you seek. He," Keeper gestures to Baby as my eyes follow, "is not what he seems."

"I know, he's a lion. One that's going to tear your ugly fucking face off in about ten seconds."

"Ah, yes. Lion. But also... family."

My eyes make their way back to his beady little ones. Family? Baby's always been family to me.

"That's right, Kayla. He's your brother."

The sounds of fighting fade, replaced with a buzzing as my head spins. That's not possible. Kyron died in an explosion when we were kids. No. Baby's not my brother. Suddenly, a face appears in front of mine. Keeper's rotten breath fans my face, my eyes snap to his.

"Your brother is a shifter. He's broken. Can't change back. And Kayla, I broke him." Baby's high-pitched whine registers in my mind as hot liquid tickles my legs. My head shoots towards Baby as the pain kicks in. Flicking my eyes down, I realise Keeper has stabbed his dagger into my stomach. "We tortured him for years, killed the children I forced him to have so that he would remain wild. Then regressed his age so that when we left him in the Wastes, he would be easy prey. Yes, he's one of my finest creations. Shame I couldn't add a fire starter to my collection, you would've made a good pet..." Keeper's rant cuts off mid-sentence as a Brute appears in front of him, a fine line of brown blood running across his neck.

Drip. Drip. Drip.

The sound draws my eyes to the end of my Katana, blood drops off the tip and onto the floor. The Brutes body hits the floor before his head does, the Brute having taken the hit meant for Keeper. Shit. When I look up, Keeper's gone. All the Brutes in the room are dead or have escaped.

A scream of pain from a voice I recognize pierces through the red haze of battle. Charlie. I flash my blade out, separating the cage door from its hinges before rushing to where Charlie's scream came from. Jumping over the bodies littering the floor, I reach Charlie fast. But not soon enough. Charlie's lying in a pool of his blood; slashes mar his upper body. In an attempt to staunch the blood flow, Crowley has taken off his shirt and is pressing it onto Charlie's chest. Dropping to my knees next to Charlie, I pick up his hand with mine. With the other, I pull the blade from my stomach, barely registering the pain.

"Charlie?" His laboured breathing echoes in the now silent room. "Heal yourself, Charlie, please!" I beg. My voice cracks and tears stream down my face unchecked. Not my Charlie, no. Not him.

He can heal.

"Heal, Charlie! **Now!** " I scream. But he doesn't even open his eyes.

"He can't, Kayla. He must be conscious. The wound's mortal," Crowley says on a sob. I turn my accusing gaze on him.

"No. No. Charlie can heal. I've seen it, this isn't the end... No." I throw my body across Charlie's, my ear to his chest I listen to his heart. Baby lays his massive body over both of ours.

Thuthump.... Thuthump...... thuthump.........
thuthump........... Thu...

BLAZE
AMELIA K'OLIVER

"L eave," the word leaves my throat burning. I push myself off Charlie's body and look Crowley dead in the eyes as Baby moves to stand by the door. "Get them out. Quickly. And far away, now!" My gravelly voice gets louder the more I speak. I need them to get out immediately. I can already feel my flames welling inside of me. Hotter than I've ever felt them, they clamber to reach the surface, to be set free.

"Kayla..." Connor begins. Just as he's about to touch my arm, flames erupt from my skin. My whole body is shaking as Crowley picks up Charlie's limp body and, with one last look over his shoulder, he leaves the room. Chris follows with Connor, Can and Cell. Baby throws me one last look, then trots off behind my guys.

Looking down, I realise almost all of me is covered in beautiful golden flames. I'm torn between doing what's right and what my heart wants to do. Spinning in a slow circle, I'm surprised to find Craven standing sentinel at the entrance.

"You need to leave, Crave. I can't…" My legs wobble and I almost fall, but quicker than should be possible for a guy his size, Craven grabs my flaming arm. "Shit, you'll burn!" I scream while yanking my arm away from his grip.

"No, I won't. See?" Craven runs his massive hand down my shoulder. He doesn't scream out in pain as his fingers go through my fire. I crane my face up to investigate his, confusion drawing my eyebrows down.

"I'm immune to your fire, Princess," he explains as I stare at his huge fingers. "It is why you chose me." He smiles sadly, revealing sharp-looking teeth. "Let's get revenge for your lover." Craven, a man of few words. But when he speaks, it's like he sees into my soul.

I nod and look around us. How the fuck did Keeper get out of here during the carnage without being seen? A wave of desolation hits me, knocking my breath away. Charlie. Fire drips from every inch of my skin. The wooden floor beneath my feet crackles and burns. I drop to a knee as another wave of grief sears through me. They killed my Charlie. They have taken his beautiful soul from this world. This fucked up ugly world is grotesque without him. I can't live without Charlie. I just can't. I don't want to.

"I am here, Princess." Craven's booming voice breaks through my pain, reminding me I'm not alone in this awful place.

I'm losing control, my flames are getting hotter. Spreading from me to where Charlie was killed, the blood there bubbles and pops. I try to fight it, the animal urge to tear this place down piece by piece. I have to find Keeper. He must pay for what he's done. He has the answers I've been searching for my whole life. I could search this building for hours trying to find him. By then, he will unleash the virus. Killing the world.

My back arches as my fire escapes from me, its golden colour slowly changing into bright white. I fall onto my hands and knees as memories of Charlie flit through my head. Sweet, loving Charlie. Torn from me just as I opened my heart. My eyes squeeze shut as I see myself from above. Charlie making love to me. Every touch, every kiss, sweet, loving. Tender. Beautiful. The heat surrounding me penetrates through the agony rolling through me. My fire's out of control. I have little desire to rein it in.

Let it consume me.

I don't want to live in a world where Charlie is not.

As I fall face-first onto the floor, I barely register my name being called over and over. Begging. Pleading.

My Charlie. Murdered. They murdered my Charlie.

"Kayla! I can't... It's too hot!" Craven's deep, resounding words vibrate through my chest. He sounds so far away. The heat flows from me. Fast and furious. I'm out of control. Falling headfirst into oblivion, I welcome it with open arms. My last thought is how I hope the others have gotten out as the building around me collapses on top of me. Bits of wood and metal crash into my body, the pain barely registering as my flames consume everything around me, even me. Finally, the pain ends, and my world goes black.

***

THE GROUND IS hard beneath my cheek. Something sharp is poking my hip and my mouth tastes like ash. Slowly cracking an eye open, I snap it shut as the white light that assaults me.

Shit, that's bright.

"Ugh, fuck." Is forced between my dry lips as I attempt to push myself up. Everything hurts. By the time I make it to my hands and knees, I'm panting like Baby does when it's hot. Sweat drips down my face and lands on the white floor. Wait, white? It definitely shouldn't be white.

"Daughter," my mother's melodic voice snaps me out of my confusion and memories stab through me like bolts of lightning.

Me running around the farm screaming at the top of my lungs. Connor, Crowley and Charlie chasing me, huge smiles on all our lips as the wind whips our hair around our faces.

The smell of strawberries and cinnamon as we sit around a big wooden table, laughing.

Craven carrying me around on his shoulder, telling everyone I'm his Queen.

Charlie picking wildflowers for me, then getting told off by his dad for wandering off the farm.

Connor pushing me on the rubber tyre tied to a blackened tree.

Crowley teaching me how to punch without hurting my fist, a wide smile on his face when I finally get it right.

My mother holding me and my brother in her arms, utter love in her gaze as we snuggled in for hugs.

Her body, oddly fluid, as she lay in one of my father's arms.

. . .

"Mum?" My head snaps up to find her standing above me, her hand outstretched like she's about to touch me. But she pulls it back at the last second.

"Yes, Kayla. You..."

"I died, didn't I?" I finish for her. I straighten out my spine as I stand upright.

"You sure did. What were you thinking? You would've burnt the entire world!" she admonishes me.

"I wanted to! My Charlie, he..." A sob breaks free. I bend over, hands on my knees, as I break from the inside out.

"I'm sorry, love. I know it's hard. But Charlie's better off- "

My head snaps up, flames crackle across my arms, the waves of heat coming from them blur the vision of my dead mother. "Don't fucking say that! Is he here? Charlie?" I shout his name, hoping beyond hope he'll appear from the white surrounding me.

"He is, but Kayla, I can't..."

In a flash, I move impossibly fast. Coming to a stop right next to the giant tree. My flaming hand outstretched, just inches from the bark. My mother lets out a surprised yip. "Give him back, and I won't burn everything to ash. I swear to you, I will blaze. And I won't even blink," I scream.

I want Charlie back, and I want him now.

"Kayla! Back away from the World Tree. Now. Please," her eyes dart around, her hands shake as she wrings them together. "Quickly! Oh, shit!" The ground beneath my feet rumbles. My stomach sinks as the feeling of weightlessness overcomes my senses.

"Kayla, Kayla, Kayla," a deep bass voice calls out from nowhere. "What is this? A tantrum?"

"Who's there?" I ask as I float through the air.

"You don't recognise my voice, child? I'm offended," the man answers back, humour lacing his voice.

What the fuck is this?

From the nothingness walks a beast so tall, I have to crane my neck to an uncomfortable angle to see his face. Blood red skin is tightly wrapped over sharp-looking bones. His head is boulder-like. Long curled horns sit atop it. Fire drips from their ends.

Oh, fuck me.

"I don't think she recognises you, brother." Another smaller but still tall as fuck man walks from the blinding light. "You're all but forgotten on her plane. What a shame." He chuckles. The red beast beside him raises his lip, revealing pointed teeth.

The shorter man is wearing what appears to be bedsheets wrapped around a plump body. Long white hair trailing to the floor is covered with all manner of creatures. Some I recognise from Earth; most I've never seen.

"Looks like she doesn't know who you are either, brother. You're obsolete," the beast counters with a smirk.

"Yes, yes. I have been absent for too long." He runs his hand over his full beard. "That'll change soon enough. Kayla," the all-white man steps forward or rather floats towards me. "It is lovely to see you again, Daughter. Oh, how you've grown!" He smiles fondly at me.

"Who are you? And him." I thrust my chin towards Red. "What fresh hell is this?"

"Not Hell, dear. Limbo," my mother provides, unhelpfully.

"I am your creator, Kayla," White guy answers.

"Jointly," the Red guy grumbles.

"Yes, jointly." The white guy rolls his eyes. "We created you in the hope that you could save the Earth plane."

"You're lucky your true powers are yet untapped; you could've destroyed the entire planet with that show. Which, by the way," Red leans in further, "I would've approved of. But," he shrugs his pointed shoulders. "Bitch tits here would've torn me a new one."

White rolls his eyes again, this time adding a tut for full effect. "Lucy, now, now. This is your doing! That virus wasn't meant to mutate like that. It was merely a culling. Not an apocalypse. It went wrong. Now we need you to fix it, Kayla." White bores his storm grey eyes into mine. I shrink under his intense gaze.

"Me? How... I... the fuck?" My shoulders sag with exhaustion. This is all kinds of fucked up. "I just want Charlie back; he shouldn't have died. Please, " I try adding a little pathetic note to my tone, hoping these two will take pity and just give me my future husband back.

Red cups his chin, his elbow resting on his other arm across his chest, "You can have the healer back, with one condition,"

"Anything!" I blurt before I've even had the chance to process what's happening. I do not know what these two things are, but really, I'm just so tired I wobble on my feet.

"Just use the blood we gave you to cure what humanity did to itself," White replies.

"Those Panda that bit you?" My mind's thrown back to the field where Chris was trapped, surrounded by Panda. The last time I ended up here in limbo was because I'd been bitten by dozens of them. "They are now cured. You must cure them all, Kayla. Otherwise, the Earth realm dies," White tells me softly while stroking his hand over

319

my flame encased fingers. "Burn the rest. Cleanse the Earth, child."

They want me to cure every Panda on Earth? And kill all the Advanced? I ask them to clarify.

"They are not human; they must be taken care of," Red utters like I should absolutely believe what he says.

"If you refuse, well... everyone on Earth will perish," White tells me. Looking around, I realise my mother's gone. As is the world tree.

"Show her, Godfrey. She doesn't believe us." Red's angry voice cuts through me.

Cure the virus? Kill the Advanced?

Save Charlie.

"But what about the innocent?" I ask them, my mind running through all my options. If I could somehow convince them not all the Advanced are bad, then maybe I could save them.

"No such thing. They are all abominations," White announces while waving his arm in front of him. From nowhere, Charlie appears.

"Charlie!" I try to throw myself at him, but I'm held by invisible arms.

"Kill them all, and you can be free." Red smiles wide and grotesquely at me. I turn my eyes back to Charlie. He appears to be asleep, his handsome face at peace.

A jolt of power hits me from behind. Schooling my face, I turn to my mother.

Take him, run. She mouths silently.

My brows draw down in confusion as I swivel my body back to Charlie just as his eyes spring open. He looks into my eyes and before I have time to react, my flames burst from my body and I'm reaching out to take his hand. Something deep within bursts free. I feel the power coursing through me like never before. Someone shouts the word, "Traitor", then suddenly, I'm falling.

The feeling of moving at warp speed makes me squeeze my eyes shut. My stomach rolls and I almost scream out as my arse hits the solid ground.

"Umph!"

A huge gasp comes from the darkness. It's then I realise my eyes are still closed. Snapping them open, I'm greeted by the most beautiful chestnut pair I've ever seen. He's still over Crow's shoulder. "Charlie?" I manage to choke out as Crowley settles Charlie to his feet. Then I'm wrapped in so many arms, I can't tell who is who.

"Fuck, Kay! We thought you were dead!" Chris sobs into my hair.

"How long was I out?"

"Long enough that we discussed where we should bury the two of you," Crowley growls in my other ear.

Wow. Felt like no time had passed.

The smell of burning hits my nose, smoke enters my lungs, making them burn. But all I can feel is the love of four amazing men saturating my every pore.

We sit here, holding each other in the ashes of the epicentre of Tri-City. A perfect circle of charred earth surrounds us. A large pile of rubble moves, all of us tense, our hands fly to our weapons. The sound of metal scraping on rock rents the air. Then Craven's gargantuan head pops out from nowhere.

"Shit, Craven! How?" I ask, overwhelmed with thankfulness. He's alive, and I didn't burn him to death.

"I found a large metal container," he says while heaving his massive body out of the ground. "I hid. That was seriously fucking hot." I push myself up and throw my arms around his waist. Steam rises from his exposed patches of skin.

"Keeper?" I ask no one in particular while Craven runs his hand over my hair.

Crowley answers me. "We don't know. We didn't see him on the way out, or when we got here. But we know the lab was destroyed. They did not set the virus-free."

Oh, thank fuck! At least that's something. I hug them all to me once again. Craven's enormous arms reach around us all.

A deafening roar I know well makes me spin around so fast, I almost fall face-first into the burnt dirt. Baby bounds over to me; his paws kicking up ash into the air behind him, giving him the appearance of a badass. Which he truly is. He crashes into me so hard we fall to the ground as he licks my face furiously. "My boy! Oh, thank God you're ok. Oh, jeez! Ugh." Slobber soaks my hair and face by the time he stops licking me. We're both relieved to see the other alive and well. I wrap my arms around his neck and use him to pull myself to stand up, my face buried in his thick fur.

My brother.

"What happens now?" Connor asks, looking out at the city without a leader.

Perhaps what's left of our island needs a Queen. One that will unite us all. Or maybe we need to do things a new way.

"We open the gates." I turn and face the gathering crowd of Advanced, my four guys at my back. "Now, we rebuild. We make Earth strong again. Together," I address the masses, the power in my voice projecting it louder and clearer than it's ever been. "We pick up the pieces of society. We open the gates and welcome our fellow man. We cure the virus and rebuild, we grow. As equals. As brothers and sisters. We take back what they took from us so long ago... Our freedom!"

A small metallic 'clink' breaks through the silence surrounding us. Seconds later, a gunshot echoes off the buildings. Screams rent the air. Then, there's only pain.

BLAZE

AMELIA K'OLIVER

Crouching down, I pluck a ripe Mato from the vine and bring it to my nose. Its sweet smell washes over my senses as I rise again. From the corner of my eye, I see a large golden beast moving through the bushes behind the field. Two years ago, Baby went on a trip with Crowley. They'd gone to collect supplies from the Underground. Baby met a lioness on the way back. She's huge and wild. Beautiful. Shortly after, they had their first litter. Five beautiful beasts were born, each of them as wild as their mother. The smallest, Justin I've called him, visits now and then. He isn't like Baby, but he's safe to have around. The sight of his fur brings on a longing to see my brother, but he rarely comes to see me

325

anymore. His protection is no longer needed. He's free now.

The heat from the sun high in the sky draws beads of sweat on my brow and the light breeze cools the droplets of liquid. I lift my face to the sky. Closing my eyes, I take a big, calming breath.

Today is the day. Exactly seven years ago, my life changed forever. All our lives did.

"We fight for what was taken from us... our freedom!" Pain. Unimaginable agony tears through my entire body as it flies through the air. I land in a heap, the smell of burning flesh making me gag. Opening my eyes, once again I'm surrounded by fire, death and pain.

Seventy Advanced died that day. Many more were injured. It was a terrible day.

Taking a bite of the mato, I savour the tangy-sweet taste as more memories assault me.

"Kayla!"

The sound of Crow screaming my name finally makes me focus. "I'm here. I'm ok! Where is everyone?" Wails of agony come from all directions. I push myself off the steaming ground and look around me. Bodies, limbs and chunks of flesh litter the area where we were standing just moments ago.

"Kay!" Crowley's face appears before mine, blocking the gruesome sight. "Fuck, are you ok?" I nod numbly, unable to process what just happened.

"Help!"

"Oh god, my legs!"

"Help me! Help me!"

"Mummy?"

The screams of the injured will forever be branded into my mind. Every year on this day, we hold a gathering to celebrate and mourn. I turn on my heel and slowly make my way back to the house, finishing the bright red mato. Stretching out a hand to open the door, another flashback takes my breath away.

"Fuck! Oh god. No!" I scream while standing over Chris. Before I can react, though, a body smashes into me from behind. "Argh! Umph."

"I will kill you!" The man on my back manoeuvres to pin my body to the ground while he grabs my hair in one hand and slashes a blade into my back with the other. A battle cry rings out and then suddenly the weight is lifted from me. Planting my hands in the bloody dirt beneath me, I stand and seek out my attacker. The move makes my back sing with agony.

"You traitorous bastard! I should have killed you years ago! Worthless clone!" Keeper yells at Connor. Spittle flies from his lips as he says the hateful words. Connor charges his father, a long sword in his hand. Just as he reaches the foul man, Connor jerks to a stop. A thud draws all our eyes to the ground.

Fire bursts from my skin, and I throw myself at Keeper. My arms go around his waist as I tackle him. We land in a tangled mess. I straddle the evillest man on our Island as flames lick down my arms and set fire to the material on his torso.

"Argh! You bitch!" He bucks and sends me crashing down, landing on my shoulder. White-hot pain lances through my arm as the sound of a bone snapping reaches my ears.

"Shit!" Before Keeper can get his arse back up, I flip from my back and land on my feet. My arm dangles at my side, floppy and useless. Ouch. "You will pay for your crimes, Keeper."

"No, I won't, you little freak! Wanna know why?" His bright red face turns a charming shade of purple as he shouts, "These people love me. I'm their king and they're loyal to me." That's when the sounds of war filters into my mind. When I turn, I'm greeted with horrors that will give me nightmares for the rest of my life. The rebels have arrived, but so have an army of Advanced.

I let my hand drop from the handle and turn back to the field of vines. So much blood was shed in the city that day. It took an age for the rain to wash it away. The sea of matos before me reminds me of how the streets ran red. Advanced", Rebels', Scraps', my men's, and mine. Our blood turned the nearby river red.

"Kayla?"

The sound of my name makes me jump while simultaneously spinning around, my hand outstretched to strike.

"Easy, Darlin. It's just me." Crowley catches my fist before it connects with his handsome face.

"I'm sorry, I..."

"I know, I know." He pulls me to him and wraps his enormous arms around me. "Today is hard for all of us."

"They'll all die, and their blood will be on your hands, bitch!" Keeper throws his body at me once again. This time, I see it coming and just sidestep. He falls to the blackened dirt with an umph. As I take a step towards him, my boot hits something, sending it skittering across the ground. Faster than an old man like him should be able to move, Keeper flips around and sits up. His hand flashes out and before I can blink, he's risen, the blade pressed against my throat.

"Now it's time to die, human." He moves to slash the steel across my throat, but I manage to get a hand up and tear the blade away. I then duck my chin and bite into his palm. He immediately lets me go, and I use the opportunity to dash away from him. Hot blood rolls down the front of my body from my neck, the wound pumping my life from within me.

The front of Keeper's body is burnt, the material melted to his blackened skin. One side of his face is destroyed. Bone and teeth poke through what little flesh is left. The air shifts behind me and my instincts roar to life. I spin only to be met with a wall of muscle. Crow.

"Let's finish this, Darlin."

A leather-bound hilt is inserted into my palm, and in one smooth move, I spin.

I'll never forget the sound of Keeper's head hitting the ground. A dull, wet thud. And just like that, the fighting behind me stopped. Weapons clanged as they were dropped. Silence enveloped me as I stood there looking down at Keeper's war-torn body.

"It's ok, love. We're here." Charlie's soothing voice wraps around my icy heart. Warming it from the outside. The door bangs shut behind him as he takes me in his arms. He plants a kiss on the top of my head and holds me tight.

The gates weren't opened immediately. We spent the next year putting together a council. Three members from each faction were chosen. Scraps, Advanced, Hands, New Panda like Chris and Evo's. And people like me, we named ourselves Mists. There are more like us, each having unique powers. One has the ability to move things with his mind, another controls earth; she can grow things using her blood. It's amazing to watch. We each have one thing in common; We all have golden hair.

Charlie, a woman named Kath, and a man called Lance, are our council members. My guys tried to convince me I should be on the council, but that's not something I've ever wanted; To be in charge. When the gates were finally opened many Advanced left the City, some started their own small communities, some just disappeared. Others objected to the new way of things. Where everything is voted on, where every faction gets their own say. Those people were forced to leave. I don't know where they went, but I'm sure we'll see them again.

"Are you hungry? Dinner's ready, let's go inside." Charlie's breath tickles my ear as he speaks. His hand playing with the ends of my arse length hair.

"Ok." I pull away from him just enough so we can walk side by side into the house.

"There you are. Did you get the matos?" Chris calls from the kitchen. His handsome face peeks around the wall and smiles at me. The black around his eyes never faded, despite the fact he's no longer a full Panda. What he is now is hard to explain. A hybrid, Charlie calls him. Half-Panda, half-human, he's the Alpha Panda on the council. Many of his brethren now live within the city, accepted as part of the people. The City scientists developed a vaccine with my blood. It was decided most Panda were far too gone to save and it would be cruel to cure them. Instead, teams were put together to brave the Wastes and give them mercy. Chris and his people are now treated well, mostly.

"I forgot, sorry," my reply is soft.

"That's ok, Connor got some." As Chris says his name, Connor comes rushing into the room, a small child on his shoulders.

"Look who I found creeping around the farm, Kay. Little Daisy decided to pay us a visit." The golden-haired girl giggles and hides behind her hands.

"Oh, did she now? Hmm. Does your mummy know you're here, sweetie?" Crowley strides towards Connor and plucks the little girl from him. She lets out a shrill scream as he lifts her through the air.

"I'm fwying!" Her voice is loud as she throws her arms out.

"I'll get her on the radio, let her know she's her. Connor, you set the table, please?" Charlie asks.

Connor throws up his arm. "I'm working with one hand here. Can't someone who has two do it?" He chuckles.

Connor lost his arm from the elbow down when he got in the way of his father. The move meant to slice my throat severed it. Luckily, Charlie healed him before he bled out, but Charlie couldn't regrow limbs. Con adapted to being handicapped quickly, even though he plays on it.

"No! Set the f..." Charlie stops and flicks his eyes to little Daisy. "fluffy table," he finishes, ever respectful when the little ones are around. Women started getting pregnant four years after what is being called The Beginning. Scientists quickly developed contraception. Of which I took full advantage of. People took notice of time passing after Keeper tried to kill us all with a bomb.

Today is New Year's Day. Year seven.

With one last kiss on my cheek, Charlie bends at the waist and presses a soft kiss to my swollen belly. "Love you, Theodore."

"Nope. Not happening," I say firmly. "He or she isn't being called that."

"Why not?" Charlie asks for the millionth time.

I'm days away from giving birth and we still haven't picked names. "I like it. But.. it doesn't feel right." My hands go to my very pregnant stomach as the baby inside wiggles. A sharp pain flashes through me. It almost brings me to my knees.

"What's wrong? What is it?" Charlie's panicked voice makes me giggle.

"I've been having these pains all morning. It's fine." I don't get to finish because another pain slices through me. This one makes me cry out.

"Ok, Con, take Daisy back to her mum. Get the Doc and tell him Kayla's in labour. Charlie, get material and water. Chris, get the plastic sheets from the cupboard in the baby's room. Craven," finally Crowley takes a breath as he bends to place an arm behind my knees and the other around my waist, lifting me into his arms. "Get Can and Cell. I want them on the door, to protect Kaleidoscope in shifts." Bossy Crowley then stomps out of the room and up the stairs, placing me on the bed I share with my four lovers.

"Are you ok? Of course, you're not. You're in labour. But..." He runs his hand through his short black hair. All the guys continue to dye their hair. They often go out into the Wastes to give aid to other communities and they say it makes them a target. Not just for bad things, but also to women. "Shit. I'm freaking out here, Darlin."

"Just breathe, Crow. It's gonna be fine. Argh!" Another wave of agony burns its way through my stomach. "Just breathe. That's it. Just keep breathing." I'm not sure who I'm talking to, him or myself, but as the pain fades, I burst into laughter.

Crowley is panting, his face bright red, and he's fisting the sheets so hard, it reminds me of the first time he and I had sex. He ripped the material on Charlie's bed then because I wouldn't allow him to touch me as I rode him.

Now, he's ripping it on our bed because I'm about to give birth.

"Don't laugh, Darlin. The first thing I'm doing once you're healed is tying you to this bed and making you cum all over my tongue," he growls seductively. Oh, my. Charlie rushes into the room. Together he and Crowley undress me, then slip a white nightie over me. Just long enough to cover my arse. That unbuttons down the front.

"Thanks, guys," I say between panting breaths. Things are happening quicker than I expected. "Ah, the pain is... intense." They both wince and Crowley begins to pace in front of the window. Charlie peppers my hand with soft kisses.

When we returned to my mother's farm, my fathers were gone. Everything was dusty, and the crops were long dead. We searched the area for signs of bodies, but we found none. Either they left, or they died. I don't know. So, we rebuilt the place, adding several more buildings for Craven, Can and Cell.

They call themselves my Sentinels. They never leave the property unless I do. And they follow me everywhere.

"Argh! Fuck! Mother fucker. Charlie!" I turn my angry gaze on my husband. "You're never to touch me again, got it?" I growl, knowing full well I don't mean it. But as more agony tries to split me from the inside, I'm on the verge of kicking him in the face.

"I'm sorry, my love. Just remember, I love you," he replies calmly. Why the fuck is he so calm? I'm being torn in two, for fuck's sake!

Charlie and I got married where his parents lived, inside a cave where the Earth gaped open. The gas that rose from the ground smelled sweet. I married Chris a year later.

Crowley claims he doesn't need to marry me, that I'm irrevocably his, anyway. Cheeky shit. And Connor refuses, claiming he hasn't set right what he did under Death's control. No matter how many times we tell him it wasn't him, we forgive him and love him; he refuses to let us unite fully.

Just as the rest of the guys and the doctor bursts into the room, I have an overwhelming desire to poop.

"Argh! It's coming!" I scream as I push down into my arse. Doctor Lance lifts the sheet that Charlie draped over my knees.

"Push, Kayla! That's it, girl. Yes. Keep going, keep going."

For what feels like an age, I push and push. My body's exhausted and my mind's is on the verge of breaking when finally, a baby's cry silences us all.

"Congratulations! It's a boy!" The doctor announces as he lifts a wiggling, screaming tiny baby into the air.

"Oh, my god!" Connor chokes out.

"Fuck, he's beautiful," Chris follows.

"Well done, Darlin. He's adorable." Crowley's voice catches in his throat.

Charlie's sobs come in time with my own. He reaches out his hands and takes our baby from Doc. He lays him gently on my chest, a look of awe in his eyes.

"He's blonde!" He chuckles, tears streaming down his face. "I'm so proud of you, my love. You're a warrior!"

"He looks just like daddy," I reply while stroking the soft golden curls on my son's head, "Oliver."

"Yes. I love that, Oliver. My beautiful son," Charlie's reply is met with a series of agreements, sighs of relief and then a round of congratulations.

"Welcome to the world, Oliver. Your Daddies and I can't wait to show you what we're building. We did it for you, son." I place a soft kiss on his forehead and look at my guys surrounding us, tears in their eyes. "I love you all so much."

THANK you so much for reading Blaze! If you are reading this, please leave me a review or a rating here. A million thank yous!!! I love you guys so much.
    Amelia xoxo

ALSO BY AMELIA K OLIVER

More by Amelia

Never Ever - Book One

https://books2read.com/u/mdGgVZ

Four Ever - Book Two

https://books2read.com/u/31GgOn

Ever lasting - Book Three

https://books2read.com/u/4AzdXd

* * *

Everything Amelia K Oliver

https://linktr.ee/ameliaoliverauthor

Sign up to my newsletter and get updates and freebies http://eepurl.com/gK6XV1

Made in United States
Orlando, FL
12 June 2023

34095371R00209